FAR FROM
A *Pleasant*
LAND

BERYL CARPENTER

In peace I will lie down and sleep,
for you alone, Lord, make me dwell in safety.

(Psalm 4:8 NIV)

To Janet Brown, my mother and first fan

AuthorHouse™ LLC
1663 Liberty Drive
Bloomington, IN 47403
www.authorhouse.com
Phone: 1-800-839-8640

Cover art by Kate Garchinsky

Published by AuthorHouse 05/21/2014

ISBN: 978-1-4918-6051-9 (sc)
ISBN: 978-1-4918-6050-2 (e)

Library of Congress Control Number: 2014908825

Any people depicted in stock imagery provided by Thinkstock are models, and such images are being used for illustrative purposes only. Certain stock imagery © Thinkstock.

This book is printed on acid-free paper.

Because of the dynamic nature of the Internet, any web addresses or links contained in this book may have changed since publication and may no longer be valid. The views expressed in this work are solely those of the author and do not necessarily reflect the views of the publisher, and the publisher hereby disclaims any responsibility for them.

Scripture quotations marked NIV are taken from the Holy Bible, New International Version®. NIV®. Copyright © 1973, 1978, 1984 by International Bible Society. Used by permission of <u>Zondervan</u>. All rights reserved.

ACKNOWLEDGMENTS

The publishing of my first book has turned out to be a long, careful process.

I'm grateful to Janice Blair, my friend and persistent motivator, who kept asking, "How's your book coming along?" She lent her support and kept me moving toward completion. So did Rhoda Russell and the Bethany book club, who all eagerly read and critiqued an early version.

Robert, my husband, became my best editor and a worthy advisor, always scrutinizing the smallest detail. Brian, our younger son, gave his expertise on English punctuation and capitalization. Brent, our older son, has always inspired me with his devotion to artistic pursuits.

Other editors included Marge McCrae, wise mentor of many developing writers, who read the manuscript the first time, and my favorite writing group and sounding board, Kitsap Christian Writers.

I'm indebted to Kate Garchinsky, who designed the cover art, bringing Sara Elena to life before my eyes. She also coached me on formatting details and marketing practices.

Many others have contributed tips and suggestions. Thanks to you all.

I now present the results to you, dear reader. I hope you have many hours of happy reading.

Best regards,
Beryl Carpenter

A Note from the Author

1492 was a momentous year, but not just for Columbus' discovery of America. Several other important events reshaped the destiny of Spain and the world forever.

Since 722 Christian forces had fought to drive Muslims out of Iberia. Finally, in the last act of Reconquest, Ferdinand and Isabella succeeded in pushing out the last Moorish king, Boabdil, from his fortress kingdom Granada. For several years before, a series of sieges and truces had foretold the end. When Ferdinand and Isabella entered the Alhambra Palace on January 2, 1492, they accepted sovereignty of Spanish lands, which would never again be controlled by Muslim sovereigns.

The Catholic Monarchs went on to make other changes to purify the religion of their country. The next was a purge, the expulsion of the Jews. Tomás de Torquemada, Ferdinand's appointed Grand Inquisitor, urged Ferdinand and Isabella to sign an Edict of Expulsion, which gave Jews three months to convert or leave Spain. About half the Jews chose to convert. The other half, about 200,000 people, left the country and headed for Portugal, North Africa, the eastern Mediterranean and the Holy Land. Spain's treasuries bulged with all the gold and property left behind. A few years later, the King and Queen expelled the remaining Moorish people, too.

Now that war was over, there was money for other purposes, including exploration. Spain needed to compete with Portugal for trade routes and commerce. Columbus seized the moment and procured permission and a few ships to head west into the unknown. Juan Sanchez and Luis de

Torres are two men listed on the ship's rosters as surgeon and interpreter. I have fictionalized their adventures.

Spain continued to modernize in other ways, too. Isabella, in fact, had already made some financial reforms before 1492, limiting the amount of money that could be minted and reducing the debt her brother Henry had built up. Ferdinand and Isabella unified the Spanish kingdoms under their rule and revised the code of laws, as well.

In 1492, the Castilian language also came into greater use and credibility. Antonio de Nebrija published a grammar of the Castilian language dedicated to Queen Isabella. When she asked, "Why would I want such a book?" he answered, "It is the instrument of empire." Spain was in the ascendancy and had much to be proud of. Future subjects would need to know the language of the conquerors.

Were Ferdinand and Isabella the first modern rulers or Machiavellian leaders maximizing their advantage, as some have called them? You decide. It's deplorable their successes came at the expense of a significant number of Spain's respected citizens. Their purges ultimately robbed Spain of its wisest advisers as well as its best administrators. Converted Jews who remained came under intense scrutiny by the Inquisition, creating an atmosphere of treachery, tattling and deception sanctioned by Ferdinand. Spain wasted its resources, tormented its people and within one hundred years slid into decline.

Sara Elena, Juan and Luis have further adventures in the New World and elsewhere in sequel novels coming soon called *Toward a Dark Horizon* and *When Doves Laughed*. Don't miss them!

Beryl J. Carpenter
May 2014

Chapter 1

❋

December 1491

Angry clouds snaked across the sky on the day of the burning. The sun struggled over the rooftops, its tepid rays failing to penetrate the bank of writhing clouds. In spite of the charged atmosphere, fear spread its sodden curtain over all. Those who came near shivered and drew their cloaks tighter.

The plaza filled with people. The holy fathers encouraged attendance by promising a one-year pardon from purgatory. Bakers, tailors, cooks, and ironsmiths closed their shops and hurried toward that most public of meeting places. Washerwomen, millers, and candle makers followed close behind. Barber-surgeons, jesters, and women of lost reputation mingled among the townspeople seeking to entertain and entice. Soldiers strutted through the throngs. Gliding at a respectable pace, clerics shoved their hands into opposite sleeves and tried not to appear eager.

A group of ragged boys assembled in the wide yard. The fine layer of dirt they kicked up sifted back over them and stuck to their sweaty faces. They jostled for position in front of the piles of wood and kindling, laughing and placing small bets on the fate of the heretics. How would the condemned face their punishment today?

Adults who came to watch knew more of what the flames could do to a human body. And still they watched flesh melt and hair crinkle and turn to sparks. Each spectator rehearsed his own response to agony. Who wouldn't? It could happen to any of them. Piercing shrieks of the condemned came straight out of hell, and that was where heretics were headed for their blasphemies against God.

In the crowd, a middle-aged man answered his daughter's questions.

"What's taking so long? I don't have all day." She tossed her auburn curls and adjusted a black shawl over her willowy figure.

"Patience, Sara Elena. You're acting more like a child than the grown woman you are. As you know, it usually *does* last all day. We'll see the condemned soon enough." He combed a trembling hand through his silver hair and stabbed the ground with his walking stick.

"I always thought the Romeros were nice enough people. I never actually met them—"

"Shh, don't let anyone hear you. A careless remark—"

"Yes, Father," she sighed. "All the same, they only read a forbidden book."

"And refused to confess. Now they must die." The man stroked his silvery beard as he would a newborn rabbit.

A cresting wave of murmurs surged through the crowd. Wheels creaked and drums thudded as the solemn procession filed through Granada's cobblestone streets toward the *quemadero*, the place of burning. Churchmen clutching rolled parchments against their scarlet-robed chests swayed in the front ranks, leading the gruesome parade. Secular authorities ambled behind, their fur-lined cloaks billowing, polished swords clanking at their hips. People looked up to catch a glimpse of the three unfortunates standing in the wooden cart, hands tied behind their backs. With head bent forward and shoulders bowed, the dark-skinned mother struggled to control her shaking body. The daughter sniffled, her lips quivering under masses of stringy, dark hair. The father kept his eyes straight ahead, ignoring his disgrace. A contingent of grim-faced soldiers formed the rear guard.

"Those *sanbenitos* are ridiculous!"

"Quiet, *mi hija.*"

"And the tall pointed hats—it's degrading."

He put his fingertips to her mouth.

"Listen to me," he whispered in Sara's ear. "The Romeros could help if you ever find yourself in a tight place. That is, if they escape the flames."

"How . . . why . . . ?" Her words fell to the ground, smothered by the roaring crowd.

The wagon pulled up to a raised platform. A soldier shoved at the condemned. They stumbled out and fell, giving the guard an excuse to kick them. Struggling to get up while shackled, the girl's tunic ripped.

"Let's see more of that shapely body," roared the soldier, pulling the bodice. The tunic split farther, revealing her white breasts, milky as alabaster.

"Stop!" screamed the mother. "Leave her alone, I beg you."

"Rot in hell," croaked her father through dry, split lips.

"No more, brute!" shouted one of the holy men. His scarlet robe swished as a ringed finger pointed at the offender. "Get away from the prisoners. This is not a festival for fools."

The soldier disappeared, and another took his place. The three prisoners listened to the charges read against them, and once again heard the crucial question,

"Do you wish to confess your sin and receive the mercy of the Church?"

"What mercy is that?" muttered the man. "You'll break our necks before laying the torch to the woodpile. We'll die anyway."

"Silence!" The Grand Inquisitor wrinkled his nose and swallowed a gagging cough. The stench of a thousand unwashed bodies lay heavily in the confined area.

"Do you now confess your crimes against the Holy Church, as you refused to do under examination?"

"You mean under torture."

"What is your answer?" His eyes burned with white-hot fury.

"Never!"

The mother and daughter gave the slightest nod in agreement.

"Enough." The head inquisitor bellowed his authority. "Guards, turn these three over to the civil authorities."

"Place the prisoners on the stacks for burning," ordered the mayor in quick succession. He brushed the fine dust off his velvet doublet and held a linen handkerchief over his nose.

A rotten tomato flew through the air and smacked the cheek of the condemned man. He grimaced and turned away, red juice and seeds trickling down into his beard. A ripple of laughter coursed through the crowd, and soon stinking eggs and flabby cabbages, mealy potatoes and kitchen peelings peppered the heretics, raising welts on their faces and slime on their clothes.

Drums throbbed as soldiers removed the garments that shamed the prisoners and lashed them to large poles set in the stacks of wood. A boom of thunder roared overhead. Black clouds now mounted up like cobras ready to strike. The crowd gasped and stopped pelting the prisoners.

"Look, the sky condemns us," the captain shouted.

"Nonsense," cried the mayor. "Keep going—"

"It's a bad omen, sire."

"Heap up more tinder. Pour on more oil."

"Rain will douse the fires."

"Be quick about it."

Soldiers sprinted to fulfill the orders. A crack of dazzling light split the sky and another thunderclap pulsed overhead.

"Light the bonfires now—and bring that scoundrel to me."

The mayor hissed at his soldiers and pointed a meaty finger toward the crowd. A salad of rotting vegetables catapulted toward him. The mayor ducked as guards encircled him.

"Set them free, set them free!" The murmur grew and swept through the crowd.

The soldiers threw torches on the three stacks of wood.

When the crowd heard the crackle of tinder igniting, some began to cheer. Others took up the chant:

"Release them, set them free."

The prisoners wailed as flames began to lick at their ankles. Another strike of lightning ripped the sky apart. Down poured millions of raindrops. They closed on the spreading flames like swarming troops. The orange-red tongues hissed and sputtered. Scarlet-robed churchmen fled for cover. Dye bled from their brocaded frocks, staining the plaza crimson.

"Look, it's the blood of the innocent." The crowd grew agitated.

"It's a sign—release them," one man yelled.

"Cut them loose! Release them!" The crowds stamped their feet and pounded their staffs on the cobblestones. Water ran in rivulets between the paving stones. Lightning licked the sky. The thunder bellowed its challenge.

"God is angry!" roared someone else. "Cut them loose." The crowd surged toward the platform where the mayor cowered. The wooden platform groaned with the pressure of bodies crushed against it.

"Cut them loose!" The crowd yelled once more.

"Very well," growled the mayor. "Guards—release the prisoners or we will have an uprising. God has decided their innocence."

The bonfires sputtered and died. Steam rose to meet the parting clouds. Few people heard the command, but a cheer erupted from a thousand throats and filled the plaza when soldiers cut the ropes off the prisoners. Señor Romero rubbed rope-raw wrists. Señora Romero ran her hand over singed hair and eyebrows. The daughter drew her tunic around her shivering nakedness. Then all three melted into the crowd.

"Leave town if you like, but we will follow your tracks like hounds," yelled the Grand Inquisitor after them. "To the ends of the earth!"

Well, we'll never see them again. They'll never be any help, thought Sara Elena.

The crowd shuffled off to their homes without a whisper. Overhead, the dark clouds slithered away, fading into deep cracks in the silent, sapphire sky.

"Hey, señorita. Going my way?"

Sara Elena shrank back into the doorway. Two soldiers sauntered toward her, water dripping off their heavy cloaks.

"Look, Miguel, she's cold." The young one grabbed her chin and turned her face toward him. A single, icy drop slid down Sara Elena's nose to the cobblestones below. She shrank from his grimy touch.

"Let me warm you." Garlic and stale beer filled the air as he leaned closer to kiss her. Prickly whiskers scraped her cheek.

Sara Elena could have been a Roman sculpture as she stood there frozen in time. It seemed she waited there a thousand years for the obnoxious soldier to pass by.

"Stop it, José. You're drunk." The old one slapped José on the side of the head and shoved him away. "Excuse his bad manners, *señorita*." He bowed then pulled the other one along with him.

"We must get to our post."

Sara Elena nodded, and watched the two disappear down the shadowy corridor, scuffling and cursing all the way. She exhaled a long, slow breath.

Maybe Margarita is right. I've felt an evil presence watching me for days.

When Sara Elena finally stepped out of her doorway, raindrops pelted her from the steely sky. They hit the uneven pavement and shattered like pottery shards. Wind rushed down the narrow lane in the Jewish quarter, and tugged at her long skirt. She drew her black woolen shawl up around her shoulders and neck.

The streets of Granada lay deserted at four o'clock this December afternoon. People kept to their homes and their beds during siesta. The misery of the rain provided another good reason. The *auto de fé* a few hours ago had marred the day beyond all reclamation. Even though the rains doused the fires and the crowds had secured the release of the prisoners, the whole experience had rattled Sara Elena. Her mind kept going back to that horrific spectacle.

Those poor tortured souls! Surely the Romeros didn't deserve to burn.

From Plaza Santa Ana, Sara Elena watched the River Darro creep along the edge of the hill, skirting the Alhambra's foundations. As Sara Elena dodged from awning to doorway along the street, she stepped lightly between rivulets of water. She felt it seep into her soft leather shoes. She frowned then rushed on to Plaza Nueva, where the market had just opened.

My shoes will just have to be ruined. It can't be helped.

"Margarita, do you have any onions today?" she called out to the older woman seated at the covered vegetable stand.

"For you, I always have onions, Sara Elena." She smiled as her eyes scanned the area. "You didn't come here alone, did you?"

"Yes, of course."

"It's not safe to be on the streets alone. Trouble could find a girl like you—so beautiful—and so willful."

"Perhaps." Sara Elena shrugged her shoulders.

Margarita beckoned. "Come sit a minute. I have something to tell you."

Margarita arranged her obsidian hair in an upsweep, pulled it back from her face and held it in place with a tortoise shell comb. She settled onto a rough stool. Sara Elena noticed a few gray hairs in her friend's elegant hairstyle.

"Granada has changed," began Margarita. "It's hard to get fresh vegetables." She took up a shriveled lemon. "Look, the fruit is old and bruised. And that's not all—"

"You didn't sit me down just to talk about oranges and pomegranates, did you?"

"Of course not, Sara. It's more than that. The streets are crowded with restless soldiers, and their stinking horses. You should stay inside."

"Believe me, I know, Margarita." Sara Elena shuddered. "But, I have to do the marketing since Ana left."

"Someone needs to caution you. Since I'm twenty years older than you, I guess it's my duty. I know your father won't. He protects you too much."

"Maybe." Sara shrugged her shoulders then grinned at her friend. "You can be my mother, then, and warn me to be careful, and complain that I don't listen to you."

"Think about it, Sara Elena." Margarita grabbed her hand. "The city has been dangerous these last ten years. Soldiers march around town—loud, coarse, and too quick to look at a woman."

"I know," said Sara Elena. "I hate how they stare at me."

"Will you be more careful?" said Margarita, hoping for a promise.

"I remember my mother,' said Sara Elena, deflecting the conversation. "I thought she was beautiful—with gentle hands and long hair dark as a moonless night."

"I'm sure she loved you very much."

"She died of the plague. It etched black spots on her fair skin and burned the life out of her. After that, we left Toledo and came to Granada. I was only eleven."

A high, piercing wail broke her reminiscence. Sara jumped. *The muezzin's call to prayer—is it dusk already?*

"My father and brothers will get up from siesta soon. They'll be hungry." Sara Elena leaped to her feet, but Margarita pulled her back.

"Sara Elena, there's one more thing. Listen to me— inquisitors are in the neighborhood. You know what that means."

"What?"

"Don't show your Jewish ways." Margarita brushed a stray wisp of hair back from the younger woman's face.

"But I'm a Christian, as is all my family. I believe in Jesus, the Messiah." She shot out her chin.

"So, promise me—"

She jumped up. "I've got to go now. There's stew to make—two onions, please."

Margarita chose two of the best she had that day and folded them into a cloth, tying up the ends to make a pouch. Sara Elena dropped a coin in her friend's hand.

"Goodbye, Margarita."

Sara Elena looked down and noticed her pendant was showing, the one given to her when she was ten years old. Sara tucked the six-pointed star back inside her neckline. *No, Mother. I will never part with my necklace.*

A sharp wind knifed through her shawl as she walked through the empty streets. She thought about what Margarita had said. *Be careful. Hide your Jewish ways. Don't go anywhere alone. I've heard it a million times!*

A sharp wind blew, cooling her heated cheeks. A few pebbles scattered across the cobblestones behind her. Hair prickled on the back of her neck. She sensed an evil presence. Was someone hiding in the shadows? *Am I imagining it, or is someone watching me? It's not the first time I've felt followed.*

Sara forced herself to think of something else—anything. *It's so easy to blame the Jews. Father says the lower-class Christians covet their money and the nobles desire their influence. And what do I think? I think the Catholic Monarchs just want to fatten their treasury.*

She glanced at the darkening sky. *It's getting late—better hurry.*

Sara Elena dropped her head and rounded the final corner before her doorway. Tripping on a loose cobblestone, she fell sideways into a black-robed figure that emerged from the shadows. Her shawl twisted around her and her pendant flew off. Her parcel bumped onto the pavement. The figure in black reeled from the collision and let out a grunt. As she lay on the ground, Sara Elena looked up into granite-cold eyes.

Is that greed I see?

Chapter 2

❋

"Don Antonio Morales, assistant to the Grand Inquisitor, at your service, *señorita*." He brushed off the mud and dust from his once-immaculate garb.

"You are Sara Elena Torres, no?"

"Yes, I am." Sara Elena rolled onto her knees.

"I have a message for you and your father, Don Alonzo." He stopped to draw a breath and look at her.

"Pardon my manners—do you need help getting up?" Don Antonio's face tightened into a mask. The veins in his neck bulged like coiling snakes, as if he was struggling to extend kindness. He offered a stiff hand to Sara Elena. It trembled.

"No, *gracias*. I can manage myself."

Sara Elena reached out her hand to scoop up the pendant that lay on the cobblestones near her. She pushed herself up into a kneeling position. Blood oozed through her torn dress sleeve. Sara's fingers wrapped around the pendant and eased it into her *bolsa*. She brushed off her skirt, grabbed her parcel and stood up. Meanwhile, she brushed her hands against her skirt.

"Why did you come yourself? Why not send a messenger?"

He tightened his lips together and said nothing for a moment.

She picked out bits of gravel from the raw, scraped skin of her palms, wiped blood off with a part of her skirt, and waited for his answer.

"I've been sent," he started again, "not by my master Bishop Torquemada, but by Her Majesty Queen Isabella's secretary. He asked me to deliver this message and await your reply."

Sara Elena sighed with relief as she took the note from Don Antonio. At least she was not being summoned before the Inquisition. The heavy parchment scroll felt smooth in her roughened hands. The crimson wax seal bore the imprint of a shield of castles and roaring lions—the royal insignia. She broke the seal, unrolled the parchment and read:

To Señorita Sara Elena de Torres,

Your father, Don Alonzo, has told me that you are skilled in copying documents. I have a special document of some delicacy that I would like you alone to work on. Please come to the palace at ten o'clock tomorrow morning, and present yourself to me. If I determine that you are well qualified, I will entrust you with this job. Ask your father to accompany you, and inform Don Antonio of your reply.

Signed, José Carlos Cabrales

Secretary to Isabella, Queen of Castile and León

"Tell Don Cabrales that we are honored to attend, at his request. Don Alonzo, my father, and I will be there without fail tomorrow morning." She curtsied.

"I will tell him." Don Antonio turned to leave, and then stopped. He peered over his shoulder and down his long, bony nose at Sara Elena. "You are a New Christian, Señorita Torres?"

"Our family has been Christian for a long time." She squeaked out the words.

"That's not true. Your family became Christians just a generation ago."

"How do you know this?" She searched his face for the answer.

"You must not wear rich clothing." He raked his eyes over her from head to hem.

"I see, however, you're wearing a fine woolen shawl and good jewelry. How can you explain this?"

Sara Elena avoided Don Antonio's eyes. "The shawl is a recent present, and the jewelry is a family keepsake. I ask your Grace's pardon." She curtsied with knees suddenly weak.

"Demonstrate true faith and character or—"

"I'll remember, Don Antonio." She closed her lips tight, her face sculpted stone.

Don Antonio's narrow smile revealed one cracked tooth, but generated no warmth. And his eyes lingered an instant too long on her countenance. After a moment, Don Antonio adjusted his cloak and walked up the narrow street that led to the broader avenue beyond.

What does he want from me?

Sara Elena watched the rain drain away. It trickled between the rows of red tiles on the roof, splashed onto the street below, and slid its way around the well-worn cobblestones.

He could make your blood freeze. Sara noticed the blood oozing from her hands had stopped. *He has!* Her lips curved up at that thought, but other ideas crowded in. *How could one man be allowed to do that to me? How many others dread his appearance?*

She kicked a loose cobblestone and yelped with pain. Sara Elena limped down the narrow lane the rest of the way home. She ducked into the door just in time to see her father enter the common room, yawning.

"Where have you been, Daughter? It's getting late—almost dark, too." He bent and kissed her on both cheeks.

"*Dos besitos* for my dear Sarita."

He pulled away from her, congealed blood staining his hands.

"You're hurt! What happened to you, Sara? And what's that you're clutching?"

"I tripped and fell down just outside—a loose cobblestone. It's nothing."

She turned and moved toward the kitchen.

"I bought some onions for the stew. Are you hungry? Would you like some bread or some olives?" Sara put down the scroll and onions on the scrubbed oak table.

"Yes, I'm as hungry as a Castilian lion—" said Father. He cupped her reddened hands in his. "But you need help. Let me get some water and a cloth to clean your hands." He drew himself up as straight as he could, as if shaking off the siesta sleepiness from his body. Filling a bowl with water, he met Sara at the table.

"Sit down here, Sara, and tell me more while I tend your cuts and scratches."

Don Alonzo's grey hair gleamed in the candlelight as he washed and bandaged her hands. A neatly trimmed beard clung to his angular jaw line. He listened and nodded.

"So, we'll see the Queen's secretary tomorrow." He stopped and clenched his fists. "Look, my hands are trembling—and it's not from fear."

"It's not so bad, Father."

"I've tried to ignore it—just a passing affliction."

"Yes."

"But the quivering increases each year."

"It's really not that noticeable."

"Will I have to give up my translation work?"

"We don't know that." She wanted to reassure him.

"What will become of the family then?" A tear gleamed in his eye.

"We'll all help you—Luis, Raul and I." Sara Elena grabbed his hands. Her own bandaged one throbbed.

"*Gracias, mi hija.* That eases my mind."

"No worries about the future, Papa. Each day has enough troubles of its own."

Don Alonzo got up. "Let me get you some bread, or some wine to drink, Sarita, while you change your gown." He smiled at her, kindness smoothing away the lines of worry.

Raul strode into the kitchen, as if an entourage were following at his heels. "I'll get the wine." Raul, dressed in fitted black hose and deep indigo doublet, sauntered over to the small alcove where cooking staples were kept.

"Where is the *tinto*? Ah, yes, here it is." He took a bottle of red wine from the wooden wine holder. He uncorked it with a flourish and swirled a swallow around in a goblet before downing it.

Next to the wine rack sat the large terracotta urn with lid. When full, it could hold many liters of olive oil. Flour was stored in another pot, and dried beans in another. Raul tapped each pot and frowned.

"These pots sound empty. We need to refill our food stores soon, Sara."

"Yes, King Raul," said Sara Elena, returning in a clean dress. "And how should we do that?"

"What happened to you?" Raul dropped the pretense and took a step toward his sister.

"Just clumsiness—don't worry." She picked up a cutting board, chopped the onions, and slid them into the cooking pot hanging over the hearth. She took a spoon and stirred the mixture of lamb, white beans, garlic, and onions. Lamb meat was scarce, but she had managed to get a few meaty bones. Taking a small taste, she turned back to the counter to find the salt. She dropped a pinch into the thick, bubbling liquid.

"We'll be able to get more of everything next Thursday," said Raul. "A caravan of traders should bring food to the market then." He stuck a spoon in the stew, blew on it, and sipped a taste.

"Little sister, you do so much with so little. This is delicious." He ran his tongue over his lips to capture all the broth.

"Thanks, I love cooking—" Sara Elena wrinkled her nose. "But not cleaning!"

"Life has become busier for you since Ana left," said Raul.

"Such a wonderful housekeeper—" Sara continued.

"But money was scarce," said Father. "At least, she could go to live with her son when we could no longer pay her."

"Yes, Papa," said Sara Elena, "but she cried at the final goodbye."

Just then, Luis swept in from the street, bringing a gust of cold air. He took off his cloak, a heavy, deep green expanse of cloth that covered him well below his knees. He unfastened the tie that held it closed, and threw the cloak onto a metal hook in the entry.

"I feel like celebrating," roared Luis. "I have a surprise for you, Sara." Although Father had trained Luis in translation, his great love was adventure. He spent a good deal of time outdoors.

"You have a voice loud enough to echo across the mountaintops." Father clamped wrinkled hands over his ears.

"It's my adventure voice—not for the translation table, right, Father?"

"What is it? Show me!" Sara Elena hopped up and down and patted his cloak.

"Not till after supper—keep away!" He held the package high over her reaching hands.

"Well, let's eat, then," said Sara, as she scurried to get bowls and cutlery from the cupboard. She dished a generous portion of stew into each person's bowl, and set a loaf of round shepherd's bread onto a plate. She gathered up spoons and a sharp knife for cutting the bread.

"Come and sit down, everyone."

"Here's the wine," said Raul. With fingers laced through the four goblets, he glided to the table.

"Be careful. You'll break the wine glasses," scolded Sara Elena.

"Yes, little mother."

"Here's a bowl of olives," offered Father, "and a few almonds." He walked slowly carrying two small bowls. The almonds clattered against the side of the bowl and one dropped out. He placed them in the center of the table and slumped down on the chair at the end. Then he took up one of the goblets and straightened his back.

"I wish to propose a toast: To Sara Elena. Although it's not customary to celebrate birthdays, I remember this time of year with fondness. You were born in December. May you always remember your family loves you, may you prosper in the coming year—" He paused. "And may you soon find a worthy husband." He took a hearty swallow.

"Papa, please!" Color crept up Sara's neck and into her cheeks, as Luis and Raul chuckled. "It's not so easy to find a husband now, and besides I am busy keeping the house and doing translation."

"It would be easier if you were willing," said Don Alonzo with a stern look. "A man needs a little encouragement."

Raul countered, "Sara's right. Blame it on politics. A generation ago, marrying a *converso* woman meant a man could expect a good dowry and higher social position. Now, Torquemada's men shove their noses into every barrio, sniffing out unorthodoxy. A good Christian man is afraid he will be tainted by a wife of Jewish heritage—no matter how devout the woman appears."

"Surely it cannot be so. Has the world changed that much?" Don Alonzo sighed and shook his head.

"Yes, Father," agreed Luis. "It's true, but I want to know what Sara meant about being busy with translation." His eyes met Sara Elena's. "As far as I know, you just help Father and me occasionally, no? What makes you so busy?"

"I have a meeting with the Queen's secretary tomorrow. It's in that scroll." Sara pointed to the rolled message on the table. "He wants me, only me, to copy a manuscript for Her Majesty." Sara Elena flipped her hair back from her face and smiled. "He called it 'a document of some delicacy.' And Father, you must come, too."

"Well, I'm glad you told me."

"You're lucky," said Raul. "You've caught the Queen's eye. That can be good or it can be bad. Just be careful not to venture an opinion unless asked. You have so many of them, you know."

Sara jabbed him in the ribs with her elbow.

"Be careful, be careful. Everyone tells me to be careful. I am sick of hearing it! I can handle myself very well." Sara Elena's eyes flamed.

"See that you do."

"Calm down, Sarita. You sound like a spoiled child."

"Let's celebrate your good fortune," Luis broke in. "Here's my surprise." He held out a small box.

Sara untied the string and looked inside. "*Tocino de cielo*—my favorite! How did you find it when the fortress is under siege?"

"You mean the off and on war? Is there a siege or not at the moment?"

"Be serious."

"All right. There is a truce now since November 25th, so Boabdil can prepare to evacuate."

"And the *tocino de cielo*?"

"I have my sources."

She sniffed the rich, reddish caramel and egg custard called 'heavenly bacon.'

"It smells wonderful! Thanks. Luis."

"Well, it seems part of my toast will come true tomorrow," said Father.

"Finding a husband for Sara?" said Luis.

"No, finding prosperity. Be humble, be pleasing, Sara Elena, and you may have a permanent job with the Queen."

Sara Elena began her preparations long before the appointed time to go. She heated water and poured it into a pottery bowl. After lathering her hands and face with a sliver of rosemary soap, she blotted her face with a piece of rough linen. Since she had only two shifts, she slipped into her best one.

Now, what should I wear? Would the Queen's secretary think me presumptuous to wear elegant clothing? I just can't meet the Queen's secretary in a plain dress.

She pushed aside her coarse black homespun dresses.

Converso dress code is so unfair!

She eliminated her green velvet gown—she had outgrown it when she was fifteen. Next to it, she also discounted the wine brocade—too frayed. Finally, in a far corner she found the lapis blue dress.

My mother's old dress—not the current fashion, but it's still beautiful. She admired the flowing satin gown. Called a houppelande, it had a high waist and low, square neckline accented with braided ribbon. The long sleeves split just below the elbow and flared out to reveal the fitted sleeves of her shift.

Now for my hair—Sara Elena attacked the tangles. Her heavy waves had to be forcibly controlled. Although young women didn't conceal their hair as married women did, she put on a close-fitting ivory cap. Her long hair cascaded down onto her shoulders, but at least the stray strands that curled onto her forehead seemed temporarily controlled.

Her soft leather shoes still felt damp from yesterday's downpour. As she finished applying pomegranate juice to redden her lips, Father came around the corner.

"You look lovely, Sarita. A bit daring, don't you think?"

"Oh, Papa, I have to look my best. I want to make a good impression for the sake of our family."

"You will." He handed her two scrolls of paper. "Sara, I have some manuscripts to return to the palace. One is a translation from Hebrew to Latin, and the other from Castilian."

Sara glanced down at her father's handwriting. The letters had wide, uneven loops, instead of narrow and oval. Alonzo noticed her scowl.

"I know, I know. My penmanship is getting worse. I will need assistance soon, to help me keep up with my work demands."

"Can't Luis do it?"

"No. Luis loves action more than translation work. He always runs after the latest adventurer, doting on their stories of new worlds and strange sights. There are some Arabic parchments due next week, and he just sits in the *bodega* talking to dreamers."

21

"I could help you. You know I understand Arabic. I've looked over your shoulder so many times during my life while you were working. I can read it. And I hear it in the streets. Please—"

"Open that small parchment in your hand. It's not Arabic, by the way, but old Castilian. Tell me what you think it says."

Sara unrolled the stiff paper with care. "It's a poem. Let's see—"

> *Calladvos, Señor,*
> *nuestro Redentor,*
> *que vuestro dolor*
> *durara poquito*

"It's a lullaby:

> 'Be still, Lord,
> our Redeemer,
> may your pain
> last but a little while.'"

"Translation comes easily for you."

"Thanks, Father, but that really wasn't so hard." She glanced at him, eyes open and waiting.

"Will you let me help you with translation, then?" She handed the roll of paper back to him.

"We'll see. Let's talk after our meeting today." He turned toward her. "You know it's dangerous to translate scriptures. The Inquisition frowns on it—"

"But if the Queen requests it, surely—"

Luis burst into the room. "I got the buggy ready. It's time you left."

"I thought you were working on translating that document. It's due next week." Father frowned.

"Fell asleep in the middle. I can't—"

"*How exciting!*" Sara rushed to the door. The buggy had been in the family forever, and showed signs of wear. But there it was! It was still impressive despite a few scratches on its finish and the much-repaired bridles on the two family horses.

Father smoothed out his best waistcoat and picked up his walking stick.

"Esperanza is getting older, but Tico will keep her going."

Luis patted the two sleek horses that lifted their heads as they heard their names. "You've brushed their coats and groomed their manes."

"It's not Queen Isabella's coach but it will serve," said Luis. "My lady—"

He bowed low and offered his arm as Sara mounted the two steps. Then he steadied Father as he stumped his way into the buggy, walking staff in hand. Father took the reins.

"I can still handle the horses." He threw his stick under the seat.

Luis nodded his head and gave Tico a slap on his flank.

"Good fortune to you, Sister."

Sara Elena waved as the buggy moved forward. The sun already promised to warm the day. Its rays reached into the open buggy and caressed her cheeks. A cloudless sky signaled a change, perhaps a new start for her and her family. The family fortune had dwindled to an alarming state over the last few years. *A steady source of income would really help.*

Father interrupted her thoughts—"Behave yourself, Sara Elena." Don Alonzo winked. "I'm very proud of you."

"I will—and thank you, Papa."

Sara Elena straightened her back as they bumped along the cobblestones. Still damp from the morning dew, they smelled of wet rocks and sunshine. She wanted to enjoy this moment. They didn't hitch up the buggy much anymore.

Father began talking, rambling about recent events in Granada—the siege.

"I can't believe it's gone on for ten years. So much hardship—so much war!"

"Yes, Papa."

Sara's thoughts floated like the few wispy clouds above. Random, not fully formed. *What will happen to me in the next few years? Life is so uncertain—do I have a future?*

The cobblestones became dirt roads as they headed out the city gates. Swallows dipped and soared through the stone portal, daring each other to a game of aerial tag. The rolling plains spread out like an old, patched blanket. It lay still and lifeless, deadened by winter and scorched by enemy sabotage. Dust curled up and made her nose itch. Sara sneezed.

"Papa?"

"Almost there." Father clucked at the horses and flicked the reins. "See the flags over there? That's our destination."

"No, I wanted to ask you—"

Sara Elena squinted and shaded her eyes. Red lions and gold castles fluttered on a flag in the distance over Santa Fe, the wartime dwellings of the royals.

"Papa, do you think I'll ever find a husband?"

"Daydreaming?"

"Yes, I guess so." Sara Elena laughed. "I was just thinking about the royal couple. They have a different kind of marriage."

"Right—they pledged to each other '*tanto monta, monta tanto*,' 'Isabella is equal to Ferdinand.'"

"So gallant."

"Yes, but remember Isabella already had power as the Queen of Castile and León."

Sara Elena's mind drifted. *A man with whom you could speak freely and express your own opinions is a rare thing.*

Are only the privileged allowed such a pleasure? Could I ever find such a man?

She shifted on the buggy seat, stiff from the ride.

"Almost there, Sarita." Father slowed the horses and let out a sigh.

The buggy drew up to the royal residence. Heavy oak doors creaked open. A man came rushing out, cutting in front of their path. Startled by the sudden stop, the horses shied and reared up. Don Alonzo's eyes started and his nostrils flared.

"Watch where you're going," he yelled.

The man glanced up, cold steel in his eyes. His compact body vibrated and his fists clenched. He shook one fist while clamping his other hand tighter against his side. Several large rolls of paper threatened to topple from his shoulder bag. The wind stirred up his wispy white hair to blown hay. His eyes blazed. Sara Elena caught at her hair and averted her eyes.

"Control your horses, sir!" He smoothed his hair in one brief motion and set out again.

"Are you coming, Juan?"

Only the ablest of men could keep up with such a stride. And he did. Flapping cloak and pummeling legs streaked past the buggy. The young man tipped his hat in flight.

"I apologize for the captain's outburst. He's under a lot of pressure."

A lean body and strong jaw was all Sara Elena had time to see. A scar on his left cheek, and green eyes. *Intriguing!*

Chapter 3

"Who was that rude man?" Sara Elena asked the footman.

"Señor Columbus, señorita."

"What does he want?"

"Has the crazy idea of finding a new trade route. He says he can navigate around the world in three months."

"Why is he at the royal residence?"

"He wants boats and men to make a voyage westward—needs money from Their Majesties."

"That seems ill-timed." Father felt for his cane in the back of the buggy.

"Sí, señor. All their money goes to the Grand Effort."

"The Grand Effort?" Don Alonzo descended with stiff movements and planted his cane for support.

"That's what I call it. Pushing out the infidels, you know."

"Oh, yes."

"I'll take your horses." A boy dressed in a striped shirt led the horses away.

"Take good care of them," said Don Alonzo.

The boy looked up and nodded. "Yes, sir. A brushing, a cool drink of water and a handful of oats."

"Follow me. Don Cabrales is waiting."

The footman, dressed in a doublet bearing the gold castles and red lions of the monarchy, led them through the entry. Sara noticed the artistic pattern of the cobblestones leading to the palace entrance. She felt the sharp ends of the embedded rocks through her soft leather shoes. The rosy sandstone walls and flowing frieze of sculpted plaster vines copied the Moorish manner of architecture. Sara Elena looked up to the roof and noticed a black bird eyeing her.

An omen of bad luck?

Sara Elena and Don Alonzo passed many guards in royal uniform before following the footman through a grand portal. They stepped into an inner tiled patio heavy with the scent of orange blossoms. Set against the walls on each side, two potted trees basked in the warmth of reflected rays and had grown full and green. Orange trees often bloomed, even as they held fruit from the past year.

A flash of light and then fleeting blindness filled her eyes as they passed from bright sunlight to velvety darkness.

"Wait here until you are summoned." The footman stopped abruptly and had them sit on a marble bench along the wall of the entry *sala*. He bent in a short bow, turned on his heel, and vanished. Don Alonzo sat down heavily.

"Come and sit by me, Sara," he said. "It won't be long." Sara Elena perched on the bench's edge. Its cold smoothness seeped through the folds of her dress. She shivered.

They waited.

"Don Cabrales will see you now."

A page pulled back the heavy tapestry curtains covering the doorway and motioned them to go through. They stood in a long rectangular room. Polished wood paneling glowed on all the walls. Carved acanthus leaves flowed up and down the legs of a solid table. A brocaded gold tapestry had been thrown over it and candelabra placed there and around the room glowed with a host of candles. An owlish scribe occupied a small table set near the one window. A copper brazier of red coals warmed the space.

"Don Alonzo de Torres and his daughter, Señorita Sara Elena."

Deep rugs and draperies muffled the page's booming voice. Sara Elena stole a glance at the figure seated at the table.

"Yes, yes, thank you," said Don Cabrales, and waved a dismissive hand at the page. He continued dictating as the scribe scratched words on a parchment.

Don Alonzo and Sara Elena waited.

"Come forward, Don Alonzo, and bring your daughter." Don Cabrales remembered his visitors.

Father gave a quick nod and a half smile to Sara Elena, and then stepped forward with head bowed. Sara Elena followed his example. She lifted her skirts just enough to keep from tripping on them.

I will not fall in the palace!

Sara Elena and her silver-haired father stopped at a respectful distance from the Queen's secretary and looked up.

Don Cabrales greeted them with a long, thoughtful gaze and indicated they should be seated. "I see that you have the same auburn hair and blue eyes, Sara Elena, as our great Queen."

Sara Elena sucked in her breath. She nodded, unable to think of a reply.

Don Cabrales looked her up and down for what seemed an eternity. He had a hawkish nose and piercing eyes. He turned his look toward Sara's father.

"Don Alonzo, have you brought back my manuscripts?"

"I have." He held out the two scrolls and bowed low. "I believe you will find them satisfactory."

"Yes, yes. I'm sure I will." The Queen's secretary glanced at the documents, and then scratched a note on a piece of paper. He summoned a page.

"Take this to the keeper of the purse. Don Alonzo shall be paid before he leaves today." The page slipped away.

"Thank you," said Don Alonzo, and dipped his head.

"*De nada*. You always give good service. Now then, tell me, is your daughter good at translation?"

"She has skill but not much experience, sir."

"In which languages is she proficient?"

"Hebrew and the Castilian idiom."

"And Arabic," Sara Elena blurted out. "I learned Arabic on the streets of Toledo when I was a little girl. I know Latin, too." Sara Elena stopped abruptly, as she saw the secretary's face cloud.

"She certainly is forward, Don Alonzo. Can she learn to hold her tongue?"

"She is an obedient girl, sir. And she will work hard for you." Sara saw his eyes narrow and his head shake.

"Are you trustworthy, child?" Don Cabrales looked straight at Sara Elena, who was trying to stifle a retort. "Can you keep quiet when required?"

"I beg your pardon, Don Carlos. Yes, I can." She hurried on, "I can be quiet as a fluttering leaf, quiet as a reflecting pond, quiet as . . ."

"Enough," Don Carlos slammed his hand on the thick table. The inkwell bounced. "I am not so sure, but I do like your spirit. Let me consider whether I can use you for my project. Leave me now, you and your Father. I will send you word in a few days." Don Cabrales waved them off and looked down at the parchments covering his desk.

"I must attend the Queen—Her Majesty is waiting." Don Alonzo and Sara Elena bowed their heads and backed their way out of the secretary's presence.

"Sara Elena, you tread on dangerous ground. Can't you learn to keep your mouth shut—especially in front of the Queen's secretary?"

"I just wanted to answer his question."

"Speaking without permission is . . ."

"He called me a child!"

"And you continue to act like one!"

"Your payment, sir," said a man coming toward them. "Don Cabrales instructed me on the amount already." He handed the small pouch to Don Alonzo.

"Please find your way out."

"Very well," said Father. "Come, Sarita."

Sara Elena took her father's arm, pushed a strand of hair into her cap, and walked out into the entry *sala*. They noticed two men of Moorish face and costume sitting on the same marble bench where they had sat earlier. The men spoke in whispered voices. Sara Elena kept her head looking straight ahead, while straining to hear what they were saying. The only words she could make out were "It's a disgrace." Father halted and listened intently, all the while pretending he had stopped to rest a while on his cane.

"Did you catch what they said?" Sara Elena asked. "I couldn't quite get it."

"I must report this to the King and Queen," he muttered.

Luis watched as Father and Sara climbed into the buggy and drove away. After the sounds of their leaving died away, he returned to his translating.

Letters soon danced before his eyes. "Why is this so tedious? I don't understand this phrase." His eyes burned like embers and rubbing them only blurred his vision.

"Ouch." He wiped his eyes with his new handkerchief and buckled down to the job before him. The heavy legal language pulled at his eyelids.

When Luis awoke, the sun had reached the rooftops.

I need some fresh air, and the latest gossip.

Luis slipped out with a cloak thrown around his shoulders. A cold December day greeted him. The Alhambra perched on the hill above Granada gleamed vermillion red. Whitewashed houses nestled in the town below sparkled like babies' teeth. The sun shone brightly, and began its daily job of penetrating the dark corners and slender streets. Set low in the winter sky, its piercing rays hit him straight in the face. He squinted and shaded his eyes with his right hand. Just then, a passing soldier saluted in reply. Luis laughed.

What will I discover today?

Luis grinned and squared his shoulders. His dark hair curled in damp weather, but today it hung in smooth waves under his black felt hat. He had a solid, compact body, with strong arms and shoulders. The biting wind reminded him it was still winter. He pulled his cloak around him. As he walked along, he became solemn again. He kicked at a lone dog sitting near an arched doorway.

Am I doomed to sit at a desk all my life? Father keeps me working like a slave on translation work. As soon as I complete one, two new scrolls appear. And Raul always points out my mistakes. Father is much better at this translation than I am. Even Sara is better.

Luis strode down the rock-encrusted walkway toward *Bodega Aventuras*. He often went there to hear the latest talk. The *cerveza* was hearty, the olives tasty, and the conversation lively. Nobody bothered him there. He was considered an equal. As he reached the door, he heard church bells chime.

Even though only a few hardy souls occupied tables at half past ten in the morning, the bodega reeked of garlic, onions, and sweat. Near the hearth sat a man in an enormous gray cape. At least it seemed to be a man. All Luis could see was steam rising from his clothing. Luis ambled over to the counter.

"*Cómo estás*, Luis," called Mico, the owner, from behind the counter. He had bowed legs and walked with a shuffling gait—an old spear wound, he claimed. With his long, hairy arms it was easy to see why everyone called him 'Monkey.'

"*Hola*, Mico. Give me a beer and a portion of *jamón serrano*."

"What's new with you?" Mico filled an earthenware cup, and walked over to a leg of ham hanging from the ceiling. He sliced four thin strips of the air-cured meat and arranged it fan-shape on a crockery plate.

"Just the usual—deciphering old manuscripts," said Luis. "Is there any news about the siege?"

Mico always had his eyes and ears open. Soldiers came in. They talked. Anything that happened in Granada, Mico was the first to know.

"There's news that the siege will end shortly. I heard two soldiers discussing it yesterday. They said Boabdil and his troops have run out of food. They've lost the will to resist. Soon there will be an end to war. We can all start living again."

"Ha. I'll believe it when I see it." Luis gave Mico a few *blancas* and took his refreshments to a small table. He sat down on the wooden stool and immediately jumped up again. "Ay! My rump! A pox on you, Mico," he yelped. "Every time I come here I get splinters!"

He reached back and pulled out the offending sliver and rubbed his posterior.

"And I say you are stealing my furniture piece by piece." Mico struggled to keep the smile from overtaking his face. A laugh exploded from his mouth.

At the same time, a loud snort and bellowing laugh erupted from beneath the gray cloak. The man turned around and dropped the cloak from his shoulders, showing a face brick-hard as a castle wall. Bright blue eyes glowed like coals at the center of a fire. Although he looked to be forty, his hair was totally white.

"You are fortunate, my friend. You cannot get very much for free in Granada these days. And such quality! That stool looks like the finest oak."

"Who are you, sir?" asked Luis, the corners of his mouth bending upward.

"I am Cristóbol Colón—Columbus—admiral of the seas, adventurer, and discoverer of new worlds." He removed his hat with a flourish and bowed his head slightly.

"And who might you be, young man?"

"Luis de Torres, translator of Hebrew, Latin, Aramaic and Arabic, and amateur astronomer."

Luis returned his gaze steadily.

"And what plans to you have for your life?"

"I don't know." Luis shrugged. "How can anyone plan? I suppose I'll continue working with my Father and brother translating documents."

"I see. But what do you dream of doing?"

"What do you mean?" Luis licked his dry lips.

"Well, take me, for example—I have a dream to get some boats, find a crew, and sail westward. I believe that I can find a new way to the East, and perhaps a new world. Yes, I believe it is possible, young man. I see your doubt. I have been a mariner for half of my life. I have studied and followed the invisible paths in the sea."

"I know there are currents in the sea," said Luis. "Is that what you mean?"

"That, and the westerly winds. Here, let me show you." He heaved himself out of his chair, bringing a scroll. He sat down next to Luis and unrolled the nautical chart.

"The ancients observed the movement of the stars—Eratosthenes is one—and concluded that the earth is round. They estimated the breadth of the oceans and land at about 27,000 miles. And twenty years ago, in 1474, Toscanelli of Florence made almost the same calculation. He concluded that if one sails to the west, he will come directly to Cipangu, Cathay, and India." He paused to draw breath.

"What? Where did you learn all this?" said Luis.

"I've been pondering the information for a long time. Picked up a little bit here, a little bit there on each voyage I take."

He scratched the coarse straw on his head and leaned close.

"It's a bigger world than we think, and full of wonders, Luis." He made a sweeping gesture. "India is a treasure of spices, for example. You can go there and return with a boatload of pepper and become rich selling it."

"Really?"

"Yes, and Cipangu is thick with pearls. There is said to be a large and magnificent city in the Orient called Quinsay. It is one hundred miles in circumference and contains ten marble bridges and other artistic treasures. Its name means 'The Heavenly City'."

"Wait. I don't understand." Luis held up his hand.

But, Columbus's words raced along as he got more excited.

"The winds blow westerly from the Canary Islands at certain times of the year," he continued. "The currents in the sea go west by the southern route and east in the northern route. Toscanelli estimated that the distance from the Canary Islands across the western ocean to the fabled

Antilia is about 1,750 miles, and from Antilia to Cipangu another 2,500 miles. A good boat in full wind can sail forty miles a day. With a short stop in Antilia, to re-supply, we can make it to Cipangu or Cathay in about three months.

"I'm totally confused. How will you get back?"

We'll return by following the easterly currents for another three months. We can carry enough supplies for such a trip on our modern vessels. I know it's possible."

What was this madman talking about? Could it be possible to travel west to get to the East? Would they indeed find a new world?

Eyes bulging, Luis looked as if a lightning bolt had shot through his body.

"Tell me more."

Chapter 4

✳

Everything about Raul was average except his nose. Raul's nose angled halfway down his face in an even line, then took a quick turn right. You could forget his oak-bark eyes that faded into brown smears under thick brows. You could forget his sallow complexion and medium build. But, that nose made a lasting impression. Everyone who saw it longed to ask how it got that way. Raul never said. Instead, he carried himself proudly. After all, he was the oldest son and heir in the Torres family.

To draw attention away from his face, Raul dressed well. Today, he stepped out of the house in green hose and slashed tunic fitted closely to his body. An elegant hat with a long feather perched on his hair like a nesting bird. He had thrown a short cape over his shoulders to fight off the cold. Leather gloves completed his costume. But people still noticed his nose because of one annoying fact. His nose whistled whenever he got excited, as it did now.

Raul pulled a scrap of paper from his sleeve and studied it.

Today is a momentous day—a day that could change my whole world. Raul drew in a long breath. "Let's see—what's first on my list of things to do?"

A person walking by just then might have noticed a hesitation in his manner and wonder to whom he was talking. In truth, he didn't know if fear or excitement would win over. Both vied for supremacy deep inside his belly.

"See Montalvo about shop space," the list demanded.

"Ah, yes. I have an appointment with Eduardo Montalvo, the man who holds the key to my future. Better hurry."

He stuffed the list back in his sleeve and strode off quickly. Calle de la Vega, just two blocks away, contained a long row of offices and shops. A tailor shop stood next to a shoemaker, a lace maker, and a bakery. A clerk's office stood at the end of the street, occupied by Señor Montalvo. Beyond it, in a quiet alcove, sat a vacant storefront.

For over two years now, I have been planning this move into the cartography business. I love working with maps. I never tire of unrolling their thick vellum and smelling the faint mustiness as they spread out on the table. I could study their features for hours and get lost wondering what lies beyond the erratic coastlines, bays and islands.

"Well, that's poetic, Raul. Let's be realistic." His nose whistled again, or more precisely, it wheezed. "My damaged nose is to blame for that annoying habit." His thoughts resumed.

It's not that I want to travel. Travel is dangerous, dirty and costly. That's why cartography is perfect. I can record the discoveries others have made without ever leaving Spain.

He continued rehearsing his reasoning as he walked toward Montalvo's shop.

"Maps have tremendous importance, providing direction into both known and undiscovered territory. Mariners need charts. I will provide them with the best. Every mariner will want Raul de Torres charts."

Raul squared up his shoulders and rapped on Sr. Montalvo's door. He heard shuffling sounds inside, then a click as the latch lifted.

"Señor Montalvo."

"Ah, yes, Raul. Come in." Sr. Montalvo, buyer and seller of properties as well as town clerk, looked at him with watery eyes. His flat nose and elongated jaw line under a head of curly white hair gave him a sheep-like look. He led the way to a polished oak desk and motioned for Raul to follow.

"Now then, Raul, sit down. I understand you wanted to see me on some business."

"Yes, sir." Raul cleared his throat. "I don't know where to start."

"At the beginning, of course."

"Yes, sir. Don Eduardo, you've been a friend of my father's for many years, haven't you?"

"Yes. How is your father?" Montalvo leaned back and picked at a ragged cuticle.

"He's well, thank you." Raul leaned forward in his chair. "My father has translated many foreign deeds and documents for you, hasn't he?"

"Yes, yes—" Montalvo drummed his fingertips on the desk.

"His translations helped settle property disputes because of accurate language, didn't they?"

"Of course. I am indebted to him for that—" He stroked his chin with thick-nailed fingers.

"And he helped you when your own wife died of the plague—" The rush of words left Raul panting.

"Yes, yes. Don Alonzo has been a great consolation to me, it is true." Creases formed in Sr. Montalvo's forehead, and his eyes narrowed. "But what has this to do with your matter of business?"

"Don Eduardo. I would like to ask a favor." Raul gulped and surged ahead. "I want to open a cartography shop, and I'd like to purchase the shop space next door."

"A cartography shop, you say? What do you propose to pay?"

"I have saved a great many *maravedis*, and hope to come by a large sum soon."

"You know the price I ask?"

"Yes, sir."

Sr. Montalvo leaned back in his chair and tapped fungus-thickened fingertips together while he studied Raul's face.

"And just what is it that makes you think you are qualified to be a map-maker?"

"Sir, I have studied drawing and chart drafting secretly for the past two years with Enrique Loza, the cartographer on the other side of town. I've also talked with him about how to begin such an enterprise."

"Where will the *maravedis* come from—your beloved's dowry, perhaps?"

Raul's neck colored.

"Your betrothed trusts you with her dowry?" Two shaggy white eyebrows leaped up over Montalvo's watery eyes.

"Yes—but of course we are not officially betrothed yet." His throat tightened.

"That makes it all the more amazing."

"Will you help me, Don Eduardo? I can make a large initial payment, and then pay you the rest, a little each month."

"What does Don Alonzo think of this?"

"He knows I want to be independent."

"Shouldn't you carry on the family business?"

"Are you my judge and accuser? My father knows I will always try to make him proud of me." Wheeze.

"He doesn't know of your plan yet, is that it?" Montalvo leaned forward, meeting Raul's gaze.

"No." Raul glanced down at his fingernails. Ink stains had etched semi-circles around all his cuticles. "But I'm sure he will approve, when he finds out."

"It's not such an easy job, running a business, Raul. You have to manage expenses, attract clients, and anticipate the unexpected." Montalvo nodded his head. "Yes, yes, always the unexpected. Add to that political unrest and it seems everything is against you."

"I can do it." Raul's voice sounded no more than a whisper.

"That's the Torres family spirit. 'I can do it.' I've heard that many times on your Father's lips."

"And he always managed to do what he said, didn't he?"

"Yes," sighed Don Eduardo, "and I expect you will, too. But you are not like your father. You don't have the same fierce spirit to succeed. And no experience."

"Will you help me or not?" Raul's nose whistled as he lifted his chin high.

"I will help you in some fashion, Raul, but before we sign any agreements, you must tell your father." Don Eduardo paused. "You still didn't answer my question. Shouldn't you be carrying on the family business of interpretation?"

"Luis can handle that. And Sara Elena wants to learn the trade, also."

"A woman! How unusual."

"What's your answer, Don Eduardo?"

"Bring Don Alonzo with you to look over the papers. I won't proceed until I know your father approves. I don't want him for an enemy. *Es claro?*"

"*Gracias*, Don Eduardo. Many thanks. I am very grateful." No sunny day could outshine Raul's face just then.

"So, you will sell me the shop space?"

"Or possibly rent it. Now, go and tell your sweetheart. It looks like you can get married, now that you're a man of business. Remember my conditions."

"Thank you, thank you, Don Eduardo. But, I hope you will sell it." Raul grasped Sr. Montalvo's hand and pumped it as if drawing water from a well. He grabbed up his cape, flung it over his shoulders and hurried to the door.

"Thank you again, I'll be back in a few days with my father. *Dios te bendiga*. God bless you, Sr. Montalvo."

"I am happy for you. By the way, how is your sister?"

"Fine, sir."

"She must have many suitors."

Raul's eyebrows slanted up at Sr. Montalvo before he flew out the door. Don Eduardo waved after him.

On the street, Raul pulled out his list again.

"Buy a red carnation," ordered the list.

"Will Don Eduardo really help me get started? His words didn't exactly discourage the plan, but I mean to move ahead with it. Should I buy a red carnation or not?" Raul hesitated.

"I must move ahead and not worry about details. When Beata sees the flower she'll know that all my plans have worked out. I mean—our plans."

Raul smiled, his decision made, and hurried to the nearest flower vendor.

Don Alonzo and Sara Elena made their way back down the sliver of a street that wound toward their home. The horses stepped faster as the streets got closer to home and stable.

"Look, Father, can I ask you something? About the Romeros?"

They left the buggy tied up in front for a few minutes.

"Ah. I thought you'd ask me sooner."

"Do you know them?"

"You might say that." Father stumped through the front door and heaved onto a bench.

"What does that mean? They've never come to our house." Sara joined him.

41

"It's complicated."

"Tell me." Sara brushed stray hairs from her face.

"There are things you don't know about our earlier life."

"Where? When?"

"In Córdoba. I did a favor for Romero, saved his life, you might say. He owes me a favor in return." His lips formed a tight red line.

"That's an answer without an answer."

"Ask him sometime. That's all I'm saying."

"That's all?" She threw up her hands. "I may never see them. They are running."

"That's all I will say. I made a promise."

Sara sighed. She hadn't learned anything yet. She changed her line of questioning.

"Now, Father—will you teach me all about translating documents?"

Don Alonzo heaved a sigh and eased a cushion under his rear. "Yes, of course."

"I need to know in a hurry. The Queen's secretary expects it."

"Do I have time to scratch my ear and take refreshment?"

Sara giggled. "I'm sorry, Papa. I guess I am a little anxious to start. Sit here and I'll bring you something. Rest a bit." She got a wooden pitcher and went to fetch wine.

"Sara, you already know a lot about translation," Don Alonzo called after her, "because you have watched me all your life. Remember how you used to come and sit on my knee while I worked at copying documents for the Duke of Alba?"

A muffled "Yes, Father" came back.

"We are living in an exciting time, Sara. You know, books are rare and expensive."

"Uh-huh."

"But now that several universities have grown up in this land, more people need professional scribes and translators. The Torres family has always excelled in translation."

"Yes, I know, Papa."

Sara re-entered with a pitcher of red wine and sloshed some into a wooden goblet. "What do they copy?"

"Usually the Holy Writings, or maybe a book of Psalms. They even make elaborate illustrations."

"Will you show me how?"

Her father gulped the wine and wiped his mouth on his sleeve. "No, Sara, the process is lengthy," he replied. "It involves drawing an illumination, embellishing it, applying gesso, and when it's dry pressing gold leaf on the gesso. It's beautiful."

"And costly," said Sara Elena.

"Yes, and it's laborious. And now, it's done less and less."

"I'm sure it would cost a great many *maravedis*. But, there is no replacement for translation work." Sara rubbed her cheek.

"Yes, that will always require a learned man—or woman."

"Now, Father," she scolded, "You were going to coach me about translation."

"I'm sorry, Sarita. How did I get off on such a wild tale?" He got up. "Let's go over to the desk and I'll show you how I go about it." He stopped—"But first a warning—"

"Yes, Father?" Sara Elena glanced up.

"The Inquisition forbids certain translation—you must not translate the Holy Writings into the current language, Spanish. It is not meant for the ordinary man or woman to read. Only priests are qualified to read and interpret God's words."

Sara Elena frowned. "Do you believe that, Father?"

They settled at the old desk. Created especially for long hours of concentration, it contained everything a serious translator might need. Don Alonzo withdrew a handful of goose quills from a mahogany box. A horn inkwell sat ready in a slot. Father took a scroll of paper and spread it out before them.

"Here's a document I'm translating for Eduardo Montalvo. You remember him, don't you?"

"Yes, I do. Our family spent many happy times with them when we were all children. Raul, Luis and I used to play with the three Montalvo children. Raul played chess with their oldest son, Ruben. Marieta, Ana and I played 'Princess and the Dragon.' We all wanted to be the princess, so we made Luis the dragon. He hated that." Sara laughed.

"We were close friends then, but since his wife also died of the Black Death, we stopped seeing them. It was a dark time in my life." Father sighed. "I still miss your mother every day."

He caught Sara's hand in his and kissed it.

"We need to work on this scroll." The sadness in his eyes melted like an afternoon cloud.

"It's an agreement between Abdel Aziz, a Moorish gentleman, and Señor Rodrigo, a Christian. The Moorish gentleman wants to sell a fine Andalusian horse to Sr. Rodrigo."

"I suppose Sr. Aziz doesn't speak much of the local language, and Sr. Rodrigo knows only a few Arabic words, right?" Sara took up the challenge.

"That's right, so we need to make it clear for both parties. Ready?" Father picked up a quill.

"Ready." Sara pulled her chair closer and peered at the manuscript.

They looked at the Arabic words, and discussed the possible meaning of several key words. After working on it for some time, Don Alonzo put down his quill.

"See, Sara, you must translate the intention of the author, even though the word is not quite the same in Castilian. In our language descriptive words come after the name words, but it is different in Arabic. They write from right to left on the page and we write from left to right. There are many things to consider, no?"

"Is it translated to your satisfaction?"

"You are the expert, Papa."

"Read it to me, please."

"Abdel Aziz, an excellent horse breeder and honest man, promises to sell a two-year-old filly by the name of Zahra, of pure Arabian lineage, to Sr. Alberto Rodrigo, of the city of Granada. The price of the horse is five hundred *maravedis*. This horse will be delivered on Friday, twenty-eighth day of December 1491, God willing, at which time the entire sum of money must be paid."

"Good. Now we copy it neatly in each language, and wait for Sr. Aziz to come. Our job is done."

"Father, I'm enjoying this. Can we try another?" She yawned and stretched.

"Very well, you choose. I have hopes, Sara, that you will soon become a fine translator."

Chapter 5

✳

"Sara Elena, you go to market all the time." Father looked up from his work.

"I need a few things for our Hanukkah celebration."

"You just want an excuse to go out."

"We've been translating for days." Sara shrugged her tired shoulders and leaned back. She tapped one foot on the floor.

"Is translating so tedious?"

"No—Oh, Father, I'm just stiff from sitting so long. You don't mind if I go, do you?"

"Go ahead. You're young—you need activity." Alonzo set down his plume, and stretched.

"Thanks, Papa." Sara Elena dropped her inkpot as she jumped up. Ink splattered and pooled on the tile floor. "Oh, no!"

"Never mind, I'll clean it up." Father reached to pick up the pot and Sara Elena kissed him on the cheek. "Take some *maravedis* from the money box before you go. Greet Margarita for me."

"I will. *Hasta luego,* Papa."

Sara Elena grabbed a basket, some money, and threw a shawl over her shoulders. She stepped into the street.

"Let's see—I need some beef and apples—and just how will I find those with all the shortages?" She passed several people on the narrow street. One or two looked up to see whom she was talking to.

"Ask Margarita," one lady responded.

"What? Oh, thanks." Sara Elena hurried on to the plaza.

She approached Margarita's empty stall. Several people stood around waiting.

46

"Where's Margarita, señora?" The tiny woman's face looked as wizened as a dried fig.

"She's often gone. So many people need her now."

"What do you mean?"

"Come closer, child." The little woman lowered her voice.

Sara Elena bent her head toward the woman.

"You don't know? Margarita goes to the prison almost every day to visit people who've been jailed by the Inquisition."

"What?"

"It's true. She brings a little food tucked into her pocket, and then sits and listens while they pour out their troubles to her."

"She never told me." Sara Elena stepped back to escape the stench of the woman's rotten teeth.

"What, you think she would tell everyone? She's not stupid."

"But I'm her best friend. I can't believe it."

"Believe it, or ask her yourself. Here she comes."

She toddled closer to the vegetable stand.

"Hello, Margarita. ¿Cómo *estás?*"

"*Hola,* Juanita. What are you looking for today?"

Margarita smoothed back her hair and put on her apron.

"Welcome, Sara Elena. I'll help you in just a minute."

"I hope you won't cheat me, Margarita. I'm just a poor old woman."

"Never, Juanita." She rolled her eyes at Sara Elena.

"Always trying to get a bargain, Juanita?"

"I'll just look around while I'm waiting." Sara Elena stepped back.

"Thanks, Sarita."

The old woman selected a number of vegetables, each time haggling with Margarita for the best price. Finally, she left with her bundles.

"You're a saint, Margarita."

"You mean Juanita? She's a tough bargainer, but she always comes back."

"You have more responsibilities now, I hear." Sara Elena looked around her, making sure no other ears could hear their words.

"What do you mean?"

"The old woman, Juanita, told me about your secret work. Why didn't you tell me?"

"Shh. It's not secret, but it is delicate." Margarita pulled her into the stall and drew an awning curtain over the opening. "I was going to tell you sooner or later. What do you want to know?"

"How long have you been doing this work?"

"It happened gradually. One day I heard the Romeros had been detained without warning. I thought, 'How would I feel if I had no chance to put my affairs in order? What if I didn't know what charges had been brought against me?' That settled it. I went to see them in prison."

"How did you find out the accusations against the Romeros?"

"I lingered around the tribunal office and overheard the guards talking about the reports coming in. You would be ashamed to hear who came in under promise of anonymity. It's disgraceful what lies are told there!" Margarita's eyes smoldered.

"Do you know where they went after the rain stopped their execution?"

"The Romeros? I'm not sure, but I hope they find a more welcoming place to live."

"Is it safe anywhere?"

"We can hope."

Hasn't anyone become suspicious of you?"

"Sometimes I send another listener."

"Who?"

"I can't tell you. Itching ears might hear. What was that?" Margarita peered around the awning curtain. She stiffened and stood up.

"Don Antonio." Margarita spoke as if addressing the deaf.

"Señora." He dipped his head a few inches.

"What vegetables do you need today?"

"Some peppers, if you please." He coughed and cleared his throat. Sara Elena became one with the pile of potatoes.

"You are troubled by a throat malady? Perhaps some medicinal herbs would help—a preparation of mint, honey and lemon juice to gargle?" Margarita thrust a spear of mint leaves at the Inquisitor and parried with a string of garlic. He retreated a few steps.

"No, just sweet peppers and some garlic." Don Antonio pursed his lips into a tight line, as if he had just chewed that garlic.

"Very well. Good health to you, señor." Margarita handed the small packet of peppers and garlic heads to the man, and took his few coins.

"Good day, señora—and Señorita Torres." Don Antonio raised his voice and looked toward the shop curtain. Sara Elena stepped out and nodded. He bowed and walked away.

"You see what I mean about listening ears?" She watched until the black figure sidled down the street and turned the corner.

"I'll say it again, Sarita, that man is trouble."

Sara Elena drew the shutters closed. Darkness crept into the corners of the room. She lit a candle and put it on the table. Yesterday's translation lessons must now be put aside. Today's preparations would be made in secret. She put papers, documents and inkwell into the closet and set out the traditional tablecloth and menorah.

Before her mother died, she had looked forward to this time of year. Each night, her parents lit another candle in the menorah until all shone brightly. The soft glow of candlelight was magical, chasing all bad things away. As they celebrated this "festival of lights," the family remembered again the time so long ago that a light had burned for eight days in the temple, though there had been only enough oil for one day. And now that they were believers, the meaning of the old traditions had become so rich and deep. All the prophecies, the Passover, the reason for the ancient sacrifices—they all pointed to Jesus. He was the fulfillment of all the old writings and traditions. Why didn't everybody see it? Maybe the present situation would never have developed in Spain.

We celebrate a miracle, but now miracles are few.

The Torres family tried to observe all the Jewish holy days, but it was more difficult since public sentiment had turned so drastically against Jews and *conversos*.

On the surface, *conversos* had a good life, enjoying all the rights and benefits of every Spanish citizen. But they were forever under scrutiny, and anyone could report them secretly to the Inquisition. Their traditions must be practiced in deep secrecy, so they would never be discovered. Tonight, Father, Raul, Luis and Sara Elena would quietly sing the ancient songs and light the candle, but in a few days they would make their way to the tiny church two streets over to celebrate *La Nochebuena*, Christmas Eve, as all good Christians must do.

I hate this double life, thought Sara Elena, *and I hate that some Christians make it necessary. Oh, yes, they proclaim that God is love, but their religion only has room for certain people. Pure Catholics—and those of certain bloodlines.*

She yanked open the cupboard door and sent it flying against the wall with a bang.

Oh, no—a gouge in the plaster. Where will we get the money to fix it? I'm becoming just as hateful as the so-called Christians.

Potato latkes, that earthy, fragrant dish fried in olive oil lay on a plate in the kitchen. A bit of tough beef simmered in the pot by the hearth. Sara Elena had found a few dried up apples at the market, and soaked them in lemon water. Now they looked good enough to eat. The lemon juice kept their pale flesh white. She chopped them, added some cinnamon and orange juice to sweeten the taste and let them simmer gently for a few minutes. Now, she was ready for Hanukkah to begin.

"What is that wonderful aroma?" Father walked slowly now. "I feel stiff as a statue—and cold as marble."

He rubbed his hands together.

"Applesauce."

"It's wonderful, but I hope the smell doesn't travel too far." A flicker of fear crossed his face. "Where are your brothers? It's time to get started."

The door flew open and in came Luis and Raul, laden with packages.

"You know how to announce yourselves." Father closed the door fast.

"Where have you been all day?" Sara Elena shook her head from side to side, a scolding jay.

"The caravan came through finally," responded Luis. "It's not often it gets through without being ambushed by the Moors or by the king's soldiers."

"Look what we bought," yelled the usually-calm Raul. "Oranges, peppers, rice, and *jamón serrano*. Also, candles, fresh cheese and a sack of flour."

"And for you, Sara Elena, a special present." Raul held out a small package and smiled.

"Open it now," chimed in Luis.

"What is it?" She fingered the small, rectangular package. "It's something soft." She ripped off the wrappings and stifled a laugh.

"Do you like it?" asked Luis.

"Yes, of course. It's beautiful. I shall tuck it in my sleeve and use it often."

"You know what it is, then?" asked Raul.

"Of course, it's a handkerchief with my initials on it."

"Yes, embroidered handkerchiefs are fashionable now, Sara Elena. We had it made especially for you. But you already know all about it—Why?"

"I'll tell you after you open your packages from me." She let out a giggle, hugged each one of them and led them to the table for their Hanukkah celebration. Afterward, she pulled out the gifts she had wrapped for her Father and brothers. They opened them and guffawed.

"I sewed a handkerchief for each of you," said Sara Elena, "and stitched each with your initial and a filigree of leaves. I thought it would be hard to get you to use them so I prepared a speech. Here it is: 'Embroidered handkerchiefs are new, but better than clearing your nostrils all over your hands and on the ground. It's cleaner and neater.' If that didn't convince you, I decided to say, 'They're in fashion.'"

They chuckled together and promised to all use their handkerchiefs. Sara Elena beamed her approval and listened to the friendly banter among them. She lost herself in thought. The night wind whispered outside, rustling a few dried leaves. Sara Elena listened and for a moment thought she heard a few soft footsteps and a low cough. Then the wind resumed and the velvet sky enveloped their celebration in a holy peace.

Chapter 6

"Father, remember when you first introduced me to the art of translation?"

"Yes, you were just a child."

"I watched you roll out a sheepskin manuscript on your desk. Then you would stare at the words so long I thought you had fallen into a trance."

"You shook my arm until I stirred and laughed at my little daughter's concern."

"'Just pondering,'" you said. "'Just pondering.'"

"I always wondered how words could be that spellbinding. Now I know."

"It goes well for you?"

"I've spent many happy hours deciphering documents these last few days."

"I threw you a nest of vipers—some nasty problems."

"You mean the yellowed manuscripts, so I have to guess at the missing letters? Or perhaps the much-folded documents, worn through at the creases that have destroyed a word or two?

Father shrugged his shoulders and grinned.

"Well—how about the coded inscriptions and Latin anagrams? Stretches the mind, you know."

"Yes, but—"

"In each case, you have the power to decide: 'What is the author trying to say?' and also, 'Does the translation capture the spirit of the original meaning?' It rouses the spirit, no?"

"Father, do you know what Queen Isabella's secretary summoned me back for two days ago?"

"No idea."

"He gave me a mysterious document, 'a manuscript of some delicacy,' he said." Sara giggled. "It's a portion from the Song of Songs."

"Oh?"

"Don Cabrales actually blushed as he discussed it. 'I'd like you to copy this document with a careful and neat hand,' he said. It's to be a present for the King from his lady wife, for the anniversary of their marriage. If I do it well, I may have another assignment."

"Of course you said yes."

"As an afterthought Don Cabrales added, 'I expect illuminations on each page.'"

"I'll help you with that." Father patted her on the back.

Sara Elena immersed herself in the language of love. She had never read that part of the holy writings. It was generally thought to be appropriate only for married people. It made her cheeks color, and a wild glow clutched her insides.

"How beautiful you are, my darling!

Oh, how beautiful!

Your eyes are doves.

How handsome you are, my lover!

Oh, how charming:

And our bed is verdant."

A booming knock on the door ruptured her concentration. Sara Elena got up from the desk.

"Who could that be?" she said. "It's barely eight in the morning." She straightened her stiff back and smoothed her skirt. Just as she reached the heavy oak door, another knock crashed on it. "*Un momento*," she yelled.

Luis staggered in from his room.

"What is it, Sara Elena?" And to the door, he said, "Who's there, and why do you come so early?" He threw open the door, only to have the Queen's footman swirl in like a blown leaf.

"*Perdón, señorita.* I must bring you immediately to the royal residence. An urgent matter requires it." He swept his hand down in a series of flourishes in front of him and tucked his head into a bow. His thick wool tabard, a kind of long vest, bore the crests of Castile and Leon. Soft cheeks and a fuzzy chin betrayed his age. Nevertheless, he was resolute, suit-of-armor stiff.

"I must get ready. It will take a few minutes." Sara Elena scurried off to tidy her appearance.

"What can be so important that you get people out of their beds this early?"

Luis stomped over and stood directly in front of the youth, stabbing his nose at him. With narrowed gaze he waited for a reply.

"Something of great importance," the young man chirped.

"How can my sister help you in political matters? She has no experience in politics."

Raul joined the group of hastily dressed Torres men, adding his questions. Behind him came Don Alonzo, yawning widely.

"I have no time to discuss it. The Queen's secretary ordered me to fetch Señorita Torres—now." He hammered the last word.

"I'm ready," she said as she scampered back into the room.

"Don't worry, I'll be fine." Sara Elena threw the improbable words at her family and closed the door on the three open-mouthed, speechless men. She followed the rapidly receding back of the footman. Her heart raced with questions as she climbed into the carriage.

The footman latched the door and sprung nimbly onto the high seat next to the driver, who clucked instructions to waiting horses. The carriage clattered through the streets Sara Elena's back jarred together. Anyone caught in their path jumped aside, for the driver slowed down for no one.

When the carriage delivered her to the Queen's residence, she found herself sprinting after palace servants to keep up. Soon, Sara Elena found herself entering Don Cabrales' *sala*.

"Come in, child," called Don Cabrales.

Sara Elena bowed her head and picked up her skirts a few inches and walked forward. In the quiet hall, she could hear her soft leather shoes tap the floor and her satin skirts swish like a cool breeze in an olive grove. She stopped a respectful distance from the secretary's desk and looked up. Her eyes met the steady gaze.

Sara Elena noticed portraits on the wall behind Don Cabrales. The king's likeness caught her attention. She saw an imposing man of aristocratic bearing. He appeared to be forty years old, and still in his prime. His strong upper arms and calloused hands showed he had wielded a sword against many a foe. Weary eyes looked out from beneath hair glossy as a raven's feathers. His face sagged, showing the sum of his many battles against the infidels. The artist had caught the king's royal bearing, but also given him a vulnerable quality.

Don Cabrales noticed where her gaze had strayed.

"Do you approve of our king, señorita?"

"Yes, sir, very much."

"He is regal, strong, and just—a great leader for this time in Spain's history."

"Yes." Sara's eyes went back to the king's face. *Such intensity.*

"What else do you see that holds your attention so—for I can see his likeness has impressed you."

"It is not my place to say. My opinion is of no consequence." Sara Elena looked down at her hands folded in her lap.

"He is a forceful man, no?"

Sara inclined her head with the slightest nod.

After a pause, Don Cabrales continued.

"Forgive the abrupt way we asked you here, but we have just received a crucial bit of information. It could bring an end to our current conflict. We've been fighting against the Moors for over 700 years, but now Granada is about to fall. They cling to our hills like leeches, tainting our land with heresy." He waved his hands in the air.

It sounds like a rehearsed speech.

Don Cabrales pressed on.

"This is what the King and Queen want to tell you: One of our spies has come back with the information that Muhammad XII—Boabdil—his support is weakening. Few remain loyal to him. Since we captured him several years ago, we have used him to our advantage. He helped us conquer the town of Loja. He also stirred up trouble in Santa Fe a few years ago, just below the Alhambra walls, and kept his uncle Al-Zagal distracted. But he is proud. He needs a way to surrender without public disgrace, or, worse yet, an attempt on his life. We wonder how to accomplish this feat."

Sara Elena wrung her hands in her lap as she listened. "Why are you telling me this?"

"We have never trusted the coward. We need someone to go up to the Alhambra and gather information. Listen to the people in the artisan village. Are the rumors true? Will Boabdil actually surrender on the appointed day?"

Sara's eyes dilated. "What?" She snapped her head toward the Queen's secretary.

"I see you caught the secret." Don Cabrales laced his fingers together. "We have already arranged terms of surrender with the Moorish king. He capitulated on the twenty-fifth of November. But, we only need to arrange a ceremony of surrender. Boabdil cowers in his palace, afraid that his subjects will kill him when they hear the news." He cleared his throat. "Is all this true? We need someone who understands Arabic excellently, someone who will become inconspicuous and listen."

He looked straight into Sara Elena's eyes. "Señorita Torres, the Queen thinks you would be the right person for the job, and I believe she has good judgment. If you wear plain clothing, you will blend into the crowd and not be noticeable."

He eyes rested on her satin dress.

"Could you put off your fancy raiment for this one occasion? Go and listen to the people. Gauge their mood for retribution."

He twirled a quill through his fingers.

"Of course, you must tell no one what you are doing, and what lies ahead. It may be dangerous. You could be captured."

"Go now and find out all you can. Tell us when you return safely, and we'll send for you to get a full report. Somehow, we must take possession of the Alhambra soon. Do this task for all of Spain."

Don Cabrales stopped, breathless.

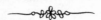

Sara Elena's mouth dropped open. *Did I hear right?*

"Señorita de Torres, what is your answer?" Don Cabrales met her eyes.

Sara's throat constricted, dry as a pumped-out well. All she could manage was a nod.

"Does that mean you will help us?" Queen Isabella's secretary leaned forward.

"Yes, sir." She gulped air to relieve her aching throat.

I need water!

"I knew Señorita de Torres has courage," said Don Cabrales turning toward her. "May God grant you success." He smoothed the folds of his doublet and summoned one of Queen Isabella's ladies in waiting.

"Maria."

"Sir?"

"Take Señorita de Torres and find a suitable disguise for her, the one we discussed earlier."

"Yes, sire." The young woman took Sara Elena by the elbow and made her way out of the secretary's presence.

"Oh, yes, and one more thing, Maria."

The young woman glanced up.

"Bring the young woman back to me for final instructions."

"It will be done." The pressure on Sara Elena's elbow told her to resume their awkward back stepping toward the door.

When they reached the door, Sara Elena wrenched her elbow from the young woman's grasp.

"Follow me, señorita." The young woman, dressed in elegant grey wool, eyed Sara Elena, her responsibility for the next hour or so. Her scornful look wounded Sara Elena, but she followed the rustling peacock down the long hall to the far door.

"Wait!" Sara Elena rushed to keep up. Her slippers fell off. She grabbed them instead of stopping to put them back on, and got to the far door just as Maria disappeared through it.

Sara Elena found herself in a large bedroom. The bed was covered with a large white cloth, and the heavily draped windows also had white cloths flung over them. Five stubby candles lit the room, their wax overflowing the brass candelabra, and several sconces reflected light onto the walls. Maria retrieved a coarse homespun dress from the big black wardrobe. An oval looking glass stood next to it.

"Remove your clothes." She turned toward Sara Elena.

"What?" Sara Elena felt like she was walking upstream against a swift current. Soon she would drown in this turn of events.

"Take off your clothes. Here, I will help you." She took Sara Elena's shoes and set them on the floor near the bed. Then, she reached up to loosen the ties that held Sara Elena's dress tight to her body. Sara Elena shrank back from her touch.

"We need to get you ready for your assignment." Maria snickered. "You're not used to being helped to dress, are you? Don't worry, I won't harm you."

Sara Elena relaxed as Maria unlaced and slipped off her gown and then her stiff farthingale. "These are a bother, aren't they?" She set the farthingale in the corner, where it stood up by itself.

"Yes." Sara Elena blushed and giggled.

"Off with your shift, too." She started to pull it off.

"No, I'll keep it on." She wrapped her hands around her body to hold the shift in place.

"But, this new shift will look out of place under peasant's clothing."

Maria frowned and tried again.

"No. It will be fine. Who will see it, anyway?" Sara Elena tightened her fists and planted her feet.

"A touch of defiance, or is it modesty?" Maria squeezed her lips into a thin line.

"Oh, very well, I suppose you're right." She shrugged her shoulders. "It won't hurt to wear your own shift."

She dropped the coarse homespun dress over Sara Elena's head.

"Ouch, that scratches." Sara Elena squirmed to find a comfortable position inside. She groaned as she saw her reflection in the looking glass.

"I look hideous—shapeless—and look at all the patches!" Sara Elena fingered the rough fabric. Her hand moved over the bumpy, uneven pieces sewn over both elbows, and in several other places on the dress. She covered her face with both hands.

"What better disguise than to be ugly and unworthy of notice?" Maria's remark stung.

"Do you hate me, making me dress like this?" Sara Elena gestured to her clothing.

"No, I don't hate you. I'm just trying to be practical."

Maria turned Sara Elena around to face her. Her eyes drifted up.

"Now let's do something about that hair—it's a glowing beacon. Sit on the bed while I decide what to do." She pushed Sara down.

Sara sat on the edge of the covered bed while Maria's hands swept over the auburn curls, combing, swirling and tucking all under a thick brunette mop of a wig. Then Maria applied powders and creams to her face.

"Look, one of the Queen's old wigs makes all the difference." She beckoned Sara Elena back to the looking glass. Sara Elena saw a black-haired peasant woman with dark circles under her eyes.

"I look like a starved Moorish maiden." She brought a hand up to her sallow face.

"Yes, the disguise is now complete." Maria smiled. "I think I've done very well by you. Now hurry, we must get back to the Queen's secretary—he's waiting."

Maria loped out of the bedroom, and Sara Elena sped after her to keep up.

Back in his office, Don Cabrales received Sara Elena with delight.

"I never would have recognized you. Your disguise is perfect." He brayed out a laugh. "Very good, Maria."

"Thank you, sir." Maria curtsied.

"Now, Señorita Torres, before you go on your assigned mission, speak with the head housekeeper and pick up the last part of the disguise. You will take skeins of yarn to sell at the local market. It will provide you with a reason to be there, and while in the market you can listen to what the people say about the treacherous Boabdil."

"Yes, sir." Sara Elena wrung her hands.

"Well, what is it?"

"Please, sir. Will you tell my family where I've gone? I don't want them to worry."

"Of course. That can be arranged. I will tell them you are under my supervision for the next twenty-four hours." He motioned to the scribe. "See to it."

The man nodded and began to scratch something on a piece of paper.

"Now go, Sara Elena. The King and Queen need the information you will gather. Report back to me as soon as may be." Don Carlos Cabrales dismissed her with a wave of the hand.

Sara Elena curtsied and backed out the door. She hurried to find the housekeeper, and then embark on her strange task.

What have I gotten myself into?

Why did the King and Queen send me to gather information? Don't they have other spies? What if I get captured?

Sara Elena took a deep breath, and then slung a reed basket over her arm. It overflowed with balls of snowy wool the housekeeper had given her to provide a justifiable reason for wandering into the Moorish quarter. She cinched a belt around the scratchy homespun dress, and threw a black shawl over her shoulders. Even with her linen shift next to her skin, she still felt the prickly fibers. If only she could scratch a million irritated spots. Instead, Sara Elena hitched up her skirts and set out from the palace, taking silent strides. She thought over her plan of action as she picked her way among the rocks.

The Alhambra crouched like a brooding vulture on the hill, waiting to devour Granada. Sara Elena glanced up and saw a single guard, marching along the edge of the vermillion tower wall high above. She stubbed her toes more than once along the rocky path that passed close to the outer brick wall, but kept her curses to herself. She hoped to avoid the guard's notice.

As Sara Elena continued on, the hillside rose up steeply. Brittle bushes clutched at the shallow soil and wind scoured the rugged terrain. The path became a cobblestone lane, straight and broad enough for two carts to pass each other. No one traversed the road now—the siege had stopped day-to-day commerce. As Sara Elena reached the Wine Gate she heard voices coming nearer. She ducked into a dark alcove near the gate.

"I tell you, Ahmad—the end is near. The Baby King will surrender soon." The guard, dressed in a thigh-length green tunic, brown hose and curved dagger, stopped at the open gate and peered out. His weathered face looked like a dry creek bed.

"How can you be sure?" Ahmad, the younger guard, adjusted his thick belt. His hand rested on a long sword at his hip.

"Because I've been inside the palace. Our baby king sulks on his pillows and twists his hands. Last week I heard him say—"

Sara Elena leaned forward to hear more. Her foot slipped. A few pebbles rattled down the hillside. She shrank into a corner, but the guards grabbed her arm and pulled her out into the open.

"What are you doing here?" He shook her like a dirty rug.

"I must see my uncle and bring him some wool," she lied. A flying carpet of Arabic words flew out of her mouth.

"And who is your uncle?" demanded the older guard.

"Ramón Moreno. He lives in the village. He's a weaver. He has run out of wool in the long siege. Please let me bring him the wool he needs so he can continue to make his living." Her lies multiplied.

She put her basket down as ordered. The guard pushed the point of his sword into the basket and prodded the skeins of ivory wool.

"All of this is forbidden," he said.

"Please, sir. Let me pass. I must go to him." Her voice escalated.

"We'll escort you to your uncle and see what he says," said the older guard.

"It's only food that's banned, Yusef," said the younger guard. "Let her pass."

"And what if she's carrying a message to someone?"

"You are too jittery, Yusef. She's only a woman, and not a very important one, it seems. What could she know?"

Ahmad ran his eyes slowly down Sara Elena's body as he spoke, her rough clothing not a detriment to his greedy eyes.

"She's pretty, though. One of us should escort her to Señor Moreno's house and verify her story."

"Ahmad, I see that look in your eye. I don't trust you. You stay here on guard."

Ahmad made noises of protest. Yusef stopped him with a cold stare.

"Come along, young woman." Yusef gestured with his sword. "Lead me to your uncle, this Señor Moreno."

Sara Elena straightened her back, tucked the wool back into her basket and set off in quick strides to her destination. The guard took her elbow.

"This pace will get us there just as well, *señorita*. My knees are weaker than yours."

She led him up the cobblestone lane that curved into the village. People settled here to sell things like chickens and vegetables, pottery and horseshoes to the Alhambra fortress and palace. It was now a lively community with hardly a distinction between Moor and Christian.

Moreno's cottage lay at the end of a small path. Fields of flax surrounded it in summer, but now the land lay at rest. An outbuilding behind the cottage served as a workshop. A loom clacked inside. Sara Elena pounded on the door.

"Tío Ramón, are you there? I've brought you some wool," she yelled to the door, which soon opened wide.

"Sara Elena, is that you? I thought I recognized your voice."

It was Ana, not the weaver. She was dressed in a frock of finely woven cloth with special detailing along the neckline and down the sleeves. She held out her arms to Sara Elena and planted a small kiss on each cheek.

"It's good to see you again, Ana," said Sara Elena, embracing her and planting a kiss on each cheek.

"What's wrong?" She stepped back, eyeing the guard.

"I demand to speak to Ramón Moreno." Yusef stepped forward.

"Who's calling me?" bellowed a deep voice.

Ramón Moreno, a tall, muscled man strode into the room, his calloused hands clenched into fists.

"Señorita Torres here claims she has come up the hill to visit her uncle and bring wool for weaving. Can you verify that?" asked the guard.

"Sara Elena often comes to visit," said Ramón. "So, if she says she brought wool this time, I say she is most welcome." Ramón crossed his large forearms and braced his legs wide apart.

"What do you make of that?"

"Just checking her story." Yusef shrugged his shoulders and took a step back.

"I—I've decided not to press my investigation. Tell your niece to stay home and out of danger. Soldiers and enemies are not to be trusted." The older guard turned abruptly to leave.

"We'll be watching your house more closely, Moreno. You can be sure of that."

"See that you do. I could use the protection." Ramon smacked his right fist into his left palm.

"Now, get out of here."

Chapter 7

❋

"What's this 'Uncle Ramón' story? I'm not your uncle. You lied to the guard. Why did you come here?" Ramón turned to glare at Sara Elena. His eyes smoldered like two red-hot coals.

"I have a good reason."

"It better be good. You took a foolish risk."

"I brought you some wool, see?"

Sara Elena held out the basket. Ramón brushed it aside.

"You shouldn't have come."

"Next you'll say it's dangerous."

"It *is* dangerous—"

"Why are you concerned? I can take care of myself." Sara drew herself up as tall as she could and faced Ramón with clenched fists of her own.

"Oh, yes, we've seen how well you handle yourself." He barked out a laugh and combed a rough hand through his unruly hair.

"But, I'm not concerned about you. You've drawn attention to my shop and my house. That could mean trouble later."

"Oh, so you're only thinking of yourself," said Sara Elena.

"You don't understand, Sarita," Ana interrupted.

"No, I don't understand," Sara Elena's voice rose higher like a steaming kettle. "I don't understand why you are making such a fuss, both of you. I've just been through enough danger to frighten a warrior."

She dropped her basket and rubbed her temples. "And I don't understand why you aren't offering me refreshment.

Aren't either of you glad to see me?" She finished her tirade by bursting into tears.

"Oh, my dear Sarita." Ana rushed over to comfort her.

"Is that your usual spoiled-child performance?" Ramón fumed. "Is that how you get your way?"

"Come and sit down. Dry your eyes. We'll talk about that later." Ana glared at Ramón.

"I'll talk to her when she has recovered herself." Ramón turned away and stalked out of the room.

Ana set out a few olives and a loaf of crusty bread and a small glass of red wine mixed with water, patted Sara Elena's shoulder and left the room. Sara Elena ate greedily and drank the wine in one gulp. She dried her eyes on a rough sleeve and let her shoulders sag.

Maybe I did make just a bit of a scene.

Sara Elena could hear Ana talking in the adjacent room with Ramón.

"She's selfish and inconsiderate."

"No, Ramón. She's just been protected all her life. She doesn't know that she's stirring up problems."

"Ha, I don't believe that. She's smarter than that. I'm going to speak with her."

"No! Let me do it," said Ana. "I know how to get to her—I'll make her listen."

"Very well. I don't think anything will make her change, but *buena suerte.* Good luck."

Ana Moreno was built like her son, stocky but considerably shorter. Her head didn't even reach the top of Ramón's shoulder. Whatever she lacked in height, however, she made up for in iron will. Ana could be strong as a Toledo sword, and twice as sharp. Sara never had been able to fool Ana with her childish excuses and schemes. Only one thing could break Ana's resolve—Sara's tears. It was the same today.

I've used that tactic more than once and I may have to use it today to win my point. Sara Elena waited for the inevitable questions from both of them.

"Now then, Señorita Torres—" Ramón pushed past his mother, and sat down next to her at the table. Ana followed and took another chair. "Why did you come here today?"

"I told you—to bring some wool." Sara Elena fidgeted. "This wretched dress!"

"Even a fool could see through that excuse."

"It's true—" she began again, but Ramón cut in.

"What's the other reason?"

Sara Elena grimaced and sat very still. When she finally spoke, she said, "Where would a person go to hear the latest gossip in your village? Is there a place where everyone meets?"

"The market, of course," said Ana. "Why?"

"Let's just say I need to catch the latest rumors in the village—it's vital to our national survival."

"That sounds unlikely."

"I can't tell you too much, except the Queen has asked me to listen and gather information."

"You're a spy?" Ramón's mouth fell open.

"Shh. I'm not supposed to tell much—" She dropped her voice and leaned forward.

"Why should I believe you? Do you really have dealings with the Queen?"

"She does, Ramón. I heard about it—"

"It began when Queen Isabella asked me to copy something for her. She knew I was Don Alonzo's daughter, and she wanted a discreet translator—a woman."

"Ha! Who is that?"

"No, Ramón, let's help her," chimed in Ana, moving to Sara's side. "Sara, if you have recovered, now would be a good time to go to the market. Today is market day."

"I'm ready. Thanks, Ana." Sara got up from the table and adjusted her black shawl. She picked up her basket of wool. "Let's go."

Ana got her wrap. She and Sara Elena linked arms and walked out of the room.

Ramón watched and wrinkled his forehead. "I'll never understand women. Just when the situation gets tense, they drop everything and go to market!"

Outside the cottage, Ana turned to Sara Elena. "You made quite a scene." Sara Elena stiffened, but kept listening as they walked.

Ana continued talking. "I know you are accustomed to having your own way, but you must think of others. Your behavior brings shame on your family and yourself—it's not at all like a woman of noble class should act."

"It's a fine thing to be noble when you have money, but our family has nothing. Remember, we had to let you go a year ago. Fewer and fewer people will spend the money for translation when they can't afford, or even find, food. And people don't want to do business with supposed Jews. So, Father's money chest gets emptier every month."

"You are not the only one to have financial troubles," snapped Ana. "Look around and you'll see everyone has suffered because of this prolonged war. That's no excuse."

Sara Elena looked down at her feet. She and Ana had walked only a dozen paces before stopping on the dusty path. A bronze beetle scurried past the toe of her shoe. She kicked it over, causing it to scramble to right itself and shuttle off even faster.

"Sara Elena, you know I love you as a granddaughter. I want the best for you, and because I do, you must listen to me."

Ana stopped speaking and looked straight at her. Sara Elena lifted her eyes to meet Ana's gaze.

"There are two things I need to tell you. First, your actions attracted attention to Ramon's home, which could bring him harm. Ramón didn't want me to tell you, but he helps outcast Moors. He gives them woven blankets, employs them, and gets them out of Granada. Boabdil doesn't like this challenge to his control. Ramón already suspects he's being watched."

Sara Elena's eyes popped. She wiped a trembling hand across her forehead.

"But, I didn't know—"

"Yes, you didn't know, but you have caused damage, anyway."

"I'm sorry."

"Sara Elena, I am glad to see you realize your mistake," Ana took her hand. "The second thing I want to say is, you must ask God to forgive you, not just for this error but for your hardness of heart. Your stubbornness grieves God. He wants people of pliable and willing spirits. Won't you confess this sin and ask God's help to change?"

Ana's earnestness caught Sara Elena off guard. "I didn't know you had such strong convictions."

"I am a follower of the Christ. Though I was born *judío*, Jewish, I have learned from Father Benito. His followers meet secretly and he reads to us every Sunday evening from the Holy Scriptures. The book of Saint Matthew shows clearly that Jesus came as Messiah—and as Savior."

"Where does Father Benito teach such dangerous beliefs?"

"It's down the road at a hidden location. But don't change the subject. Will you stop and pray with me, and ask God's forgiveness of your hard heart?"

"Oh, Ana, I'm a difficult case. I have such resentment against the Church. They have forced us to convert, but it just makes me want to rebel."

"The Church is not God himself, it's just people—human, fallible people who have lately twisted God's message. Remember, Sarita, God loves you deeply and wants you to return that love."

A loud boom split the calm. The two women recoiled and clapped hands over their ears.

"What was that—a new assault beginning?"

"Sounds like it came from the plaza," said Ana, her voice hoarse with fear.

"*Vámonos*," said Sara Elena. She turned and ran down the path toward the square, the basket of wool clutched tightly in her hand.

"Wait for me, Sarita. You need a chaperone." Ana watched Sara Elena's form disappear down the path. She sighed. "Another rabbit chase." Knotting her shawl securely around her neck, she gathered up her skirts with both hands, and dashed after Sara.

Chaos overpowered the plaza. Neat piles of oranges and figs had toppled and smashed into sticky puddles. Eggplants once glossy as giant amethysts now became purple mud. Fowl condemned to fill a stewpot flew around in sudden reprieve. Frantic merchants trying to salvage the remains of their merchandise from hundreds of trampling feet ran around in circles like the chickens. Shrieks and yells careened off the plaza walls.

"What happened?" Sara Elena shouted to a woman holding a squawking chicken in each hand.

"A cannon ball just exploded. It might be an act of sabotage or an old rusted relic—who can say?"

Chickens feathers swirled around the woman and landed in her hair as she shrugged her shoulders and spit bits of hay from her mouth.

Ana entered into the wild scene and immediately began to help. Sara Elena, however, retreated to a corner.

I need to be inconspicuous. Nobody would want my help if they knew I was the enemy.

All around her, tongues danced with furious speculation. Sara Elena listened.

"Ferdinand wants to provoke us again."

"It's the final assault."

"Boabdil staged it to gain our sympathy. He's scared."

"He's at the end of his reign."

"He's nothing but a collaborator with the enemy. Let him rot."

A rough hand clapped her on the shoulder.

"What are you doing here, young woman? Haven't you gotten into enough trouble already?" It was Yusef, the guard, followed closely by Ahmad.

"Perhaps you caused this incident."

Sara's face became a whitewashed wall as the cold hand gripped her harder. Just then, a bleating sheep skittered between Yusef's legs. He relaxed his grip for a moment. Hitting him with the wool basket, Sara took the only chance she might have and ducked out of their sight and into the swirling crowds. She heard their disapproving roars above the ongoing commotion and heard thudding footsteps come after her. She worked her way up a short side street off the plaza. It was pockmarked with doorways and portals leading to inner patios and workspaces. Desperate to find a hiding place, she dove behind a pile of rice sacks in an alcove. Her temples throbbed. She heard the two guards arguing at the mouth of the narrow street.

"She must have slipped into one of these doors."

"But, which one?"

"How would I know?"

"Start searching. I'll take the left, you take the right."

Sara Elena peered over the top rice sack just in time to see each guard disappear into opposite doorways.

Thank God for the labyrinth of ancient city streets!

Sara Elena jumped up and flew back down the street she had entered. She skirted around shouting people, wove among booths and piles of rubble and paused now and then to hide and look out for the persistent Yusef and Ahmad. She worked her way out of the village and down the hill. She didn't stop running and hiding until she swirled into her own door and shut the latch an hour later.

"Where have you been?"

"You've been gone all day."

"We've been worried about you." Father and her brothers greeted her, noticing the great heaving breaths she gulped.

"Nowhere," she gasped. "I'm fine."

"Now that's a mysterious and not convincing answer."

"We deserve a better answer than that, daughter."

"Did you receive a message from the Queen? She promised to let you know where I was."

A look of disbelief crossed Don Alonzo's face.

"You mean she didn't send you a note?" She looked from one to the other for an answer.

"Daughter, daughter. Don't fret." Father gave her hand a squeeze.

"I did receive a message you had a task to perform for the Queen. The message included no details, however."

"Tell us what happened," said Luis. "Was it dangerous?" His eyes glowed.

"Did you go alone?" Raul jumped into the interrogation.

"Listen, everyone," said Sara Elena. "I'll tell you as much as I can, but it's really a secret."

She lowered her voice. They leaned nearer.

"Sit close while I tell the story, I must speak so only you will hear. It's complicated." All three men pulled out a chair and sat down at the table, heads close together.

"Promise you won't tell anyone."

"We promise." They leaned forward like dogs eager for a meaty bone.

"Well, here is what happened since this morning." Sara Elena lowered her voice to a whisper, and related the saga of the day's events. She left nothing out, and at the end of the tale, she felt limp as a wrung-out rag. Luis let out a low whistle. Raul massaged the bridge of his nose. Don Alonzo studied his shaking hands.

"*Hija*, I am afraid for you. You are involved in high politics." His eyes met and searched hers. "What does the Queen intend?"

"I don't know all of it, I'm sure, but she said she and the king wanted information about Boabdil."

"This is dangerous in the extreme," said Raul. "Has she offered you protection—guards, perhaps?"

"Not really, but I doubt anything will happen to me. The siege is nearly over."

"This Ahmad and Yusef won't come after you?"

"I doubt it."

"I'll watch over you, little sister," said Luis, making sword play in the air.

"I need to report to the King and Queen within twenty-four hours. What time is it?" She looked past Luis to the window to see the shadows lengthening. "Oh, dear, I must at least get a message to the King and Queen before nightfall." She jumped up to find a scrap of parchment to write on.

"I'll take it to the palace, Sarita." Luis strode over to the wall hooks and retrieved his cloak. "Can I take Tico?"

"Of course," said Father. "Go quickly and return as soon as possible. Remember, it's New Year's Eve."

"I'll go saddle the horse." Raul dashed out.

Sara Elena looked up from the letter she had written. "I'd forgotten what day it was. There's much to be done." She folded the parchment corners diagonally to meet in the center, forming a neat envelope. A few drops of sealing wax completed the task.

"Here, Luis. Take this to the head chamberlain at the court. He will know what to do. I doubt if Queen Isabella will see me tonight, but if she does, come back fast and let me know." She handed the note to Luis. "I hope this is the right thing to do."

Luis nodded and fled out the door. A short whinny and the sound of galloping hooves, then Raul entered.

"He's on his way." Raul slid onto a chair.

"Why are you two sitting around?" said Sara. "Don't you know we have work to do before Luis returns?"

"We've already made most of the preparations ourselves, because we didn't know when to expect you back." Don Alonzo's look of concern melted Sara Elena's heart.

"I'm sorry, Father. I forgot about the coming holiday. Forgive me. I had something very important to do, but nothing as important as spending time with my family."

She pulled off mud-caked shoes and rubbed her feet.

"You're forgiven. I understand now."

"Well, if there's nothing to do, tell me what's been happening today?" She leaned back in her chair and crossed her arms. A yawn escaped.

"Let me get rid of this silly wig," she said, yanking it off and throwing it on the table.

"Haven't you heard the news?" Raul broke in. "Boabdil surrenders day after tomorrow." Raul's words bubbled up like a stream in springtime. "And, there's more"—

"Raul is betrothed to Beata," said Don Alonzo. "And, he's going into business as a mapmaker. Apparently, Señor Montalvo will sell him some shop space."

"You approved?"

Father's answer was a grimace.

Sara Elena didn't know which piece of news was more staggering.

If anyone should know about Boabdil, it ought to be me. Why didn't the King and Queen tell me about this? I thought there was some doubt about it all.

"Congratulations, Raul," said Sara Elena after a pause. "God bless you both."

"Thank you, sister." A smile glowed on his face. "I'm very happy."

"Luis has something to tell you when he returns," said Raul.

"Seems he's met an interesting man named Columbus. Something about a plan to sail west to find the eastern lands. He's a great sea captain and can prove it will take no more than two to three months to get to Cipangu and Cathay." Raul rolled his eyes. "So the man says."

"Why did Luis tell you this?" said Sara Elena.

"He's very interested in the venture."

"Oh, no. Surely this is madness."

"That's what I thought," said Father. "It seems the whole world changed today."

His eyes met Sara's, and for a moment she saw a piercing sadness there.

"He vows he'll go as soon as a ship can be outfitted."

"What else could happen today?"

Sara Elena slumped into a chair by the window and dreamt of struggling to escape a pursuer until someone yelled,

"I think I see Luis coming back. That was quick."

Sara hauled herself up and stretched every sore muscle. "Let's get ready for our celebration."

"The world has intruded into our family today with both feet." Father sighed.

"Come get the food, and bring the wine," said Sara Elena. "Let's be ready when Luis comes in. We have much to look forward to in the coming year."

She hobbled to get tableware and goblets, legs burning and blisters stinging. The men went off to retrieve the special foods they had bought.

"Their Majesties don't need you to come to the palace," said Luis striding into the house. "They are pleased with you, of course. They will send for you somewhat later."

"What does that mean?"

"Who knows? Let's worry about that tomorrow. Tonight we celebrate."

All four raised their goblets and their hopes high to the coming year.

Chapter 8

✳

The second day of January 1492, dawned bright and clear. Sara Elena heard the church bells of Granada toll their clanging ring as she cleared away a few olives, dirty goblets, and a dry crust of bread from yesterday's celebrations. The long peals pulsed through the town and rolled up the mountains, their insistent voices declaring the importance of this day. People emerged from their homes and lined the streets waiting for the news. Sara Elena could hear their distant chatter.

The sound of victory.

At this very moment, Ferdinand and Isabella, resplendent in their brocades and velvets, meet with Boabdil to accept his surrender.

The royal monarchs had kept it quiet. Very little pomp and ceremony meant less chance of an uprising by the people. Usually, the fighting men on both sides gathered around their leaders to view the proceedings. The defeated ruler handed over his sword and scepter and any other symbols of power he possessed. A gracious victor would allow the vanquished leader a dignified departure, but most often he would be humbled and humiliated by paying public homage to the conqueror. There was no evidence any of this was happening today. No news at all.

Don't they want everyone to know the enemy is finally subdued? The bells betray them. The secret will come out.

"What more earth-shaking news can there be?" said Sara Elena. She gazed out the window. The morning sun colored the walls with dancing light and shadow. She noticed

80

an older man making his way toward their home, head bent down. The familiar form soon reached their door. They heard three loud knocks.

"That should be Señor Montalvo," said Father. "He said he had two important matters to discuss with me. Let him in, Sara Elena."

She opened the door, as Father ushered Señor Montalvo into his study.

"Raul, stay close," he called over his shoulder. "I'll bring you in later after Don Eduardo and I discuss a few matters." He closed the door behind him, not waiting for Raul's answer.

"I'll be right here, Father." Raul sat down for a moment, but then jumped up. He started pacing back and forth. Luis jumped up and joined him.

"Raul and Luis, calm yourselves." Sara Elena saw both brothers had reached boiling.

"I'm leaving," said Luis. "This house is busier than a beehive. I need to get away." With that pronouncement, he rushed out the door. Raul turned to her.

"And you, Raul?"

"I can't help it, Sara Elena. The discussion they're having is crucial to my future. I need to be in there. What are they discussing without me?" Raul scratched one side of his head then pulled at his collar.

"Confound these uncomfortable clothes."

"Relax. I'm sure Father will let you know soon." Sara Elena offered him a cup of wine. He pushed it away and kept pacing.

"Very well, don't listen to me." Sara Elena walked into the kitchen and busied herself with preparing the next meal.

I spend half my day buying, chopping and stirring. What drudgery! How I wish Ana were still here.

81

After Señor Montalvo conferred privately with their father and protector, Raul received his summons.

"We need you now, son. Come in and help us work out important details."

Raul leaped into action, bounding into the study before Don Alonzo had finished talking. Sara Elena heard the drone of male voices through the heavy oak door, but couldn't make out the particulars. When Raul emerged later, he wore a smile wide enough to swallow a whole melon slice.

"Thank you, sir. You won't be sorry you invested in me." He gripped Montalvo's hand until the older man winced.

"You're most welcome, Raul." He rubbed his hand.

"I have every confidence in you. Now, if you'll allow me to discuss one more idea with your father—"

"Of course." Raul pulled away and closed the door as he exited. He ran into the kitchen and twirled Sara Elena around.

"You're making me dizzy, Raul."

"I can't help it. Father and Señor Montalvo have agreed to my business plan."

"Wonderful!"

"It's better than that. Now I can marry Beata." He let go of Sara Elena and rushed toward the front door. "I've got to tell her right away. *Hasta luego.*"

"*Hasta la vista*, Raul. See you soon." Sara Elena leaned against the wall until her spinning head returned to normal.

Back in the kitchen, she cleaned up the vegetable and meat scraps she had made while preparing tonight's stew. She heard Father and Señor Montalvo emerge from the study, and Father said, "I'll speak with you soon about your new proposal." She turned in time to see them shake hands. Señor Montalvo exited before she could clean her hands and come say a proper good-bye.

"Sara Elena, I need to speak with you."

"I'm coming." She plunged her hands in a bowl of clean water, and then dried them on her apron as she removed it.

"Come into my study. Sit down, Daughter." Alonzo moved a chair next to his.

"What is it, Father? You look so serious." Sara Elena smoothed her skirts as she sat down.

"Eduardo Montalvo has been thinking of his lonely condition. He's been widowed for many years."

"Yes, I know. That's nothing new. His wife died over ten years ago."

"Lately, his thoughts have strayed to a possible remedy." Father leaned forward and grasped Sara Elena's hands.

"As he said in his own words, 'My thoughts have wandered often to the fair graces of Sara Elena.'" Father looked into her eyes. "His second matter for discussion was a marriage proposal."

"I don't believe it." Sara jumped up, pulling her hands away from her father.

"I am as surprised as you are. He made a generous proposal, quite fair under the circumstances."

"This is not just a surprise. It's a disaster! How could I ever marry Señor Montalvo? He's old!" She began pacing the floor.

"Now, Sara Elena. It's not such a bad offer Wait till you hear it. Sit down."

She complied. Don Alonzo stroked her hands.

"He is a family friend. And, he is generous. I think you should consider his proposal. He's patient. He'll wait while you decide."

For once, Sara kept silent, but inside she knew: *I could never love him.*

Sara Elena ached to speak her mind. Two days, ago, her future had looked hopeful. Adventure beckoned. Now, her whole world lay shattered. The deception of King Ferdinand and Queen Isabella stung worst.

They asked me to embark on a mission of espionage. They commissioned me to gather facts about the likelihood of Boabdil's early capitulation. I risked my life trying to find the truth. Then I heard from my brother that the Moorish king has already surrendered, and it was no secret to anyone.

Sara Elena punched the dough again. It felt good to knead all her frustrations into the satiny ball of flour, yeast, and water. Rough handling improved bread, but how did it improve people? Lately, life had delivered unexpected punches—an unreasonable royal request and also an unwelcome marriage proposal.

I feel worked over and beat down just like this bread dough.

Keep calm, Sara Elena. There is no possibility of complaining to Isabella and Ferdinand. As a subject of the Spanish monarchy, I cannot go to the palace unless summoned. I just want to shout out a great big Why? But such an outburst would only get me into trouble.

Sara Elena kept pulling and pushing the yeasty lump as she thought about the other part of her current predicament.

Eduardo Montalvo is good and prosperous—and he's a religious man. But his soul dried up like a fig long ago when his wife died. He rarely smiles and never laughs. The furrows in his forehead deepen every year, and that droopy mustache of white, wispy hair around the corners of his mouth looks ridiculous. White hair! He must be fifty years old!

Sara Elena formed the well-kneaded dough into two long loaves and slashed the tops with a sharp knife. She set the loaves aside to rise and her thoughts drifted back to another proposal—her first. She was barely sixteen. Diego was twenty-five and intended to make his riches with a military career. He and her father struck an agreement. Diego was nice enough and handsome enough, and kissed her hand as he rode off to war. He said he would return to marry her after the next battle. Instead of a siege, the battle raged hot and deadly and Diego came back to Sara Elena wrapped in a shroud slung face down over a horse.

I'll never forget staring at that chalky face as Diego lay in the church. I felt as lifeless as he—not a flicker of emotion, not a tear, no regrets. Shouldn't I be crying copious tears? But, I hardly knew him when he left. Did he prefer strawberries or cherries? Did he favor blue tunics or green? What about his hopes for the future? I don't know. We only had those two polite conversations—nothing to reveal his character or passions—nothing to make me care for him.

What a strange and difficult time—that year of mourning. Half the time feeling guilty for not experiencing more grief, and half the time wishing I could feel something. Never going out, except to church. Just like a loaf of daily bread, hardened and cracked on the outside—and no softness inside.

If it hadn't been for Ana drawing me out, I don't know what would have become of me—the real me. But each day she came with a request. "Sara Elena, get up and sweep for me." Another day, "Wash the dusty floor" or "Shake out the linens today." Yes, dear Ana's blunt orders got me moving again. Most often, the order was "Knead the bread dough, Sarita. My hands are stiff and old, but yours are strong."

Sara Elena remembered her present problem and froze with fear.

What am I going to do? I don't love Eduardo Montalvo.

Sara Elena fell to her knees and covered her face with floury hands. Tears streaked down like spring rain on dusty ground, etching rivulets through the white powder. Her body rocked back and forth with each sob. The world was tilting out of control. Her life might break off into pieces at any moment and go flying in a dozen directions, and she had no way to stop it.

God—help me!

"Sara, what's the matter? Are you sick? You look terrible." Luis strode in and came over to take both her hands and help her up.

"I'm sorry, Luis. I have a lot on my mind." Sara Elena got up, freed her hands, and then swatted the flour out of her hair and off her skirts.

"You have flour on your face, too, little sister." Luis brushed her cheeks.

"I wonder how long I was sitting on the floor."

"I don't know, but you look as though you've been doing battle with the bread—and I think the bread won."

"Making bread gives me time to think, and the rhythmic pushing and folding of fragrant dough soothes me."

"Really?" Luis fingered the ring on his index finger.

"Yes, it reminds of that peaceful feeling I would experience as a young girl. I used to run out to the olive orchards whenever I was sad or angry. I'd lie back on the ground next to the oldest tree and look up through the silvery-green foliage to clear, cobalt skies. A breath of summer wind would stir the tiny leaves of the olive trees.

They'd flutter and click together. With rarely a cloud passing by, you could look deep into the blue and, you know what?"

"What, Sarita?"

"Well, I thought I could see God."

"You never told me that before," said Luis, touching her cheek.

"You know how sometimes painters put the Virgin Mary on a cloud with stars and the moon around her? I prefer to imagine God in a blue velvet robe with a silvery lining, looking down, smiling back at me, and saying, 'I love you, Sara Elena, You are mine.' That's a king you could love forever." Sara smiled at her brother.

"That's a beautiful story, dear sister." Luis's eyes held a hint of question. "So, you're feeling fine now?"

"I'm all right. What's—?"

"Listen, Sara, as you know, the Moorish king has surrendered. Those bells we all heard a while ago signaled his formal capitulation."

"I don't understand. Why didn't the King and Queen announce it beforehand? It's usually a triumphant time."

"People say it's because the Moorish monarch, what's his name?—"

"Boabdil."

"Yes, that's it. Boabdil insisted that the final surrender ceremony be private. He's afraid his subjects would mob him for giving up."

"What a coward," said Sara Elena.

"You seem to know a great deal about many secret things."

"Don't tease, Luis. This is an important day. Just think— no more foreigners ruling our country! We can live in peace again."

"Let's celebrate tonight. How about getting some stuffed olives? Do we have almonds?"

"Yes, a few handfuls. I'll go to market and look for a bit of mutton, too." Sara Elena jumped up, grabbed her shawl, and waved as she swirled out the door.

"Always ready for a celebration. That's my sister." Luis laughed loud and long.

"See you tonight."

Chapter 9

✴

March 1492

"Everything has changed for the better in just two months," said Raul, leaning back on his stool. "Sabotaged roads and bridges get repaired. Shortages disappear daily. People emerge from their homes like spring rabbits and want to buy things. Business has doubled in the last month. I suppose even Ferdinand and Isabella are turning their energies toward more profitable projects."

"The King and Queen are desperate for money these days," said Father more to himself than anyone else. "Too many years of war have drained the royal treasury. Remember, Queen Isabella had to sell her jewels a few years ago." He looked up from a manuscript he was working on, nodding to Raul who sat next to him.

"What can be done?"

"They'll be looking for money-making ventures, or maybe put a new tax on the people."

"We don't need more taxes."

"I know, I know, but that's out of our control." He winked at Raul.

"I suppose you want to marry Beata soon, now that war is over."

"Yes, Father." Raul's neck reddened. "And I have some additional details for you. Is this a good time?"

"Yes, tell me your plan." Don Alonzo put down his writing plume and looked at his oldest son. He alternately nodded then scowled as Raul explained his ideas again, adding the latest details about when he wanted to marry Beata.

"It's not like you to be so daring, Raul. Are you sure Señor Montalvo supports your enterprise? Or is he just trying to gain favor with our family, and win the hand of Sara Elena?"

"If Sara Elena refuses, she will be laughed at by everyone in Granada."

"But it is a difficult proposal."

"Not many women get two marriage proposals."

"She wants freedom to make her own choice. And she's right—Señor Montalvo is a musty old ram."

"To say no is a disgrace."

"Enough of that," said Don Alonzo, laying his hand on Raul's shoulder. "Let's hope Beata and her parents accept the latest details of your marriage proposal."

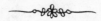

Later that day, Luis buzzed into the room like a fly seeking trash.

"Sara Elena, are you here?"

"I'm in the kitchen. Just a minute."

Luis didn't wait. He raced back to find her. Someone was with him. He stayed back, obscured by Luis's closeness.

"Guess what's happened?"

"I don't know—is it good or bad?" Sara Elena wiped her hands on the apron covering her front and brushed a wiry strand back from her forehead.

"Good. It's the best news ever."

"*Dígame.* Tell me." Sara Elena looked over Luis's shoulder and saw a shock of ebony hair, two intense eyes—*and a scar on the man's left cheek.*

"Remember when I told you about that ship's captain looking for a crew?" Luis continued.

"You mean that lunatic who thinks he's a great explorer?" She flinched as she realized she had been gazing at those green eyes much too long. Sara turned back to Luis.

"Yes and no. Yes, he's looking for a crew. No, he's not mad. He's a visionary."

"So you say."

"He's received approval from King Ferdinand and Queen Isabella to make his voyage, and I'm going to be part of it."

"What? Where's he going?"

"To find the New World."

"Where's that? Are you *loco*?"

"Columbus wants to sail west from Spain to find a shorter way to the East. He'll follow the trade winds west, find the new lands, and then return by the northern easterlies. He's been promised a reward and part of the land he discovers."

"Who promised—the King and Queen?"

"Yes, and he needs to arrange a crew and several boats. We'll sail this summer."

"I wonder how the King and Queen will finance this trip."

"Taxes? Private donations? Who knows? But, we'll all be rich when we return, and Columbus will prove his theory to the whole world."

"What will Father say?"

"That's the hard part," admitted Luis. "Could you help me?"

"How?"

"Talk to Father. I told him already, but he's skeptical. You are good at approaching him." He squeezed her arm. "Maybe you could persuade him."

"No, Luis. You don't need to risk your life by going off with a madman."

"Please, Sara Elena. I must go. I've always wanted to do something like this."

"Maybe, Luis. I'll think about it."

"*Mil gracias,* a thousand thanks, sister. I truly appreciate it. You'll see. It's the best thing that could ever happen." Luis embraced her, and then remembered his companion.

"Oh yes, I want you to meet Juan Sanchez. He's signed on as the ship's surgeon. Maybe he can help convince you, too. And that's not all. He has a project for you."

"*Encantado, señorita.*" Juan Sanchez stepped forward and bowed. "I am happy to meet you." His smile spread into a wide crevasse above a rocky chin.

"I'm happy to meet you, too." She took a towel and wiped her hands.

"By the way, Sarita," said Luis, "Your Señor Montalvo is coming to dinner in two days. Father says you should be ready to answer his proposal then."

"He's not *my* Señor Montalvo, Luis."

"If you say so. I'll leave you and Juan Sanchez to negotiate." Cloak in hand, Luis disappeared out the door.

"Wait, Luis," called Sara Elena, to her brother's disappearing back. "It's not proper—"

"To be left alone with a man," finished Juan Sanchez.

"Yes."

"I'll leave." Juan Sanchez turned on his heel and reached for the door latch.

"No!" Sara Elena's sudden response stopped him. "Come back, please. We can conduct business. My father is in the next room—"

"Sara Elena, is that you? Do you need me?" Don Alonzo called from the study, as if reading his lines on cue.

"No, Father. It's just a new client with a translation task. I can take care of it."

Please don't come in to help me. That would be embarrassing.

"Very well, Sarita. I'll leave it to you."

"How may I assist you, Doctor Sanchez?" said Sara Elena. She swept back a stray curl from her forehead. "Please come and sit at the table."

"I have a medical document I'd like translated from Arabic," said Juan Sanchez. He came back over toward Sara Elena, threw his cloak on a bench and pulled a parchment out of a leather sheath. Spreading it on the table between them, he sat down.

"I need to take a look to see what's involved." Sara Elena leaned over the pages just as Sanchez moved closer. His head brushed her forehead.

"I'm sorry," he said, pulling back. As he shifted his weight, he stepped on Sara's foot under the table.

"Excuse me, again."

Sara's cheeks grew warm.

"You see," Sanchez rushed on, "It's an essay about how to treat tropical diseases. I'll need it soon as you can get it done."

"I understand. I can—"

"I need to study every available treatise on the subject, since Captain Columbus' expedition will go to the Orient. We don't know what we'll find there. I must be prepared for anything."

"I'll have it ready for you in two weeks," said Sara Elena.

"Two weeks? That's too long."

"It has a number of medical terms I'll need to work out."

"One week. I must have it in one week," said Sanchez.

"You're very demanding."

"One week."

"I'll do my best, but it will cost extra." *I can be as stubborn as you.*

"Very well." Sanchez got up and threw his cloak around his shoulders. "I wish you and Señor Montalvo a happy marriage. But, with a temper like yours, perhaps I should wish him courage."

"I do not welcome your comments," said Sara Elena through clenched teeth. "You know nothing of the situation." *What a maddening man!*

"As you say. I will return in one week for my document."

"It will be ready."

"Until then, Señorita Torres." He tipped his head slightly toward her and walked out the door.

Her conversation with Dr. Sanchez had brought on a throbbing headache, but Sara Elena went to her worktable and spread the medical treatise before her. This parchment was old. Frayed corners and discolored edges kept rolling back into a cylindrical shape.

This will be difficult to work with, and not just because of its owner. Some of these words are not even used anymore.

Sara reached for a smooth rock, one of several she kept to hold back curling edges. *True, the Arabic characters undulate from right to left in neat rows, but look at all these medical terms. So—*

"However will I translate this in one week?" Sara said out loud, just as Father shuffled into the room.

"Is that the manuscript that just came in?" he asked.

"Yes, Father. Take a look."

"Hmm, a medical document—tropical diseases—and just look at these archaic words—"

"Yes, and Dr. Juan Sanchez wants it translated in one week—impossible. Absolutely impossible!"

"I'm surprised at you. You usually like a challenge," said Don Alonzo.

"Dr. Sanchez is *orgulloso*—full of pride. He made me angry. I wanted to show him the Torres family can do anything. Now, I'm not sure I can."

"Nothing is impossible, Sarita. May I help you?"

"Oh, would you, please?"

"Yes, of course, anything for my beloved daughter." A smile moved across his face, smoothing out the deepest wrinkles. He dropped onto the other end of the bench.

"Let's get to work."

Sara Elena received a royal summons to appear the following day. Again, she dressed in her finest clothes and climbed into the carriage when it came. The driver guided the horses in a different direction.

"Where are you taking me? This is not the way." Sara yelled out the window.

"We are going to the King and Queen's new palace—the Alhambra."

"When did they move there?"

"Soon after Boabdil surrendered."

"Oh."

At the top of the hill and through a horseshoe-arched gate, the carriage stopped.

"Get out, please, señorita, and follow him." A court page stepped forward and led her along a cobbled street. Low-growing myrtle bushes had been planted at intervals along the walkway. Sara Elena glanced at them, noticing that on this late winter day they clutched their dried-up black berries.

In summer, white flowers on those bushes will lavish a sweet aroma on passersby.

Sara Elena followed the page through a series of open patios planted with tropical flowers and vines of endless variety. Pomegranate shrubs held out their red fruit like tiny castanets. Swaying yews, veronica, geraniums, roses and trumpet vine swirled like gypsy dancers throughout the garden beds. Although not everything was blooming, movement and airiness permeated the area. Box hedge sentries surrounded the formal garden beds. And even at the end of winter, water danced in fountains, trickled through narrow channels, and dripped down to lower pools, filling the gardens with its watery music. Its merry noise enchanted her.

At last, the page led Sara Elena through an arched doorway. What she saw next took her breath away.

"Oh," she said. "I've never seen such a beautiful place."

"Yes, señorita, this is a special place. It's called *patio de los leones*, Patio of the Lions. Do you see the fountain in the middle?"

"It has lions supporting a large basin."

"Yes, twelve lions, and each one in turn spurts water from its mouth to tell what hour of the day it is."

"Intriguing."

"Señorita, please sit here and wait until you are called." The page led Sara Elena to a chair shaped like a large, upturned roof tile. She sat.

Sara Elena looked around the courtyard. A host of slender columns held up the tiled roof. Everywhere she looked, trailing vines and branches sculpted from white plaster adorned the walls. Light splashing over it made the raised surfaces gleam and shadows recede into the carved-out spaces. Sayings in Arabic lettering bordered the lacy designs. It was hard to make them out.

What is that word? Oh—praises to Allah.

She looked at a line of lettering closer to her. As she studied it, another page approached her.

'*There is no conqueror but God.*'

"The King and Queen will see you now."

Sara Elena followed the page to the throne room, hands trembling.

"Señorita Torres," announced the page in the throne room.

"Your Majesty," murmured Sara Elena, curtsying, eyes lowered.

"Come forward," replied Queen Isabella. "The king isn't here just now, but I need to speak with you."

Candles sputtered brightly in the golden candelabra placed around the room. Damask cloths covered wooden tables laden with scrolls and books. A scribe sat at one, quill in hand, waiting for his Queen's next command. Sara stepped forward onto the many-colored wool carpet, which had been spread over pale marble floors. Her foot sank into it. The heel of her shoe caught in the thick richness. She stumbled and lost her shoe. Without looking down, she felt for it with her bare foot.

"Come, child. Don't dally."

It was still under her skirts. Sara Elena pushed her foot back into the wayward shoe and moved close to Isabella.

"Much has happened lately," said Queen Isabella. "As you know, we have completed the re-conquest of our beloved land, *España*, wresting it from the hands of the infidels. Praise to Almighty God and His Holy Church." She made the sign of the cross and kissed a jeweled rosary hanging low from her neck.

She's not what I expected. Hair the color of terracotta pots, sagging chin—

"We called you here to thank you for your service. You have proved yourself loyal and brave."

The Queen's face chiseled onto every public building's façade would diminish its artistry. But her force of will permeates the throne room.

"Thank you, my Queen, but you didn't need my help." Sara averted her gaze.

"Oh yes. We are most pleased with you. We would like to reward you in some way."

"I don't want a reward—I want an explanation." Sara Elena panted and caught her breath.

"What did you say?" Isabella clutched her throat and rose out of her chair. Her cheeks flamed brighter than her wavy auburn hair.

"Your Highness, w-why did you send me as a spy into enemy t-territory?" Sara Elena choked on her words. Fear, a heavy suit of armor, weighted her chest, but the need for answers made her continue. "You already knew the answers to your questions about Boabdil."

Queen Isabella paced back and forth in front of Sara Elena, waving her arms.

"I could have you thrown in prison for your impertinent remarks." She raised her chin in a regal pose. "You must never question our decisions."

She stared a moment at Sara Elena, and then sat down. She leaned her head back against the throne, and closed her eyes. Her mouth, like a taut bowstring, quivered, prepared to unleash destruction. Sara Elena bowed lower and braced herself for a reprimand—or worse.

At last, Isabella opened her eyes and exhaled loud as a blacksmith's bellows. She looked straight and long at Sara Elena. "You have trespassed all decency and courtly manners by addressing Your Queen in such a manner. Subjects have been sentenced to the dungeon and worse for what you have just done. Oh, yes, much worse. And there you stand without a hint of remorse. I don't understand you." She pointed a long, jeweled finger at her. "You deserve punishment."

"Forgive me, Your Highness. I—"

"But I feel disposed to treat you with leniency. Perhaps I am getting soft, but there is something about you—I will answer." The color faded from Queen Isabella's face as she relaxed.

"I rely on my advisor, Bishop Torquemada, to advise me on current religious and social affairs. What you may not know about our recently-resolved conflict is that spies had infiltrated our land. They were everywhere—and heresy against our Holy Catholic Church continues to rise steadily. How can we protect our country and our land from insidious threats such as these?" Queen Isabella paused, her cheeks flushed and eyes bright. She plunged on.

"Everyone's loyalty is suspect—no one is above scrutiny. So, we must devise tests of loyalty to our Royal Persons."

"I have always been devoted—"

"How could I be certain?" Queen Isabella cut her off.

"Torquemada, and his advisor, Don Antonio, suggested the task I sent you on. It could be a way to gauge your devotion, they said. I'm glad to say that you performed well." She motioned for a goblet and sipped the wine.

Sara Elena bit her lip and made another curtsy. "Your Majesty doesn't know what I learned on that mission."

"The information is of no importance. What matters is you behaved courageously and advanced our royal cause. A reward is due. What do you request?"

"I have no need for compensation," said Sara.

"No, but I am sure there is something you would desire of me."

99

"Your Highness, I must think about it. Please give me some time to consult my Father."

"Very well. I will give you seven days. You may return and convey your wishes to me then."

The Queen got up and walked over to the scribe's table. She picked up a parchment. "You may leave me, Señorita Torres. I have an important matter to deal with now."

Sara Elena bowed low, and backed out of Queen Isabella's presence, being careful not to trip again. As she reached the back of the room and turned around to exit, a short man with hawk's beak nose, floated in, a scarlet cape draped over his shoulders. His ample silk robes rustled like wheat at harvest time.

"Master Torquemada, come in," said Isabella.

Sara Elena left the room, but her aroused curiosity overpowered her. With the page nowhere in sight, she turned around and crept back into a shadowed corner of the throne room. Standing behind a column and drapery in the rear corner, she began to listen.

"I am tormented about this document," began the Queen.

"How may I assist you, my Queen?" said Torquemada. "Surely we have examined the arguments sufficiently."

"Yes, yes. But tell me, is this really the wisest course of action?"

"What do you mean, your Royal Highness?"

"This proclamation—this edict—will change the course of our country forever."

"Yes, and it is a necessary step. Heresy and unorthodoxy pollute our society, our streets. Who can we trust? Certainly not the infidels, who believe in their strange god, Allah. That's why we thrust them out."

"Of course, I see that. But what about the Jews? Some of them are my best advisers. Isaac Abravanel gives me excellent advice on money matters, for example. There are others, as well."

"Ah, yes, but don't you see, Majesty, that the Jews cannot be relied upon. They keep to themselves. They perpetuate their strange practices. They defy the teachings of our Holy Mother Church. We must deliver Spain of this great sickness!"

Sara Elena sucked in her breath.

What does this mean?

"Then, there is no other way?" said Isabella, fingering her rosary again.

"None," said Torquemada. "Your Majesties must sign this edict, which will force the Jews to convert to our holy faith within three months, or leave the country."

Sara Elena gasped, clutched the drapery and leaned against the pillar.

"What's that?" said Torquemada. "I heard something."

Queen Isabella paused to listen.

Sara Elena recovered herself enough to let go of the drapery. She slipped out of the throne room without a sound. Dodging an approaching court attendant, she raced out of the Alhambra. Skirting around the Patio of the Lions and hurrying past the garden beds, she disappeared down the path to the village. She slowed down and let the news trickle into her head.

This knowledge is too heavy for me to bear, but who will believe what I've heard? What am I to do now? What are we all to do?

Sara Elena buried these thoughts deep in her heart as she hurried home.

Chapter 10

"Delicious," Sara Elena pronounced after taking a small taste. The large white beans, called *alubias*, simmered in a thick, creamy broth, along with pieces of spicy sausage. She sprinkled paprika on the bubbling mixture, and stirred it once more.

Have I forgotten anything?

She went over the details again—the first course would be a platter of cooked, cooled white asparagus with crumbled bits of *jamón serrano* and boiled egg. The second course consisted of the bean stew with chorizo. A plate of figs and oranges would serve as dessert.

No matter how distracted I am, I want this meal to bring honor to my family.

Señor Montalvo had arrived on the scheduled day and now sat in the main *sala* with Father, Luis and Raul. The low rumbles of her brothers' and elder father's deep voices contrasted with the bleating of Señor Montalvo's nasal replies. They discussed their favorite subject—plans for a bright future after the war.

If you only knew what's coming, your conversation would take a different turn.

She checked the table service—all the plates and bowls sparkled. Fine silver cutlery gleamed as it lined up like attentive servants next to the plates. A tall decanter of wine and smaller one of sherry caught the sunlight, throwing splashes of red and gold about the room. A loaf of fresh crusty bread lay on a tray.

"Come to the table," Sara Elena called to the men. "All is ready."

Except me.

"As I was saying," said Señor Montalvo, "the climate for business is favorable again. Now that the great conflict is resolved, people will be ready to resume their lives. They will want to buy and sell."

"That may be true," said Don Alonzo. "But they have no *maravedis*. Where will the coins come from?"

"Trade," said Luis.

"Starting new businesses," said Raul. "Father, I think—"

The men continued their conversation while Sara Elena served them.

I have news that will stop all your voices, she thought. *But I can hardly believe it myself.*

"Sara Elena, could we have more . . ." Father handed his empty bowl to her.

"Sarita, you look so serious. What troubles you?"

"Perhaps she is considering her answer to my proposal." Señor Montalvo's smile revealed flat, yellow teeth. A bit of *jamón* stuck between the two middle ones. He had started talking with some food still in his mouth, so he'd pushed it into one cheek. Now, he shifted it back with his tongue and gnashed on it again.

"I have thought carefully on it, señor," she said. Sara's forced smile barely lifted the corners of her mouth.

"We will have a private meeting in my study soon," said Alonzo. "A little more patience, Don Eduardo, and you will have your answer."

"What about my business proposal?" said Raul. "Do you have an answer for me, Señor Montalvo?"

"It all rests on the shoulders of your sister." When she gives her answer, I will give you mine."

"This is unbearable. I thought it was already settled."

Montalvo grinned and glanced toward Sara Elena.

Yes, unbearable, thought Sara Elena. *A burden too heavy for me.*

She closed her eyes a moment.

Help me, God. Give me the words to make it plain. And help them all to understand.

"Would you all like dessert now?"

She served the fruit and cleared the table afterwards. Dishes would have to wait.

Luis excused himself and Raul went off to his sleeping quarters.

"Now, then," said Father. "Come to my study, Señor Montalvo and Sara Elena. We must have a talk."

Alonzo Torres, dressed in a dark blue tunic and black hosen, led the group to a quiet room. Señor Montalvo followed. His grey hosen sagged a little at the knees and a misshapen ochre tunic covered his ample torso. Sara Elena wore a ruby-colored gown over a small farthingale, and drew her black shawl over her shoulders as she completed the parade. In the study, they all sat down, except Alonzo. He got up and paced back and forth as he talked.

"Don Eduardo, you have been a family friend for many years. We value your friendship and loyalty." He tipped his head in salute.

"I thank you, Don Alonzo." Montalvo returned the nod.

"As you know, a marriage proposal from you has a number of advantages. You are established in business and have monetary assets to support my daughter well. You have proved yourself a faithful husband already, in your first marriage. Your social standing in Granada is impeccable. Do you have anything you would like to add?" Father sat down and motioned to Don Eduardo.

Señor Montalvo bowed his head in acknowledgment. He stood up and addressed his comments to Sara Elena, but looked at Don Alonzo.

"I have been widowed many years, and earnestly desire a companion in my later years. I have very regular habits. I am dependable and pious." Color flushed his cheeks crimson. "And I have a great affection for you, Sara Elena." He sat down abruptly.

Alonzo directed his next comments to Sara Elena.

"Daughter, *hija,* you and I have discussed this before. The Torres family is of proud heritage and social standing. However, the war years have depleted our resources. We are not able to provide a large dowry to a suitor. Many potential husbands may have stayed away for this reason alone. And since you have been betrothed once before, but not married—"

"Father, my intended was killed in battle. It was not of my doing. Why should it reflect unfavorably on me?"

"I know, Sara Elena. Nevertheless, your acceptability presents a problem since the marriage arrangements didn't reach completion. Don Montalvo has told me he would not require a large dowry, since our families are on good terms."

He looked at Don Eduardo to confirm this, and received a nod.

"He also understands the circumstances of your first betrothal, and assures me he has—"

"I have the highest regard for you, Sara Elena. I hope one day you will return me the favor of your affection." Don Eduardo's nose glowed purple, accentuating the revelation. He retook his chair.

"What is your answer, *mi hija*? Here is a prosperous man who cares for you and would see to your best interests. Don Eduardo has revealed his heart to you. I beg you not to break it." Alonzo turned toward Sara Elena and slumped into his chair.

Sara Elena sat there for a long time, face devoid of expression and hands folded in her lap. A single fly buzzed on its back, dying on the window ledge.

I feel just like that fly—powerless.

"Don Eduardo, I have considered your marriage proposal carefully." Sara's voice rang out steady and clear, and she held her head high. "You are an honorable man, and someone I have known for a long time. I would feel very secure in your household."

Don Eduardo began to look hopeful. Sara Elena looked away from him.

"Father, I know that you desire the best for me, and want me to accept this proposal. There are many reasons I should accept this arrangement."

Alonzo began to smile.

"However—certain circumstances, recently set in motion by King Ferdinand and Queen Isabella, make it impossible for me to accept." Sara Elena gulped and went on.

"Soon you will hear about it, and the whole country will be put in turmoil. All of our lives will change forever. It would not be wise to enter a marriage agreement at this time. I am sorry, Don Eduardo."

Sara Elena's shoulders slumped and she looked down at her hands folded in her lap.

Don Alonzo's face changed like a dark cloud rolling in from the sea, converting his smile to a black frown.

"I don't understand, Sara Elena. That's dangerous talk. Where does it come from?" He folded trembling arms over his chest and pushed out his chin.

"Most people I know give me more respect." Señor Montalvo slapped gnarled hands on his gray hosen, and clinched them so hard his knuckles turned white and his veins bulged.

"Just a minute, Montalvo," said Father.

"No, I will not be cast aside like stale bread." His breath came in ragged gulps.

"Father, Señor Montalvo, please listen—"

Sara Elena looked from one to the other trying to find words that would make everything clear and simple.

"No, you listen," sputtered Don Eduardo. "What does this fantastic speech mean? Surely, you don't expect me to believe such a feeble excuse? What could you possibly know that no one else knows? Where do you find such lies?" He threw his arms up into the air.

"It's true. I beg you to believe me. Let me explain. I heard it at the palace." Sara's eyes pleaded with her would-be suitor.

Don Eduardo's anger boiled over. "You have made light of my proposal by inventing a silly reason to refuse. You discredit yourself and your family." He stood up, adjusted his belt around his sagging middle and looked directly at Sara Elena.

"You are—" He stopped to find the right word to convey his hurt and humiliation.

"Don Eduardo, please don't be hasty." Don Alonzo intervened.

"You are a frivolous and foolish young woman." Señor Montalvo finally exploded. "I withdraw my marriage proposal. Furthermore, I refuse to support Raul's business plan. Since you find me so disagreeable, Señorita Torres, you and your family will never see nor hear from me again." With a nod toward Don Alonzo, he turned and stormed out of the room.

"Sit down and don't cry," said Father, for by this time Sara Elena had burst into tears. "We need to have a talk." He drooped in his chair and covered his eyes with a shaky hand. Sara Elena sat down, and wiped her face. She had never seen him look so old and dejected.

"Papa, let me explain."

"Quiet. How can I trust anything you say? You seem to be full of lies. Don Eduardo was right."

"What I said is the truth."

"Truth? Do you know what that means? Lately, you have forgotten the meaning of truthfulness. You sneak off for hours and come back saying you are helping the national security. Or, that you have been visiting a friend. Now, you say you cannot accept a sincere marriage proposal because our country, España, will soon be set in turmoil. I ask you, do these sound like truthful sayings?"

"I'm sorry, Father. These things do sound fantastic, I admit. But, they are all true."

"Of all people, you should not lie to your own father. I raised you to honor your family and the truth. I am disappointed in you, Sara Elena."

"I swear to you I am not lying." Deep creases raked across her forehead and grooved the corners of her eyes.

"Then, how do you explain all these claims you have made? Please tell me—I'm listening." Don Alonzo leaned forward, gazing steadily at Sara Elena.

"I'll tell you everything. It would be a relief to share it with someone—it's been a terrible weight on me." She covered her face with both hands before beginning.

"It all began after we were summoned by the Queen." Sara Elena met her father's gaze, gathered her courage, and began to explain all that had happened in recent weeks. Alonzo listened intently, sometimes raising his bushy eyebrows, sometimes frowning, and once letting out a thunderclap of laughter as Sara Elena related how she got away from the two palace guards.

"And so, Father, when I was at the Alhambra palace two days ago, I heard Queen Isabella discussing a new law with Torquemada. This edict would require all Jews to convert to the Catholic faith or leave the country. I think they said it would be announced by the end of March, and take effect the end of July."

"That's a devastating matter to overhear," said Alonzo.

"Yes, it's worse than anything I've ever imagined. It's the end of our lives. You know *conversos* will be looked at, too."

"Now, Sarita, don't despair. This kind of thing has happened before to our people."

"But I feel so responsible."

"No!" said Alonzo. "There is no way it could be your doing. But perhaps your eavesdropping does serve a purpose. Of course, you know that was a foolish and reckless thing to do. You do know that, don't you?"

"Life isn't always safe."

"Have the King and Queen signed this law yet?" Father looked at her, a curious expression overtaking his face.

"No, I don't think so. I believe Isabella was just considering it. Why?" Sara Elena shot back a questioning look.

"Do you remember the story of Esther, one of the bravest women in the Holy Scriptures?"

"Yes, of course. She was courageous and saved her people from annihilation by the king of Persia—"

"You do see the similarities, don't you, Sara Elena? An unjust law, a beautiful Jewish woman who intervened, the saving of the Jewish people—what do you think?"

"Oh, Father. That's different. Don't even suggest it!"

"Perhaps the Almighty One has brought you to the present peril 'for such a time as this' as the Scriptures say."

"I can't. It's too much for me."

"Of course it is. It was too much for Esther, too. But, you have a unique connection with the Queen. She likes you—you look like her—you are loyal, clever, and courageous." Father grabbed her hands and squeezed them. His piercing eyes locked on hers. "If you don't speak with her, who will?"

"There's no way I can go without a summons."

"Search your heart. Trust in God. He has helped you much lately, it seems."

"Father, no. I dare not. The Queen was angry with my outburst, my 'impertinence' she called it. She warned me that people had been sent to the dungeon—or worse—for such behavior."

"I know, I know, dear daughter, but please consider it. Pray—search your heart for the next day, and then tell me your answer." He looked away and shuddered.

"I recoil at suggesting such a perilous thing of you, dear Sarita, but I know you are capable. And our situation is desperate. Will you consider it?"

She pulled away from her elderly father and ran for the door.

"You don't know what you're asking. How can you even think of such a horrible thing?" Sara Elena burst from the door, dashing out into the hot spring sun.

I just want to hide and forget everything that's happened. I've got to get away!

"She's nothing but selfish," ranted Raul. "My one opportunity is ruined. How will I find another shop space?" He paced the floor and stopped to look at Father.

"When will Sara Elena understand she is not the *infanta,* and we are not here to bow to her whims?" Father had explained, but Raul had not taken it well.

"Señor Montalvo's marriage proposal and my business contract tied so closely together—that's unfair pressure on me."

"Maybe it's unfair pressure on Sara Elena, too," said Don Alonzo. "Sit down, Raul. There's more involved than you can imagine." When Father explained about the proposed new law, Raul sobered up considerably.

"This changes everything. "I must go tell Beata." He excused himself.

Father grabbed his shoulder. "Keep this to yourself. Tell no one, Raul." He locked eyes with his oldest son, but then blinked.

"All right, tell Beata—but no one else. Understood?"

Raul strode out without a word, his cloak flying, leaving Don Alonzo to wonder.

Sara Elena ran out of the house after her big disaster with Father and Señor Montalvo. She raced all the way down their street, past the plaza and finally stopped at the bridge over the River Darro. She crawled down the grassy bank and hid in the shadows of that Roman structure. Bracing her back against the chiseled rocks set in place so long ago, Sara Elena slipped off her shoes and let her toes mingle with the sparse grass and warm dust. She listened with her eyes closed to the trickling, carefree sounds of the water flowing by.

Did Father really ask me to plead with the King and Queen for the future of all the Jews of Spain? I can't do it—I won't!

Behind her eyelids Sara Elena saw the palace, dazzling like polished alabaster. But something was wrong. A disturbance, an angry turmoil of bodies, people yelling and clamoring. A woman dressed in purple robes and a scarlet-caped priest stood above them all, wagging their fingers at the crowd. 'Get out! Get out! You don't belong!' Suddenly, the crowd parted and a young woman appeared, clothed in blue, voice clear as a running stream, each word full of wisdom and prudence. She reasoned long and forcefully with the two towering figures. They saw her desperation and her determination. Would she convince them? It almost seemed possible if—

A trickle of water landed on Sara Elena's face and woke her from her dream. She got up and brushed off her clothing. Putting on her shoes, she started the long walk back to her home and her situation. Nothing was clear. The whole future of Spain and especially her own future lay in disarray, but Sara Elena was no nearer to a decision about what her role should be. Who could ever talk the King and Queen out of their cruel scheme?

It will take a miracle.

Chapter 11

"I have only two more days to finish the translation for Juan Sanchez," said Sara Elena. "He'll return for it, and it won't be done." She pushed her shoulders back to relieve the tension and looked up at Raul, who paced back and forth in front of her.

"Write this down on your list, Sara: candles, lots of olives, garlic, shrimp, dates and figs, and all the ingredients for that good chicken and rice dish you make." Raul stopped and grinned at her.

"You're enjoying this, aren't you?" said Sara, scribbling the information as fast as she could.

"Of course. It's for my wedding—*Las bodas de Raul y Beata*. We will be married in only two weeks. There's a lot to be done, but I have spoken with Father Miguel at the cathedral and scheduled a wedding mass, as is required of good *conversos*."

"Congratulations," she said again, "but your preparations are making me panic. I'm busy, Raul. I have much to do."

"What I'm wondering is if you could help us prepare for a proper Jewish wedding canopy and all? We don't know what lies ahead for us, but we surely need your love and support." Raul was breathless after such a long speech.

"It would be a pleasure and an honor," said Father, rousing from his thoughts.

"I have a great new recipe for *pasteles*," said Sara Elena. "Just remember, I have other work to do besides planning your wedding." She pointed a quill at her brother.

"But nothing as important," said Raul and winked at her.

"You're happy today." She looked away so he wouldn't see her grinding her teeth.

"Yes, I'll marry my lovely Beata soon, and leave this intolerant wasteland."

Raul clapped his hand over his mouth.

"What did you say?"

"*Lo siento*, I shouldn't have told. Beata and I wanted to tell you all together tonight. If it's really true that all true Jews will be expelled from Spain, then we intend to leave the country soon—before general panic sets in."

"But where will you go, Raul?"

"Italy accepts Jews, I've heard. If not there, then we'll go directly to the Holy Land."

"Jerusalem? That's a long journey. It's dangerous. And it's expensive. Do you have the money?"

"Remember, I've been saving for some time."

"Why go? You're a *converso*—you'd be safe to stay."

"Beata and I have talked hours and hours about this. We want to be free to practice our religion without hiding all the time. One never knows when the political winds will blow another direction."

"It's no worse for *conversos* than before," said Sara Elena.

"It's already intolerable, as far as we're concerned," said Raul. "Beata and I want to raise our children in freedom."

"You're talking about children already?" Sara Elena grinned at Raul.

"Yes, of course." Raul blushed. "It's only natural."

"We this, we that. You sound like an old married man."

"Yes. We—I—can hardly wait." Raul laughed and gave Sara Elena kisses on both cheeks. "I'll see you later, *mi hermana*. Beata wants to talk over some more arrangements today."

"Yes, run to Beata. I'll stay here and do the hard work of translation."

"Sorry, Sara Elena. I'm too busy now—goodbye."

"*Hasta luego.*" Sara Elena sighed, put the list aside, and took up the manuscript again. She and Father had made progress, but the work had stopped since she revealed the bad news of the coming expulsion.

Father yawned. "I think I'll go lie down—there's too much going on—makes me tired." He shuffled out of the room and down the hall.

Father had become silent lately. Occasionally, he said things such as "What are my people to do?" or "España has forsaken its history of tolerance," so you knew he was ruminating about it all. But mostly, he sat in his special chair and worked his hands, wringing one and then the other.

Sara Elena translated another few sentences, and then shoved the medical treatise aside.

"Who cares about swamp ague and yellow fever? I have other problems right now."

She got up from the desk and crossed over to a shelf of books and scrolls. Father had accumulated them over the years, or made copies for himself from documents left for translation.

"Isn't there a scroll of the sacred writings?" Sara Elena said to herself. She scanned the shelf for titles.

"No, no, no—here it is." She selected a scroll covered with a soft leather sheath, and inscribed with the Star of David.

Sitting down again, Sara Elena unrolled it and ran her finger across the roll until she came to what she wanted.

"Yes, here it is—" The familiar story jumped off the parchment as she pored over it, looking for answers.

Esther became Queen after King Xerxes deposed Vashti, the beautiful wife that had not obeyed his command to come and be displayed in front of his dinner guests. His anger resulted in a decision that all husbands should rule their wives with firmness—no favors granted, no requests considered.

Will Ferdinand and Isabella grant me a favor after I have so recently challenged the Queen? She sighed and read on.

Mordecai, a Jew and Esther's uncle and guardian, refused to bow down to Haman, a proud high official of Xerxes. Haman planned his revenge—murder of all the Jews. Mordecai asked Esther to go to King Xerxes without being summoned, which by law could mean death.

Sara Elena shivered.

I could receive the same punishment from Queen Isabella. Will the Queen accept me if I come for an audience without a summons? How did Esther cope with the situation?

First, Esther made herself as attractive as possible. Then, she acted with patience and tact to win the goodwill of the king. Eventually, in spite of the ever-looming possibility of banishment or death for disobedience, she went to King Xerxes and persuaded him to save her people, the Jews.

It's just like my current situation. However, I am not royalty like Esther. It's not certain that Ferdinand and Isabella favor me over anyone else. If I go to them, I risk their anger. Would they have me killed? I don't think so, but I can't be sure. If I ask them not to sign the law, I reveal that I overheard a private conversation. What will I accomplish—anything at all? Would they listen? Perhaps I should seek an audience only with Queen Isabella. She likes me a little—and she wants to grant me a favor.

Sara Elena rehearsed all the possibilities many times, never quite certain of the outcome, but in the end she knew:

I must try. For the sake of my people, the Jews of Spain, I, Sara Elena Torres, must go to the Queen and ask her not to sign the proposed law of expulsion.

A rap on the door interrupted Sara Elena's thoughts.

"Who's there?"

"Don Antonio Morales, señorita. May I come in?"

"One moment." Sara Elena rolled up the scroll and put it away. She straightened the papers on the table and pushed an ever-straying lock back under her hair cap.

"Come in, sir."

Don Antonio glided in, his long black robes rustling. Sara Elena closed the heavy door behind him.

"Good day, Señorita Torres. I trust you are well."

"Why have you come, sir?" She bobbed her head and performed a cursory curtsy.

"Could we sit down first, señorita?" His outstretched hand surprised her more than his sudden visit.

"If you've come to bring an Inquisition summons, just tell me so plainly. And why the courtly manner? Last time you displayed all the grace of a corpse."

"Patience, please."

Don Antonio installed himself on a nearby bench in the *sala* and directed her to another one. Sara Elena settled like a dry leaf gliding to the ground.

"I hope it won't take long—and keep your voice quiet. Father's sleeping and shouldn't be disturbed."

"I assure you, I will not overstep my bounds, dear woman."

Dear woman?

"I'm listening." She rubbed her hands together.

"Señorita Torres, surely you are aware of the current state of affairs in Spain."

"Yes. Go on."

"Our country stands on the verge of greatness. We have finally conquered our foes. Now we must strengthen our inner core. As you know, I work along with the Grand Inquisitor to uncover unorthodoxy."

"How does this concern me, Don Antonio?"

"I came to warn you. Your family has come under our scrutiny. You must be watchful."

"You've already warned us many times before. What more can we do?"

"You need an advocate, a protector—someone of influence." He met her eyes.

"Like you, perhaps? Why would you care, sir?"

"Since you ask, I'll tell you." Don Antonio shifted his weight and leaned closer.

"Sara Elena, you show great promise. You are young, possessed of quick intelligence and pretty. It would be a shame to see you waste away in prison."

"So you want to come to my aid and be my protector. Why?" Her face hardened into a sandstone sculpture.

"Always so direct, I like that about you. I'll be direct, too." He reached for her hand. "Sara Elena, you intrigue me with your courage and recklessness. I'm a lonely man and over forty years old, but I can offer you protection and a comfortable life."

"How can you propose marriage—you're a clergyman?" Sara Elena tried to free her hand, but he gripped it tighter, ignored her comment and continued on.

"I am proposing an arrangement that could benefit us both. I will use my considerable influence to save you from the Inquisition. You will provide me the pleasures of your company, as I desire. You'll have everything you want—fine gowns, jewelry, feather beds." He looked intently at her face, his eyes glistening steel balls.

"Please think it over. It is a generous offer, no?"

"No! It sounds more like a threat." She yanked her hand free.

"I mean the proposal sincerely. You do see—"

"I see that you are an odious man, Don Antonio. You—"

"Say whatever you like, but you know in the end you must accept. There is no other way for you." Don Antonio's thin lips curved like an upturned tile. He stood up and straightened his back. He looked a stiff stork, with thin legs and a long beak of a nose.

"You horrible man! You disgrace your office and the God you represent."

Sara Elena's voice rose up the scale as she marched over to the door. Opening it wide, she said, "Get out!" She swept her arm wide.

There stood Juan Sanchez, tensed and ready. Juan Sanchez grabbed Don Antonio's black vest and shook him.

"Let me speed your departure."

Don Antonio wrenched himself out of Sanchez's grasp and shoved his chin out.

"You'll be sorry you treated me this way."

"The lady said to get out." Juan Sanchez planted his feet and jammed his fists on his hips.

"Señorita Torres, think about my offer."

Don Antonio screwed up his face like a dried date. He opened his mouth to speak but then snapped it shut. He eased himself around Sanchez and out the door. Juan slammed the door shut and Sara slid the lock beam in place. Sara collapsed onto the nearest bench and let out a groan.

"Señorita Torres, is everyone in love with you?" A grin split his face like an ax on wood.

"I don't find it amusing." Sara Elena wrapped her arms around her shaking body.

"Every time I come here you have another marriage proposal to consider."

"It's a horrible offer."

"Sorry. I overheard only part of the conversation. I'm sure it is a serious matter."

"He promises to keep me from the Inquisition in exchange for certain favors." She looked up and rubbed her temples. She pinched back the tears stinging her eyes.

"The rat! I should have run him through when I had the chance." Juan Sanchez pounded a fist into his palm. He draped his angular body on the bench next to Sara Elena and leaned toward her.

"What can I do to help?"

"Don't endanger yourself. There's not much either you or I can do." Her shoulders sagged.

"By the way, why are you here?" She caught his gaze. "Your document isn't ready yet."

"I didn't come for it. I came to offer my services."

"Not you, too." She rolled her eyes.

"No, it's not a marriage proposal. I think that would not be welcome, correct?"

"What, then?"

"Your brother Luis told me about your father's illness the other day. I'd like to examine him and see what I can do to treat his malady."

"We cannot pay you much."

"I don't require payment, except for the medicines I give him."

"Why are you interested in our family affairs?"

"It's professional curiosity. I have heard of this shaking palsy, and would like to see if I can find a treatment for it. There are herbal potions that could lessen the shaking."

"Oh, so Father is an experiment, a professional case?"

"I said that poorly, didn't I? Forgive me."

"Do you always apologize to everyone this much?"

"No, just to you. Maybe it's because you always take my words wrong."

Sara Elena heaved a great sigh, and then her face brightened.

"Your offer is the best one I've had today," she said, face brightening. "We certainly could use your knowledge. My father seems to grow weaker year by year."

She offered her hand to him. "Thank you, Doctor Sanchez. I welcome your help."

"*Con mucho gusto.* I'm pleased to help. Call on me anytime." Juan Sanchez gripped her hand in his own strong one.

Sara slipped her hand out of his.

"Now, señor, if you'll let me return to my translating, maybe I'll have your document ready on time." She beamed a smile at him warm as the rays of summer. "Come back in two days and your document will be ready."

"Until then. Goodbye, Sara Elena." Juan Sanchez's sword clanked against the bench as he stood. Without another word, he turned on his heel, lifted the lock beam and disappeared.

Chapter 12

The holy writings Sara Elena read earlier said Esther, the beautiful maiden, took beauty treatments for one year before appearing before King Xerxes—six months with oil of myrrh and six months with perfumes and cosmetics.

Well, I can't do that, but I'll do my best to prepare.

Sara Elena soaked her elbows and feet in warm water and rubbed off the dead skin with a porous stone. Into her hands she dropped a mixture of beaten aloe juice and olive oil, and smoothed it over all the rough parts of her body. She buffed her fingernails with a cloth wrapped around a rosemary sprig. The prickly aroma made her nose twitch. She massaged her face with a soft linen cloth, put on a shift and stretched out on her bed.

I wonder what Esther thought so many years ago before she went to the king? The risk of losing his goodwill? The danger of daring the unknown? The near certainty of failure? She must have felt a crushing responsibility—like I do now.

Inside of her, the faint sensation of a little mouse nibbling grain reminded Sara Elena of the other part of the Holy Writings she studied yesterday. Esther had fasted and prayed for three days before requesting an audience with the king. She herself had eaten nothing since last night.

I can do the fasting, but praying is—All I can say is ayúdame, Señor. Help me, God.

Sara Elena closed her eyes and relaxed for the first time that day. A gentle sleep enfolded her.

After her siesta, Sara dressed and made her way to Margarita's house. Tucked behind a plain façade, the golden warmth it radiated had nothing to do with the sandstone bricks, but everything to do with Margarita's supportive ways. With Margarita you always felt secure and tranquil. Confident in her own life, she encouraged the same in others.

"Margarita, do you have a gown I could borrow for tomorrow?"

"And just why do you need a gown, Sara Elena?" Margarita looked up from her mending.

"It's difficult to explain."

"I have time to spare. Sit down, child."

"If I tell, you can't mention it to a soul, Margarita. Promise?"

"Yes, I promise. Now tell me everything."

Sara Elena plopped down on the nearest chair and poured out her story. Margarita listened with no comment but an occasional raised eyebrow. At last, Sara Elena finished her tale and sighed.

"*Es increíble.* That's an incredible story—is it true?"

"Yes, of course, Margarita. It was my curse to overhear the worst possible news."

"And now you must do what you can to alter the course of history."

"Do you think so? It's foolhardy and impossible, but that's what Father said, too."

"He's right. Who else of our people could persuade Isabella and Ferdinand?"

"Many of Isabella's advisors are Jewish, I'm told."

"Of course, but they have long gray beards. You are young and like a daughter. Yes, you could influence her."

"Will you'll help me?"

"Let's find the perfect gown for your court visit." Margarita dropped her sewing and moved toward Sara.

"Oh, thank you, dear friend. I knew you would help me."

The two women embraced. Then Margarita took Sara's arm and led her off to the wardrobe.

"There's just one more thing, Margarita."

"What more can I do for you, Sara?"

"Pray for me tomorrow. That's when I go to the Queen."

"You shall have my prayers, and mightily."

Sara Elena arrived at the Alhambra by mid-morning and immediately requested an audience from the steward of the gate.

"What is the nature of your request, señorita? You are haughty to expect an audience with the Queen."

"Please, sir, just tell her that Sara Elena Torres requests a short audience. I need to discuss a personal matter."

"You and countless others would bother her all day long. See how many people are waiting already?" He waved his hand at a group of people lined up in the entry *sala*. The steward squinted at her from watery black eyes. Hunched over as he was in his black tunic and cape, he looked more crow-like than human.

"Please, sir, it's terribly important."

"Very well." The steward shifted his weight, and then grimaced as if he had tight shoes. "I will convey your message. But I can't promise anything. Stand over there and wait." He pointed again to the group of people. Sara Elena walked silently over to the side of the room. Two men and a woman waited there. One man, dressed in black tunic, hose and brocade cape, wore a golden chain with jeweled pendant around his neck. He drummed his fingers on one thigh. A heavy pouch hung from his belt, and he clutched a rolled manuscript in his free hand. Another man and woman wore well-made but worn clothing, and talked together of measurements and fabrics.

Like an arthritic raven, the steward hobbled down the hall toward the throne room. Sara smoothed the folds of Margarita's wine-colored dress and shifted her weight to one foot. *Waiting was not in my plan. I need to see Queen Isabella now, or I'll lose my courage.*

But before she had waited long, the steward returned.

"You are fortunate, Señorita Torres. The Queen will see you."

"Thank you, sir." Sara Elena moved forward to follow him.

"Not yet." He stopped her with an upheld hand.

"Don Abravanel, you must come now. The Queen awaits."

He peered down his pointed nose toward the man in black, who stepped forward with a swish. He followed a page down the hall and into the throne room. Sara Elena could hear the murmur of voices from where she stood—first a confident treble and then a rich baritone. Sara couldn't hear what they said.

The steward busied himself looking at a list of names at his desk.

Isn't Abravanel one of the Queen's chief advisors? And isn't he Jewish? What business does he have with Isabella today?

Curious to know, Sara Elena drifted toward the throne room door. She took a few more steps, and then a few more, and sat on a bench placed next to the doorway.

"My Queen, I beseech you," said the baritone voice.

"Your offer is generous."

"I beg you to reconsider the edict you have before you. Expulsion of the Jewish people would only work a hardship on your court. You consult many of my people on matters of business and politics."

"Yes, I know that's true."

"We support your wars with our currency."

"True again. I have always relied on the good counsel and treasuries of Jews."

"Then, please accept this purse as a pledge that more will come. We beg you to honor your good feelings toward the Jews by letting them continue to live peacefully in your kingdom."

"Although the King's mind is set, you have almost persuaded me, Don Abravanel."

"Stop! What's this rubbish I hear?" A commanding tenor voice interrupted. "Do not give in, my Queen!"

"Don Torquemada." Don Abravanel's voice grew loud. "You are not needed here. This is a private matter I'm discussing with the Queen." Sara Elena leaned closer to the door.

"Your Majesty," said Torquemada's voice. "Must I remind you of your solemn vow to rid our holy nation of infidels? Anyone who follows another creed than our holy Catholic faith must be purged from our society." His voice shrieked louder with each word. Sara Elena sprang off the bench and moved away from the door, afraid of what might erupt any minute from the throne room.

"What are you doing? You should be sitting over there." The steward glared at her and pointed to the proper place. Sara Elena walked down the hall with measured steps. Just as she seated herself, the man in black rushed out of the throne room. He sped down the hall, brushing past her, cape flying and his face pomegranate red. The steward glanced up as if nothing had taken place until now.

"Señorita Torres, it's your turn. Follow me." He limped toward the throne room door and motioned for Sara Elena to follow the court page into the room.

Tension simmered throughout the room like a boiling cauldron. Torquemada, puffed up like a strutting rooster in his scarlet chasuble, circled the area near Queen Isabella's throne, his hands clasped behind his back. Queen Isabella's face, frozen to a vacant stare, showed no sign of recognition that someone had entered the room. Isabella's thoughts pulled her somewhere else, away from the present conflict. Sara Elena composed herself and waited.

"Señorita Torres, Your Majesty," ventured the page with a deep bow.

"What's that?" The Queen shook her head and blinked her eyes. She focused her eyes on Torquemada, who had just stopped pacing. He frowned, just waking to the unexpected interruption. Then he gazed at the Queen with glowing eyes and bobbed his head. She hid her face behind a lacy fan, folded it in her lap. With a now composed face she looked toward the page and nodded her acknowledgment of his announcement.

"Señorita Torres, come in. We need a breath of fresh air."

"Your Royal Highness." Sara Elena moved forward and curtsied deep and long.

"What brings you here? I don't remember calling you to the palace." She wiped a bead of perspiration off her cheek.

"If it pleases Your Majesty, I came requesting an audience so I could discuss a personal matter." Sara Elena glanced toward Torquemada, who stared back with squinted eyes.

"Now, Sara Elena, there is little that I keep from my advisor, Bishop Torquemada." At the mention of his name, he dipped his head in a shallow bow, while his cobra eyes inspected Sara Elena's personage, assessing his prey.

"Señorita Torres." He acknowledged her with arched eyebrows and a nose lifted so high Sara could see thick dark hairs growing out of his nostrils. She curtsied back.

What can I say now? The king already rejected a request to reconsider the edict. Sara Elena shifted her feet and clasped her hands tight.

"Go ahead, Sara Elena." The Queen smiled with encouragement.

"Your Majesty, I've come to ask a favor." She gulped as an idea began to form in her head.

"Yes, I promised you a favor for your service to the monarchy. Go on." Isabella nodded. Torquemada's coal bit eyes receded behind creased eyelids.

"If it wouldn't be an imposition, and if you would consent to it, I would like to come and show you my progress on the copy work you gave me."

Where did that idea spring from?

"What an attractive idea!" cried the Queen, clapping her hands together like a little girl. "Such courage, such resourcefulness, young lady. I commend you." She beamed at Sara.

"I would be delighted to have you come tomorrow. And, please, stay for the afternoon meal. I may want to commission another manuscript to be copied for someone I admire. Perhaps we could discuss that as well." Her eyes darted around the room.

"Bishop Torquemada, you and your assistant, Don Antonio Morales, are invited, also."

"If that pleases you, Your Highness."

That's like inviting a vulture to lunch—nothing but trouble.

"You do me a great honor, Majesty," said the beaky advisor, bobbing his head several times, his chest fully expanded, a smile sliding over his face.

"I accept and will send Don Antonio, since I am obligated to the King tomorrow." He curled his upper lip like an arching snail.

"Tomorrow, then, at two? Scribe, send a message to the chamberlain." Queen Isabella's question was more of a command.

"Thank you, Your Highness."

"Sara Elena, my carriage will bring you to the palace. Watch for it." She smiled and looked down her nose.

"You are a remarkable young woman, Señorita Torres."

"Thank you. I'll take my leave then." She bowed low and began back-stepping to the throne room door.

"Thank you, my dear," called Queen Isabella. "I look forward to our next meeting."

Torquemada smirked and returned to his pacing.

Chapter 13

"Margarita, guess what happened?" Sara Elena trotted up to Margarita's vegetable stand in her friend's wine-colored gown, panting and brushing sticky curls off her forehead.

"Tell me. I can hardly wait to hear." Margarita ushered Sara Elena behind the baskets of fruit and vegetables and into the curtained coolness in back.

"Sit down. I'll be right back after I put up my 'back in a few minutes' sign." She soon scurried back.

"Now then—"

Sara Elena spilled her story to the older woman, keeping her voice low. Margarita added a few well-placed exclamations. When Sara got to the end, Margarita said, "You are either crazy or God has inspired you."

"Tell me how to dine with a Queen. I know I'll embarrass myself." She withered on the stool, a flower out of water.

"You can't do this on your own. Let me teach you courtly manners."

"I wish you would. May I wear your dress again?"

"Yes, of course, I'll help all I can, Sarita. Come back after siesta and we'll work on proper etiquette. Now, go tell your family." Margarita patted Sara Elena's back and ushered her out into the sunshine and flurry of the marketplace.

"*Vaya con Dios.*"

"Thanks for the encouraging words. See you soon." Sara Elena waved and ran down the lane.

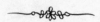

"You're crazy," said Luis and Raul together.

"You're a courageous young woman." Father shook his head in wonder.

"The wedding's coming up soon," said Raul. "What were you thinking? Don't we have enough to think about?"

"Look at it this way—my visit to the Queen will be over before the wedding." Sara looked from face to face, hoping someone would agree with her. "And it's for a higher purpose. I will dine in the highest circles tomorrow."

"And what company! None other than the Queen of Spain." Father stroked his silver beard. "Do you have a plan to make this work?"

"Listen, everyone—in one hour, I go to Margarita's for a lesson in courtly manners. Before and after the dinner at court tomorrow, I'll get everything ready for the wedding. All we have to do is get the house clean, and see that the kitchen and pantry are stocked well." She put on an apron.

"Raul, you go out and buy the best wines you can find. Luis, I'm sending you to Margarita's stall to get some fresh things. Here, I'll make a list."

Sara Elena sat down with a scrap of paper and scratched down a few items. She gave the list to Luis. The two brothers dashed out the door. She called to them as they disappeared—

"Just buy plenty of all the things we need for the wedding. It shouldn't be so hard." Sara Elena sat down next to Father and wiped her brow.

"You look more like a limp linen towel than my daughter. Are you sure you can handle this?" Father's concern warmed her heart.

"Oh Papa, I'm not worried about the etiquette of dining at court. I'm concerned about convincing Isabella to abolish the edict. Just before I went into the Queen's presence today, I heard Don Abravanel offer the King and Queen a huge sum of money to change their minds. She refused, after Bishop Torquemada interrupted, bellowing at her not to waver."

"Oh, dear."

"Yes, anything I could have said after that would have been ineffective."

"So, that's why you devised another plan."

"Yes, and now I'm afraid. Somehow, I got myself invited to the mid-day meal. I didn't know what else to do." Sara Elena's eyes clouded and she turned away.

"We don't know the workings of the Almighty, Sara Elena. Perhaps this plan will work for our overall good." He patted her hand. "Thank you for trying your best."

"Now, all we have to do is get the house spotless, put on our best clothes, and prepare for the wedding. Let's get started."

Sara Elena ran to get a bucket and water.

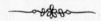

When the knock came, Margarita answered the door. With her black hair combed back and caught up in a glistening ebony comb and dressed in her finest gown, she looked the picture of refinement and decorum.

"Welcome, Señorita Torres," she said, opening wide the creaking door and bowing low. Sara Elena, again wearing Margarita's wine-colored dress, curtsied and waited for Margarita to cue her on the next bit of diplomacy to perform.

"Queen Isabella will inquire about your family first. What will you answer?" Margarita cocked her head and waited.

"Your Highness—my father Don Alonzo and my brothers Raul and Luis are in good health. They send their greetings."

"Very good. Do not inquire after the Queen's health. She is the one who must initiate every bit of conversation." Margarita tapped the table in front of her.

"Now sit down, and let's practice using the proper eating utensils."

"Not again, Margarita." Sara Elena folded her arms and started tapping her foot. "We've gone over this three times already."

"Nevertheless, you must have perfect manners. One mishap and you'll irritate the Queen and lose your opportunity."

"Very well," sighed Sara Elena, "but only once more. I'm tired."

"A final dress rehearsal, and then you may dine with the Queen." Margarita gestured toward the table as Sara Elena glided toward her place.

"Don Antonio Morales, you will represent Bishop Torquemada today, but I do wish to concentrate on Sara Elena and her translation work." She waved the scarlet-clad bishop aside.

"I'll call on you in a moment, Don Antonio, when I need your advice. You will make yourself available, won't you?"

"With pleasure, Your Majesty." Morales peered down his arched nose at Sara Elena.

"Follow me," said the Queen as she glided toward the dining room. "And bring your translation work."

"Thank you, Your Majesty. I hope you will approve of what I've done." Sara Elena followed Don Antonio and the Queen at the proper distance and soon found a seat at the long, elegant table. Inlaid with squares and triangles of pine, maple and ebony wood, the design glowed under careful waxing. A huge glass bowl in the center contained blood-red geraniums and white roses. Several other courtiers had been invited to share the mid-day meal, but most of the dozens of seats remained empty.

"The King is off attending to some matters in Aragon and has taken Bishop Torquemada," said Queen Isabella from the far end of the dining room. Servants hovered like hummingbirds, placing full plates onto the table and returning later to remove empty ones. After several courses, the servants brought in a dessert of melons of all kinds—the meltingly sweet green and yellow fruits of the Canary Islands, of Andalucia, and of far-off Africa. Sara Elena savored their delicate scent and even more their delicious, cool taste.

These melons are so juicy, I'll stain the table and Margarita's gown!

After a leisurely lunch, Queen Isabella dismissed everyone except Father Morales to the large marble-lined parlor for sweets and more wine.

"Come and show me now how the copy is progressing." She gestured for Sara Elena to move closer. Don Antonio observed in quiet concentration from the far corner he occupied.

Sara Elena took the next half hour showing Queen Isabella her copy of the Song of Songs passage. The Queen exclaimed over the intricate illuminations Sara Elena had painstakingly wrought on each page.

"Just like the old, traditional style," she commented. "Marvelous—and your calligraphy is elegant." At the end of the discussion, Queen Isabella folded her hands in her lap and smiled at the young woman.

"Señorita Torres, I am exceedingly happy with your work. Don Antonio, come and see this."

"Thank you." Sara Elena blushed as she bowed her head toward the Queen.

"You still have not requested the favor I promised you."

This is the moment!

Sara Elena took a deep breath. "My Queen I do have a request of you." She met the Queen's clear blue eyes, so much a mirror of hers.

"I know that you do. Ask me anything." She returned a smile. As Sara Elena opened her mouth to answer, Father Morales burst into the conversation.

"Here I am, My Queen. How can I be of service?"

"Just a moment, Sara Elena. We'll continue in just a moment. Let me speak with the Holy Father." She motioned to Morales as Sara Elena moved back a few paces into a corner where she could watch them.

"Come here and look at Señorita Torres' exquisite workmanship." The black stork stepped over to the desk and peered at the parchments.

"Very good, indeed." He teetered back a pace.

"Now, sir, instruct me what portion of the Holy Scriptures should be copied for someone I wish to honor."

"How shall I advise Your Majesty unless I am acquainted with this person you wish to honor?" A smile slid across his oily face. "Do I know this favored one?"

"I believe you do. He's a learned man—a scholar—and well esteemed." She sniffed.

"Then, perhaps a portion of the Prophets—Isaiah—or the Ten Commandments. A devout man would also welcome the Psalms." His dipping nod did not hide his proud eyes. Sara cringed.

"Yes, good suggestions. How about a portion of the Psalms, perhaps Psalm 100? Sara Elena, could you copy and illustrate that for me?"

"*Con mucho gusto*, Your Majesty." Sara Elena scurried closer and gathered up her translated papers.

Is this to be for Don Antonio, the Cruel?

"I will provide a copy from the royal library. Let me know when you have completed it."

"And who is the book for?" Sara Elena asked, not really wanting to know the answer. Morales leaned his ear closer.

"Why, that is a secret for now. All will be revealed in due time."

Don Antonio Morales stuck his hands in opposite sleeves like a humble priest, and closed his lips in a demure smile. Queen Isabella shrugged her shoulders and looked around.

"Sara Elena, I fear this interruption's taken too long. I believe it's time for my next appointment." Queen Isabella patted the young woman's shoulder, stood and glided out of the study. "I'm sorry."

"Your Majesty, if we could talk once more in private, I would appreciate it."

"What?" Isabella paused and looked back. "Can't you ask me now?"

"I'd prefer to tell you in private." Sara Elena curtsied low.

"Oh, very well, we must still hear your request. Come next week to get the book to copy. I will see you then and hear your personal request."

"You are most gracious, Your Highness." Sara Elena bowed.

"Thank you, dear," said Queen Isabella. "It's been a most delightful day. I look forward to our little talk soon."

"So do I." She curtsied as the Queen floated out of the room, her brocade gown rustling like leaves in a summer breeze.

Will you be as delighted when I make my request?

Chapter 14

❋

Raul felt perspiration running down his back and beading up on his forehead as he gazed at Beata in her soft sky-blue wedding dress. A lacy white veil encircled her face and shoulders and her pale hair like fine flax threads hung down beyond the veil to her waist. He recalled the day he met her.

Beata's delicate features and quiet manner had first attracted him five years ago. The daughter of one of their clients, she had come along with her father to deliver a manuscript for translation and copying. She was thin of body then and just growing into womanhood—only fourteen, he had discovered later. He sought her out, and they became acquainted in the usual way, with chaperones smoothing the way.

Not that the road had been stony, just the usual difficulties of getting to know someone and learning each other's ways. Their love had grown like a tender rosebud, blossoming into something pure and beautiful. They both recognized the need to nurture and cherish it.

Last night's traditional Jewish ceremony had unfolded like that rose, with each turn revealing another lovely vista. Raul's family had hosted the wedding, since it was too dangerous to hold it in the synagogue. Their home was larger than Beata's, with space for the relatives of both families to gather round the *chuppah*, the wedding canopy. However, it provided only enough room to stand around the perimeter.

Sara Elena, Luis and Father organized many delicious foods and drink for the feast—roasted lamb, giant bowls of tangy olives and almond torte. Beata's family brought a host of candles and a fiddler. Instead of the usually boisterous celebration that was traditional, it was held in quiet simplicity. Old Rabbi Ibrahim presided over the occasion. His skin looked like tree bark and his beard hung from his chin like trailing gray moss. In his dark robes, he seemed more like a gnarled olive tree than a man.

"It will be hard to keep from dancing tonight, children," he began, "but remember we are living in an evil time. We are being hunted down once again. As children of Israel, let us hold fast to our faith, and re-enact here the sacred ceremony of marriage. With quiet reverence we wish Raul and Beata a wonderful life together."

The Jewish wedding ceremony included a covenant of unconditional love pledged by each party as they said their vows. With quavering voice and nearly overcome with love, Raul said, "My beloved one, I love you. I love you. When you awaken, let me await you. And when you walk, let me tell the whole of the worlds that you are coming. And should you weep, let my hands upon your face hold your tears, to count each one, that you might know that what has hurt you will be remembered forever. And wheresoever you shall go, let me go. And whomsoever you shall love, let me love.

"My beloved one, I have waited from the beginning unto forever that I may hold you. And so what is insignificant here is anything but that I love you. Let me be quick to give you love that you might know you are loved. Let me be quick to be gentle that you might know you are loved. Let me be quick to be patient that you might know you are allowed. Let me love you more. Let me love you more than I seek to be loved.

"The journey home is filled with struggle, peace and love. For it has been noted before and is a forever truth—the greatest of these is love.

"I love you. So be it." Last night, Raul leaned forward and grasped Beata's hand. It felt warm and moist. She looked up at him, shaking her long golden mane away from her eyes.

Light from all the candles in the room cannot outshine the glow in my Beata's eyes. My heart is overflowing. Oh, my Beata—blessed one. Surely God has given me a great blessing.

"Beata," he whispered into her ear. "I will always try to be worthy of your love. I will be a good husband."

"I love you, Raul. You are all I need." Her warm breath floated past his ear. His heart and body soared with a painful longing.

"Couldn't we be together tonight?" His hand drifted toward his belt and the ache he felt below.

"*Querido*, dearest. Tomorrow, after the Christian ceremony, we can begin our life as husband and wife. Our behavior must bear up under the strongest scrutiny. Spies may be watching us tonight, hoping we will reveal that we are already married in the eyes of our ancient faith."

Raul sighed. The fiddler spun a few plaintive melodies. The relatives sampled Sara's good food. Beata went home to her Father's house one last time, and Raul alone to his bed.

But tomorrow will be different. Ah yes, tomorrow night—

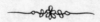

The Catholic ceremony began at ten in the morning. The intoning of the priest put everyone in a subdued mood as he said mass, served communion and led the couple in the exchange of vows.

Raul looked up to the soaring arches of the church and smiled. *Such fine craftsmanship honors God. This vaulted ceiling grows up to God and makes me think of his glory and might.* Raul quickly banished the unbidden thought from his mind as the priest finished his litany.

Raul and Beata filed down the long aisle and out to the street. It was traditional to walk to the church, and then walk to the wedding feast afterward.

"These double ceremonies mean double expense," said Raul. "I hope your father can afford it."

"Don Alonzo kindly consented to provide some of the food." Beata beamed at him. "Now we are doubly husband and wife."

"The end of the celebrations can't come fast enough for me. Then we can be man and wife in reality." He shuddered as he fought to control his rising physical desire.

"Patience, *mi querido*," said Beata, blushing and squeezing his hand. "We'll soon begin a lifetime of love." They walked along the cobblestone streets toward Beata's family home. Guests followed behind as a hired guitarist strummed a wedding tune. A black, cloaked figure peered out of a narrow side street, coughed and then retreated.

Life took a new turn after the nuptials, although at the beginning all seemed ordinary enough. Beata and Raul set off for a *pensión* for her bridal week, and like a cat curling up for a nap, the house settled into quiet again.

Father shuffled down the hall to take a siesta as he did more often now. Sara Elena cleaned up the dishes, stray crusts of bread, chicken bones and olive pits. She scrubbed and swept to divert her thoughts, but fear crept in like a gnawing rat. By late afternoon, her insides churned and acid boiled up from her stomach into her throat.

What will happen when I finally put my request to the Queen?

"Stop worrying!" she scolded herself under her breath.

Sara Elena sighed and put away her cleaning rags and broom. Picking up her favorite quill, she resumed working on the Queen's manuscript. She was down to the final touches.

"Perhaps I can finish this document and take it to Queen Isabella when I see her tomorrow."

She pressed on with the last page—a title page with a large illumination covering most of the parchment. Painstakingly, she applied ink of different colors to fill in small details of the penned drawing—a young man and woman clad in flowing garments, hands held out to each other and clasped. Each looked at the other with adoration and longing. The leafy tree spread over them and birds sat on several branches. A low hedge of lavender circled three sides. A rabbit and a deer browsed among the foliage. It was a private garden, a secret meeting place for the two lovers, and Sara Elena poured all her efforts into the tranquil scene.

"Sara Elena, what are you doing? It's late." Don Alonzo came padding closer toward her, only hosen covering his feet. He yawned and stretched his arms.

"What?—" Sara Elena blinked and put down her quill. Sara saw long shadows spread across the floor tiles. "Oh, no, I hope I haven't dripped ink on the parchment. Let's see." She examined the page. One spot of green spread out near the base of the tree trunk. Sara Elena drew some spiky grass spears around it and set down her quill. "There, it's finished."

"I've slept through supper," said Don Alonzo. "It appears you missed supper, too. Come and eat some bread and cheese with me." He shuffled to the kitchen and put some bread and a hunk of cheese on a tray. Sara Elena followed, and planted herself at the table.

"Where's Luis?"

"Said he had business to attend to—left hours ago." Father sliced a few ragged slivers of cheese and pushed the platter toward Sara Elena. He poured some wine into wooden cups. "Here, eat something. Then you need to go to bed. Tomorrow you see the Queen."

"Yes, I know." Sara Elena sighed. "Let's pray Queen Isabella will listen to reason and abolish that infernal edict."

"My thoughts will be with you—as they always are." Alonzo patted her hand.

"Good night, Father." Sara Elena shook crumbs from her skirts and wandered down the hall to her room. As she prepared for bed, Sara Elena heard the creak of Father's bed next door. She climbed into her own bed and pulled up the cool, white coverlet.

In the darkness, night sounds magnified—a dove calling from the roof, a lone dog barking far off, Father's deep, resonant breathing from across the hall. After a long time she heard the front door open, quiet steps toward the kitchen and a low curse as Luis bumped into something.

A great sense of peace washed over Sara Elena. At the same time, her stomach tightened as she remembered she might soon influence the course of history.

How can peace seem so strong when disaster lurks just around the corner?

She drifted off to sleep just as the cool night wind rose and swirled down the sleeping streets of Granada.

Tomorrow . . . tomorrow. It all depends upon tomorrow.

"Sara Elena, how splendid to see you." Queen Isabella beckoned her to draw closer.

"The pleasure is mine, Your Majesty." Sara Elena curtsied and advanced in a deep blue gown she had chosen for today's meeting. "I've finished the Song of Songs document, and brought it to you." She presented it with both hands.

"Wonderful! I'm pleased." Queen Isabella glanced at it and motioned for the scribe to take charge of it. "You shall have payment today for your fine work." She nodded toward the scribe.

"I have the new document for you to copy, my dear." The scribe got up and brought a leather-covered sheaf of papers to Sara Elena, which she accepted and clutched to her chest. Her fingers tightened around the bundle.

"Don Antonio, and perhaps even Torquemada, I think, expects the document to be for them. I want you to know, however, I intend to give the document, when you finish it, to your Father, Don Alonzo. He's been a faithful and humble servant to me. A few months ago he alerted me to an assassination plot. Said he heard it discussed right in the palace courtyard."

Sara Elena thought back and remembered something odd about her first visit to the Alhambra palace.

I remember Father muttering he should report something to the Queen. Is that when it happened?

Isabella lifted her eyebrows and smiled. "Let's keep it a surprise for now."

"He will be so pleased," said Sara Elena and curtsied low.

"Dear Sara Elena, I have such positive feelings for you. You are like a daughter—and resemble me even more than my real daughter, Juana. How I wish I could grant you the favor you most desire—even up to half of my wealth." Queen Isabella sighed and leaned back in her throne.

Sara Elena drew in her breath at the implied promise.

"Now, Sara Elena, at long last, please tell me what is your request—a favor so personal that you couldn't say it in front of my trusted advisors." Queen Isabella gazed at the young woman with interest, her hands folded in her brocaded lap.

"My Queen, I come to ask a favor not just for me but also for a great host of people—and your subjects—the Jews." She paused and drew a deep breath.

"Oh?" Queen Isabella's eyebrows shot up.

"Yes, Your Majesty. I have heard you and the King plan to demand conversion or expulsion of all the Jews. That an edict will be signed to this effect."

"It has already been signed." The Queen's demeanor cooled.

"Then I ask you, if you value my services to you and if you value the resources of knowledge and ability of the Jews of Spain, please grant me this favor." Sara Elena gulped and bowed low. "I beg you most humbly to repeal and abolish this ugly law."

Silence permeated the court. Queen Isabella gazed at the rings on her hands. Finally she spoke.

"An impassioned request, Sara Elena, but one I cannot grant. His Majesty and I are resolved to purify the holy faith of Spain." She shifted her weight forward and stood.

"Look at me, Señorita Torres." She waited to continue until Sara Elena complied. "You shall have 1,000 maravedis for your services to the crown." She paused. "But we are sorry we cannot grant your special favor." She bowed her head and folded her arms over her chest.

"And now, good day."

Chapter 15

✳

Everything was against her! That horrible law, the Queen's refusal and even nature conspired to undo her. As Sara Elena walked home, she noticed vines climbing up walls to spread out their pale green leaves. She saw bold wisteria grabbing at railings and throwing its lavender shawls everywhere. The fresh air swirled its scented breath along the cobbled streets. It was spring and a time of new life and new hope—but not for her and her people.

Sara Elena walked home and embraced her father, Don Alonzo. He listened with hope at first, and then as the full story unfolded, he touched her moist cheek and said,

"Sara Elena, I am proud of you. You have done your very best to persuade the Queen. Please be content with that knowledge. God has shown us his will. Repeal of the edict was not meant to be." He placed a kiss on each cheek and rubbed her arm.

"But, Father, I am desolate. Think of what is coming for us, and all the Jewish people." Her shoulders sagged and she twisted a part of her shawl around a finger. "I think I'll go and rest a while." She lay down on her bed but slept little and for the next few days worked with none of her usual energy.

Is there no way out of this dark discovery, God? It's a gathering storm that will sweep us all away.

Raul and Beata returned a few days after Sara Elena's disastrous day, dreamy-eyed and in a world of their own.

"You two have the look of the recently married," said Don Alonzo. "Beata, you have stars in your eyes, and Raul, you're glowing." They blushed and exchanged a secret look.

146

Beata soon came to live with Raul at the Torres residence. Father moved out of his large bedroom to let them use his furniture. "This wide bed suits a new husband and wife. My parents gave it to me when I married my wife," he told Raul. "I will sleep in your old room now, since I am a *viudo*, an old widower."

"Thank you, Father. We will stay here only until we make arrangements to leave Spain."

"I hate to see you go. It tears at my heart."

"Father, what can I do to make your life happier?"

"Don't worry yourself about me. Sara Elena is a good help. If you want to do something for me, just love your wife, Raul."

"I will do that."

"Remember that the Holy Scriptures say that a new husband should make his wife happy during their first year of marriage."

"I can promise you, Father. I'll make it my solemn duty to keep that commandment." Raul's lips parted in a sudden smile, and his eyes met and held his father's for a long moment.

"Never take advantage of your wife's love, Raul. Treasure it. Guard it with diligence. Promise me you will be good to Beata always."

"Yes, sir. I will." Father patted his son on the back.

"*Muy bien*, then will you please help me move my books and clothing to your old room. My old body isn't strong anymore."

"With pleasure," said Raul, gathering up a stack of books and rolled parchments.

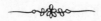

Later that evening, after shuttling all of Don Alonzo's tunics, cloaks, boots, hats and writing equipment out of the large bedroom, and bringing in all of Beata's gowns, shifts, shoes and shawls, Raul took a moment to rest. He wiped his brow.

"Surely a woman doesn't need all this clothing. Where will I put my things?" he said to no one in particular.

"These are just the essentials," said Beata, breezing in with a box of gloves, necklaces and scarves. "I left two farthingales at my Father's house."

"If you ask me, those contrivances that hold out a lady's skirts to two meters on each side of the waist merely disguise a woman's natural shape."

"It is the fashion. Any respectable lady must wear one. The Queen does."

"I know. But I still say they are ridiculous." He grabbed her hand and kissed it. "By the way, how are you getting along with Sara Elena?"

"We're doing well. I tried helping her with meal preparation just now. She is an excellent cook—better than I. When she said, 'Cut the carrots,' I did. When she said, 'Boil the potatoes,' I did. When she said, 'Sprinkle rosemary on the chicken,' I did."

"*Bien*. You will learn from Sara Elena. She has been cooking for many years."

"I hope so. I came to tell you both, dinner is ready." Beata placed a kiss on his cheek and swept out of the room.

Raul followed behind her and caught her by the waist. He planted a kiss on her moist lips. "I love you, Beata, *mi esposa*."

"And I love you, dear husband." She caught his hand and kissed the back of it. They held hands and walked into the living room just as Luis exploded through the door. Sara

Elena ignored everyone—she stirred the bubbling pot on the hearth.

"Hello, lovebirds. Guess what has happened."

"Do you always rush into a room like that? Where are your manners?"

"Sorry, older brother. Good evening, Beata." Luis bowed low to his new sister-in-law and tossed a short nod toward Raul.

"Good evening. Now what's your news, Luis?"

"Margarita has been arrested by the Inquisition."

"What did you say?" Sara Elena dropped the spoon she was stirring with and grabbed Luis by the arm.

"I stopped at the *bodega* today on the way home for dinner. Everyone was buzzing like bees around a hive. The Inquisition has detained several people for suspicious activities. One of them is Margarita."

"How do you know it's true, not just gossip?"

"I saw posted notices on several walls. Here—I brought one home." He unfolded a leaf of paper and read it out loud—

"Be it known that certain persons have committed acts of a suspicious nature against Their Majesties and against our Mother Church, namely aiding and giving comfort to persons detained for questioning by our Lord Inquisitor, Torquemada. If anyone has information about the activities of Pedro Gomez, Rosa Gonzales or Margarita Martinez, you are commanded to inform the tribunal. Your testimony will be kept in strictest confidence. Signed, Don Antonio Morales."

"That's impossible." Sara Elena snatched the piece of paper from Luis and looked it over. "It says the trial is planned for the first of August. That's barely three months from now. Why the rush? They usually prolong inquiries for years."

"I'll tell you why," said Luis. "They want to accomplish it before the edict takes effect."

"But Margarita is not a danger to the King and Queen—or the Church. She's just a generous woman who cares about people. She takes blankets and food to people waiting for their Inquisition trial. Sometimes she finds out what they are being charged with and lets them know. She's a saint!"

"I'm sorry to bring the bad news. I know she's your friend. What will you do?"

"What can I do but go and visit her."

"And be arrested like she was?" said Luis. "That's unwise, Sara Elena. Sit down and eat dinner. Take some time—think about what it all means."

"Yes Sarita, sit down," interrupted Father. "Let me get the chicken and vegetables. We will eat now, then pray for wisdom and make our plans." He tottered over to the hearth to retrieve the stew pot. "The world has turned inside out again."

"Margarita?"

"Sara Elena, is that you? I'm over here in the corner."

"Where?" Sara Elena's eyes throbbed as she picked her way through the darkness of the prison toward her friend's voice. Three pairs of red eyes glowed in the murky blackness, and then Sara heard scurrying sounds retreat across the prison floor.

"Over here, Sarita, where there's some light by the window. Maybe we can see each other."

"I'm so glad to—"

"You shouldn't come here." Margarita turned her face toward Sara Elena. Tear streaks etched crevices in her dusty face.

"I had to find you. But, oh, Margarita, you look awful."

"Never mind me. The inquisitors will notice your presence. They have their spies everywhere."

"Have you slept? Have you eaten?" Sara dropped a basket of food into Margarita's lap and sat beside her. Dirty straw covered the earthen floor, but dampness soon found its way into her skirts. The stink of urine and sweat stung her eyes and made her gag.

"Thank you, dear Sarita. I am starving. I've been here three days. Alfredo brings me what he can, but he's no good at cooking." Margarita took a bite from the empanada.

"How is Alfredo doing?"

"He may be arrested soon. Usually they detain a whole family at once, but he wasn't home when they came for me."

"Where is he staying—at home?"

"No, at his shop, but we know that's not safe for long."

"What else is he doing? Can he still work?"

"Life is complicated. We don't know who we can trust. He works some, but nobody comes to the shop—afraid they'll be tainted by suspicion, also."

"I've been making quiet inquiries about your case."

"Bless you, Sara Elena." Margarita took a sip of the wine. "I've been so thirsty."

"There are two oranges in the basket, too. Keep one for later."

"What have you found out during your inquiries?" Margarita dug a thumb into the orange's rind, releasing a bittersweet burst of fragrance into the stinking room.

"Not much. Your sole fault seems to be aiding people under investigation by the Inquisition."

"That is my calling and duty—not a fault."

"I agree, but you know the authorities want people to betray their friends and neighbors—not help them.

They want to hear bad things about people's habits and shortcomings."

"Outrageous."

"I know—I don't like it, either."

"In the name of truth, the Inquisition extracts information from people of dubious reputation or spiteful inclination and then convicts good people of heresy using false testimony. It's shameful!" Margarita's voice echoed in the small alcove.

"Shh. Keep your voice down. Someone will hear."

"I don't care. There's no way out of here alive."

"Don't say that. Some people are cleared of suspicion and released."

"When have you heard of that happening? You're dreaming." Margarita wiped her hands on her stained skirt.

"We can hope and pray."

"I do pray, my dear Sara Elena. I pray that I'll stay true to my mission of helping the unfortunates here. I guess God has brought me a little closer to them." She grasped Sara Elena's hands.

"Dear Sarita, go now. You must not stay any longer."

"I'll come again, and bring more food." She took the basket and got up from the moldy straw.

"Be careful not to be seen coming or going. Take the short, angled street behind the prison and keep your head covered."

"I'll see you next time—soon."

"*Adios*, Sarita. God bless you."

Sara Elena took Margarita's advice and ducked under her black shawl. She kept her head down, walking as inconspicuously as possible past the guard at the prison gate. Her feet plodded silently over the old cobblestones of the narrow back street. She didn't breathe until she slipped around the corner.

Finally, I'm out of sight of that horrible place.

She took a breath then noticed something different on the main street.

What's happening out here?

Dozens of people filled the wide avenue, clutching purses in their hands. Three men ran into a moneychanger's, only to be pushed out by the manager closing the door. Whole families carried dishes and chairs, candlesticks and tapestries in their hands. The babble of voices assaulted Sara Elena's ears. She squeezed through the throng of bodies.

"What happened today? What is everyone doing?" she asked a middle-aged woman next to her.

"If you haven't heard, you're the only one in all Granada who doesn't know."

"Know what?"

"Edict of Expulsion. Their Royal Majesties want all Jews out of the country."

"When?"

"In three months. It was announced today in the plaza."

"Why are people carrying around all their possessions?"

"To get money for passage out of Spain. What use are valuables when we've been displaced from our homes."

Several people crowded in between, so Sara Elena lost sight of the woman. Someone ripped the basket out of her hand. Sara Elena grabbed it back and held her arms up in front of her. She pushed through the crowd. People stepped on her toes and pulled at her clothes. Once, someone tugged at her shawl. Finally, she reached her front door and swirled in out of the confusion.

"The Edict—"

"Yes, we know," said Beata, reaching for her. "Sara Elena, you're trembling."

"People have gone mad. It's all fists and elbows out there."

"We know," said Raul. "We just came through the crowds a little while ago. The royal heralds announced the proclamation an hour ago. Where were you?"

"At the prison seeing Margarita." Sara Elena brushed back a lock of hair. "I look and smell like a prisoner." She wrinkled her nose.

"I wasn't going to mention it," said Beata, "but you could use a washing."

"Thanks, Sister," grinned Sara Elena. "Where's Luis?"

"Luis said he had some business to see to."

"By the way, I hope you've booked your passage already."

"Yes, we have," said Raul. "Praise be to God, we got it yesterday, paid for by some of Beata's dowry."

"Just another reason to love your new wife, Raul." Father had come into the room without anyone noticing.

"Yes, that's what I was thinking." He reached for Beata and encircled her with his arms.

"Where are you going?"

"We booked passage on a ship bound for Naples. From there, we will travel to Jerusalem."

"Ah, the Holy Land," said Father. "I heartily approve. Go to the heartland of our faith." He grimaced and rubbed his temple.

"We'll miss you," said Sara Elena. "When do you leave?"

"The first of June, well ahead of the imposed deadline. Thanks to you, Sara Elena, we were able to get a good vessel with an honest captain."

"Yes, thank you, Sara Elena." Beata kissed her on both cheeks, and then pinched her nose.

"But you still need a bath."

"I will go now, if you—"

"It's the beginning of the end—do you hear? Spain will never recover—" Father's voice rose to an angry howl.

"I don't feel well." He clutched his head. "Can't see—can't feel—hand—foot." He crumpled to the floor in front of them and lay still.

Chapter 16

"Papa!" Sara Elena reached him first. She loosened the narrow ties around the neck of his doublet.

Raul and Beata supported him under each arm and helped him into the bedroom. Sara Elena went ahead, taking off the coverlet and spreading back the blankets. They propped him on the edge of the bed. Raul pulled off Father's boots, and removed the belt from around his waist.

"I feel weak." Droplets of sweat poured down Don Alonzo's flushed face.

"What did he say? I can hardly understand him."

"His voice sounds far away, like he's not really here."

Sara Elena leaned down and put her ear next to his mouth. "What is wrong, Father? Where do you feel pain?

"Head—pain like a knife. Can't feel arm—leg—" His words faded away like a wispy summer cloud. His head sank into the pillow.

"Beata, get some hot water and a cloth. Raul, go find Juan Sanchez. He may be with Luis, since they are preparing to go with that Columbus fellow. Tell him we need them both now." Sara Elena barked out the orders, surprised at her own fierceness.

The two hurried to fulfill her commands. "I'll be back as soon as I can. Pray that I can find them," said Raul as he slung his cloak over one shoulder, kissed Beata and sped out the door.

Beata raced to the kitchen for a bowl and towel, and then sped to the water kettle heating over the hearth. She splashed the steaming liquid into a pottery bowl and returned before Sara Elena could let out a breath.

"What new evil has come upon us?"

"Beata, help me take off Father's doublet," said Sara Elena. Together they worked at easing his limp arms up and through the ample sleeves, one after the other. Sara Elena lifted Father up so Beata could pull the garment over his head.

"He looks so ashen. I'm worried," said Beata.

"You're right. He's as pale as the bed sheets." She wrung out the wet cloth and placed it on the old man's head. "Father, I love you. You need to rest. We've sent for a doctor." She stroked his hand. His eyes flickered open for a moment, then closed.

After she smoothed the blankets up around his shoulders, Sara Elena turned toward her sister-in-law and saw the deep creases carved into her face.

"What more can be done? Tell me, and I'll gladly do it."

"Don't distress yourself. You have done all you can for now. Wait for Juan Sanchez and see that your father rests quietly."

Beata approached Sara Elena and wrapped her arms around her. Sara Elena pulled away.

"I can't let myself give in to emotion. I need to watch, not get clouded by sentiment. I'll go now and wash up." She walked out.

"I understand," said Beata, shrinking back as though she didn't. She retreated to a corner. Raul, Luis and Juan Sanchez burst into the room a few minutes later. Sara Elena came running from the kitchen, wiping her face and hands with a towel.

"I'm here. Tell me what happened," said Juan Sanchez, flinging his cloak over a nearby chair and unbuckling his sword. He rolled up his sleeves. "Hot water, soap and a towel," he snapped.

"Father came down with a strange malady less than an hour ago. He complained of weakness in an arm and leg and a sharp pain in his temple. He's also feverish."

"Can you think of anything else?" Juan Sanchez fixed his intent eyes on Sara Elena.

"His speech is clouded," Sara Elena murmured.

"Hmm." Juan Sanchez plunged his hands in the hot water Beata had fetched and proceeded to scrub his hands carefully. "Clean hands for touching patients," he said. 'I read that in an old manuscript. Now, if you'll all excuse me, I need to examine your Father." He motioned for them all to leave the room.

Luis, who had come in with Dr. Sanchez, led the procession out of the bedroom. The others followed him to the dining room. They settled onto benches around the oak table.

"What does he plan to do that we cannot see?"

"Perhaps a more thorough exam. I've heard some doctors look at the unclothed body. They can see physical signs of illness when a patient can't describe how they feel." Raul drummed his fingers on the table. Beata nodded.

"That's disrespectful. We need to go back in." Sara Elena moved toward the door.

"Stay here, sister." Luis thrust out his arm. "I trust Doctor Sanchez. He has a very good reputation, according to Captain Columbus. Said he was glad to have him on the voyage."

"Are you still pursuing that nonsense?" Raul glared at his younger brother.

"Yes, I am. I'll be leaving on one of three ships at the end of the summer. Columbus is making the arrangements and getting his financial support now."

"You are foolhardy, brother."

"No, just pursuing a dream." Luis straightened his shoulders and raised his chin.

"Stop arguing," said Sara Elena. "We should be praying for Father." She clasped her hands together and bowed her head, but Raul interrupted—

"We also should think about the future. Who will take care of Father? How long will it take for him to recover?"

"We don't know any answers until we speak to Doctor Sanchez."

"I can't cancel my voyage." said Luis. "I've already signed up for at least one year, or until Columbus successfully returns."

"*Igualmente*. It is the same for us. We booked our passages to Naples, and cannot get our money back. We must leave June first."

"Father won't be well by then. His injuries are too severe, can't you see that?" Sara Elena's voice rose higher and louder.

"Should I mention it—we don't even know if he will survive," said Luis.

Raul punched his brother in the nose. "How dare you say that?"

"Pardon me, but it's the truth." He dabbed at blood dripping from his reddened nose.

"What's the truth?" said Juan Sanchez as he came out of Alonzo's bedroom.

"We were just discussing—it's nothing." Luis looked down at the floor.

"How is Father? Can you tell us anything?" Sara Elena searched Juan Sanchez's face for clues.

"His condition is grave, as you've probably guessed. I've seen this affliction in others, especially older people. A sudden pain, weakness of an arm and leg on one side of the body, and sometimes speaking is affected. We know so little about the malady."

"So what can we do to help him?"

"Our medicines can do nothing but relieve the pain. I'll give you some poppy juice to calm him and let him sleep. Other than that, keep watch over him. Rest and then give him clear broth when he awakens. It will be many days before your Father returns to his former self, if he ever does. I'm sorry."

"Can you give us no hope?"

"His body is still sturdy for his age, in spite of his other ailments. Perhaps his fighting spirit will prevail in this struggle." He opened his bag and took out a small vial. "Give him several drops in the morning and the same at night." He handed it to Sara Elena.

"Señorita Torres," he said, letting his hand linger on hers. "May I speak with you a moment—alone?"

"Yes, of course. Let's step outside."

"Beata, could you sit with Father and tend to his needs?"

"Gladly." Beata turned to go into the sickroom, while Juan Sanchez followed Sara Elena outside. The two brothers stood in the hallway.

"Señorita Torres—Sara Elena—the duty of caring for your father will fall to you, I fear. It will not be easy. You will need to stay with him day and night, to see that nothing further befalls him."

"I understand."

"This illness has come at a bad time. All your family is leaving the country. The political situation is desperate. I fear your financial stability will suffer, as well. What will you do?"

"I will stay with Father as long as he needs me. We will manage."

"How?"

"We have some savings, and I can continue the translation work."

"You don't know how much work it will be to care for your sick father. Promise me you will get someone to come and help." The scar on his cheek pulsed.

"I'm not afraid of hard work."

"I know that. And you have such courage—it's one of the things I admire about you." He grabbed her hands in his. "But the responsibilities of nursing an invalid are heavy. Who do you know that could come and stay for a while?"

"Perhaps I could ask Ana, our old housekeeper. She lives up the hill."

"Send Luis to get her, Sara Elena. Promise me." The intensity of his feeling found its way into a tightening grip on her hands. She winced and pulled her hands free and then wished she hadn't been so hasty.

"I promise."

"Good. I must leave now, but I'll return in a few days to check on my patient. I'll see you then, and will have more to tell you."

"Thank you, Doctor Sanchez. I'll get your cloak." She turned to go inside the door, but stopped. "My brothers and I are grateful."

"You are welcome." His eyes met hers. "And please—call me Juan."

The following days blended together like simmering soup. Each day's tasks, threatening to overpower, melded into a blur of misery and obligation. Sara Elena's movements felt thick and sluggish. She rubbed her arms and shoulders and often let out a yawn worthy of a coddled cat.

The minute Luis burst in upon her and Ramón, Ana went to pack a few things in her shoulder bag, then put on her shawl and followed after him.

Ana said, "I knew something was wrong even before you came."

Luis brought a horse for her to ride. He lifted her up, tied the bundle to the saddle and led horse and rider down the steep hill back to the Torres house.

"Ana, I'm so glad to have you with me again." Sara ran to embrace her, tears streaking her face. "I'm so nervous now. I can't do the simplest of tasks anymore. Yesterday I sliced a deep gouge in my finger while chopping onions." She held up her bandaged finger. "See? It bled everywhere! I'm still finding orange spots on my clothes and on the floor—I need your help."

"I'll do the marketing, cooking and cleaning," Ana said, her face a steely mask.

"I can help you—"

"Come now, Sarita," said Ana. "Let me take over the kitchen duties. Your mind and heart are with your sick father, as they should be. Go and tend to him. That's where you belong." Ana washed Sara's streaked face and re-wrapped her finger with a piece of clean linen.

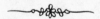

Sara Elena retreated to Father's bedchamber. "The worry never stops. It makes me into a simpleton. My hands shake. I forget what I should do next. I can think of nothing but Father. So, that is what I'll do."

Sara sat down and took Father's hand in hers. It was the one least affected by this terrifying sickness. Maybe he would feel her warm hand around his. She watched him sleep, felt his forehead and smoothed out the linens over his shrunken body.

Day after day she remained in close attendance, frequently changing bed linens and bathing her patient. Many times a day, she lifted Father's head to get him to swallow a little water or clear broth. Sara talked to Father and tried to get him to open his eyes, to blink or shake his head—anything to engage his mind and move his body.

"I'm so tired," Father usually indicated and closed his eyes again. His body was heavy and as supple as an anchor. Sara's arms and back muscles burned at the end of each day. She tried to resist the temptation, but often she fell asleep in the chair next to his bed. Exhausted from a long day of care, she said to Ana, "It really doesn't matter to me if the world swirls out of control beyond our door or not. My world is here in this sick room."

"Sara Elena, you must get some rest. Sit and eat now. I'll get Beata to take a turn."

Sara Elena woke up with sharp pains in her shoulders. She got up from the chair and walked over to the window, massaging the sore spots she could reach.

"Another night, another doze in the chair. I feel like a tailor's pincushion—are the needles sticking out?" She looked herself over. "Don't see any." Sara winced as the rusty latch creaked. The sun shot its dusty rays through the open shutters. The morning air trembled with a pungent, piney scent.

"I smell rosemary—or is it thyme? The kitchen garden must be in full flower." Sara looked toward the bed, now brighter with the early light.

"Father's face has regained some of its color. For weeks it's been pale as a mourning dove's wings." Sara looked at him now and saw an eye lid twitching.

"Father, do you remember the song you sang to me when I was a girl?" She spoke loudly. "At bedtime you sang it. How does it go?" She began singing as she tiptoed toward the bed.

"Sleep Sarita, *mi bonita . . .*"

Was he stirring?

"On your little bed. Sleep and dream—"

"Shleep—" Sara Elena leaned close to his ear.

"That's right. Keep singing."

"Sleep and dream, the angels guard you, all through the night."

"Sala mala ballalah."

Sara Elena scowled, her face grotesque as a griffin on a castle wall.

What does that mean? It's just nonsense.

"Thank you for trying to sing, *Father.* You rest now." Don Alonzo sank deeper into the pillow and closed onion-skin eyelids. Sara Elena straightened the covers over his bony body. His once robust framework had wasted away these past few weeks. He had become fragile as a dried tree branch.

One false step and snap, he will shatter.

She closed her eyes and leaned her head back against the wall.

Dear God, protect him, please. Is Father regaining his speech, or is he losing his mind piece by piece? Such strange babbling language came out of his mouth today. I need to ask Juan about it. I wish he would come today. But there's no reason to expect him. Doctor Sanchez comes twice a week. Didn't he just come yesterday? It's hard to separate the days— they all run together in a mind-numbing sameness.

Sara Elena's thoughts wandered from one thought to another, in a maze without an outlet. After a while, she heard noises and voices. Exiting the room, she saw Raul and Beata, breathless and rosy-faced.

"Hola, *amantes*, how are you?" She kissed them both.

"Tired," they said together, and laughed. Beata mopped her forehead.

"What's the news out there on the street?" asked Sara. I hear noise—"

"Not good."

"People are everywhere, clamoring to get passage on a ship out of Spain."

"What ships are available?"

"Nothing. Every one is completely full. There's no room left but space in steerage or on deck. Their Majesties had to extend the deadline for leaving till August second because of the shortage of boats."

"How can people take along their belongings if they're forced to lodge on deck? And won't it be dangerous for them to carry their life savings?"

"Haven't you heard? Oh, of course you haven't—" Raul paused.

"Heard what?"

"Their Majesties proclaimed that Jews may take all portable goods with them—but no gold, silver or currency."

"That's barbaric." Sara Elena raked her fingers through the wisps that once again sprang to her forehead.

"It is true, unfortunately." Raul tweaked his chin. "After the Edict of Expulsion proclamation, the richest people went about trying to arrange for shipping of their goods. For those without money, however, it's a much different situation."

"Can't they sell everything here and take currency?"

"How much are household goods worth if everyone's selling them? And, as I said, if you're caught leaving the country with more than a few *maravedis*, they will be taken away." Raul paced the floor as he talked. "I'm grateful we are leaving tomorrow—thanks to you."

"Is it time for you to go already?"

"Yes, tomorrow is June first."

"Last week you told me the Fontanas just walked away from their home, and rode their two horses toward Portugal."

"Yes, and now looters have ravaged their home. That's happening everywhere."

"Have people forgotten their sense of honor?"

"It's all confusion and pain and a scramble for survival."

"Speaking of survival, how's Father today?" said Raul.

"He's resting quietly. Sometimes I think he's making progress, but then he does something strange and I lose faith."

"I know it's a slow process. Have you gotten him out of bed yet?"

"Oh, no. He's too weak."

"Sara, it's been a month or more since he fell ill. Shouldn't he get out of bed sometime?"

"Perhaps—maybe—I don't know." Sara Elena covered her eyes and shook her head. "Tell me what to do. I'm worn out with thinking. I can't think!" She slumped onto a bench.

"You're exhausted." Beata reached out and laid a hand on her shoulder. "Let us take care of him today, so you can go out for a while."

"I don't know what I'd do."

"Sister, don't despair." Raul patted Sara's back. "I'll send a message to Doctor Sanchez right now. Let's see what he says." Raul drafted a note, sealed it and looked outside.

"Here, boy," he said to a boy playing on the street outside. "Take this to Doctor Sanchez, quick as you can, and wait for his reply. Bring it back immediately. Can you do that?"

"Yes, sir."

"Here's a coin for you, and there will be another if you do it quickly."

"*Gracias, señor.*" He dashed off and disappeared around the corner.

"Now then, Sara Elena. Let's put our trust in Doctor Juan Sanchez. He'll help us." Raul sat down next to her and put his arm around her shoulders. Sara sighed.

"*Quizás.* Perhaps. Besides God our Father, the doctor's our only hope right now."

Chapter 17

Instead of the boy's return, a quick knock on the door produced Juan Sanchez. "Your note sounded urgent, Raul."

Sara Elena ushered him in, while Raul offered a glass of wine. He waved it aside.

"Has your father's condition changed since yesterday?" He stood against the wall, facing Sara.

"Not for the better, if that's what you mean. Tell him, Sara Elena." Raul turned toward his sister.

"He keeps getting weaker. His mind wanders. Today, I tried to get him to speak, and he did, at first." She looked up to see Juan Sanchez studying her face.

"That's good."

"I thought so, and I urged him to keep going. His next words, if you can call them that, were nonsense syllables meaning nothing. I worked so hard to get one word out of him, and then he retreated to babble. It's hopeless." Sara Elena rubbed her itching eyes.

"Why do I always cry? I'm tired of it!"

"How often have you gotten out of the house since your father fell ill?" His concerned look melted her fragile composure.

"Once or twice, I think. But we're not talking about me."

"An illness like your father's requires patience and endurance. The one who cares for the invalid must be protected as much as the ill person. You are on the verge of collapse."

Juan walked over to Sara Elena and lifted her chin. He turned her face from side to side, cradling it as if it might shatter at any time. "Your eyes are red, your face though pretty, is pale, and your disposition is brittle. This doctor prescribes a respite for you."

"Don't be silly, Juan Sanchez. I am perfectly well." Sara Elena flicked a tear from each eye. She got up and wobbled toward the kitchen.

"When did you eat last?" Juan's hand came to rest on her shoulder, and its gentle pressure forced her to sit back down.

"I don't know. This morning, I think."

"*La enfermera* needs rest and a day away from her responsibilities."

"I agree," said Luis, who had just come in. "You look terrible, Sara."

"*Gracias, mi familia* and Dr. Sanchez, for your concern, but—"

"We insist on taking care of Father this evening and tomorrow," said Raul, as Beata nodded her agreement.

"Get some rest tonight," ordered Doctor Sanchez. "I will return tomorrow to discuss some new treatments for Don Alonzo. And, if you would accompany me to the plaza, we'll look for some special herbs I've been reading about that might help improve his condition. That will also get you away from the sickroom."

"But, I'm not a child—" *I sound like a whiny little girl, though.*

"The doctor orders it. I'll see you tomorrow at ten."

"Very well." Her mouth curved into a weak smile.

"*Hasta luego.*" He left as quickly as he came.

"Sara Elena has her own personal physician, doesn't she?" said Luis shooting her a grin.

"That's not true! He's here to take care of Father."

"Your care seems quite important to him, also, dear sister."

"Tell me, Luis, how fares your Captain Columbus with outfitting his boats?"

"Oh, so you want to talk about the voyage, Sarita? I'll go along with the abrupt change of topic." He winked at her. "Well, *Admiral* Columbus—you know the King and Queen made him an admiral—He hoped to leave the end of July, but that doesn't look certain now."

"Why not?"

"All the available boats have been put into service to escort Jews out of the country. Even dilapidated hulks command a huge price for passage. I don't know how Columbus will get ships ready in time." He scratched his head.

"How many does he need?"

"Three, he says. The King and Queen have commanded the city of Palos to furnish the vessels, and others in the south here must make provisions available. They've been hoarding things to sell to the Jews—more lucrative, you know."

"Why must he leave the end of July?"

"To catch the prevailing winds west. He calculates when they will change with the seasons."

"How big is the crew?"

"Admiral Columbus wants ninety. We have most of the officers. I'll be interpreter and Juan Sanchez will be the ships' surgeon, of course. It's been hard to get the regular crew—they think Columbus is a little *loco.* And they resent being forced to help him."

"How will he get everyone in time?"

"Did you hear Ferdinand and Isabella offered to pardon anyone who completes a voyage with Columbus? So, at least we can get some criminals on board."

"Could be a disagreeable bunch."

"Actually, it's not so different from how it usually happens. We'll see results soon enough, I think."

"Luis, I worry about you. Is this trip safe?" Sara patted his cheek.

"If I wanted to be safe, I wouldn't have signed up for this expedition." Luis leaned over and embraced Sara Elena. "Don't worry, Sister. I can handle anything that comes my way. I will be fine."

"Just remember, wherever in the world you find yourself, your family loves you."

"*Mil gracias*, Sarita. Now, I must be off—there is still much to prepare. *Adios.*"

"Promise you won't leave without saying goodbye."

"Of course not. Goodbye for now."

"*Hasta la vista.*"

"I'm here as promised," said Juan Sanchez as he strode in the next morning. His mottled green eyes glowed bright with anticipation. "I have much to tell you, Sara Elena. I read a long time last night—"

"Good morning to you, too, Doctor Sanchez." Sara Elena made a short curtsy.

"You always demand the best manners. Good morning, señorita." He grasped her hand, kissed it and bowed. "How are you, my lady?"

"I rested well, thanks to Beata. She sat up with Father during the night."

"You look exceedingly fine today—better than you have for weeks." Juan smiled.

"It's amazing what a clean gown and a scrubbed face will produce. I'm glad you approve, Doctor."

"I mean, it's good to see you refreshed." Juan Sanchez looked away to hide his warm face.

"We're wasting time, Doctor Sanchez. You've come to help me deal with Father. What have you learned in all your reading?" She led him to the living room *sala* where they sat down.

"I had a patient once with an illness like your father's, an old man, a farmer who supported a wife and invalid son. In spite of my warnings to stay in bed and recuperate slowly, he got out of bed after just two or three weeks and went out to the fields a little bit every day. He worked until he got tired—but every day he could work a few minutes longer."

"Wasn't that a great risk?"

"I kept telling him that, but he always replied 'How else will I feed my family?'"

"What happened to him?"

"In spite of all my warnings, he got stronger and his mind more alert. He still had some weakness and limping, but I'd say he recovered better than others who waste away in bed."

"Why are you telling me this?"

"The human body can heal itself, often without a physician's intervention. Medicine is only beginning to study its mysteries. Although I read last night through some of the best writings of the ancients and current thinkers, I found no answer to your father's treatment. It was only as I thought about the old farmer that I received insight."

"Yes?"

"Would you allow me to try a similar routine on your father? I think it could make a difference."

"He's terribly weak right now. How much would you require of him?"

172

"Whatever he can manage. It will be a long, slow process, but he needs to get up each day. He will have to learn how to walk again."

"I'm afraid he will fall."

"That's why he will need encouragement. I plan to come every day from now on. You and I can support him, one on each side, and help him to get stronger and walk."

"What about his speech?"

"I cannot promise what will happen. His words may become clearer or not at all. But perhaps if he hears conversation again, some of it will seep in. You may be surprised—he might say intelligent words again."

Sara Elena sat still as if staring into a deep pool. "I will do what you say," she finally said. "It's the only positive suggestion I've heard for many weeks. Shall we get started?"

"Courage and action, always. You amaze me. Sara Elena."

"Let's begin." Juan followed Sara Elena through the hall and into Don Alonzo's bedroom.

"Good morning, Beata. Doctor Sanchez is here to try a new treatment on Father. Why don't you go get something to eat from Ana, and take a *siesta*."

"Thank you." She yawned. "I don't know how you have done it all these weeks, Sara. I'll be back after a while." Beata retrieved her blue shawl from the back of the chair and drifted out of the room.

Juan and Sara Elena spent the rest of the morning working with Father. Doctor Sanchez explained what he wanted to accomplish. He and Sara Elena coaxed Father to sit up on the edge of the bed and then move to the chair. Each movement, hesitant and slow, showed that his muscles had forgotten how to move. When Dr. Sanchez suggested he stand, he balked.

"Enaah," he said. "Blalah." He shook his head.

"Very good, Don Alonzo. We'll try again tomorrow. You are a good student." He and Sara Elena eased Father back under the covers. He sighed and immediately fell asleep.

"He looks innocent as a child," said Sara.

"And weak as a babe." Juan gazed at Don Alonzo.

Beata met them as they exited the room.

"How's the patient?"

"He tried his best to follow my instructions," said Juan Sanchez.

"Father has so little strength. Even if your program works, it will take a long time." Sara Elena paused and rubbed her lower back. "I'm tired, too."

"Come with me, Señorita Torres. Let me take you to the plaza now. We'll get something to eat, and then look for new herbal remedies."

"All right, if that's part of the regimen. I think Ana will want to accompany us as chaperone. We'll see you later, Beata. Can you manage?"

"I'll be fine. I expect Raul to return soon."

Juan and Sara Elena walked along the narrow street and toward the plaza. Ana followed behind them a few paces. They strolled along for a while in silence. The uneven cobblestones dug into Sara Elena's soft-soled shoes. She tried to match Juan's long strides.

"Working with a person who cannot support himself is difficult. You handled him well, Sara Elena." Juan glanced sideways at her, his mouth curved up in a crescent moon.

"We did it together. You're right—there's no other way. But, our family cannot ask you to come back every day."

"It would be my pleasure. Your father is stubborn, and courageous—a family trait, perhaps?

"Do you mean he's like me, or maybe that I'm like him?"

Juan shrugged his shoulders in reply. "There are worse characteristics to have." They passed by a *cantina*. "I smell something wonderful. Would you like to eat here?"

"Of course. They make a good meatball stew here."

"Wonderful. And while we eat, we can discuss more treatments and remedies for your Father." They found a table. Ana sat nearby.

"I do appreciate your concern, but—"

"But what?"

"Luis thinks you have other reasons for being so helpful."

"Does he really? What reasons?"

"He wouldn't say."

"I do. Can't you guess, Sara Elena?" He took her hand. "You take my breath away. I hadn't thought I—"

"Juan Sanchez, I hope you aren't considering offering me another marriage proposal." Sara Elena raked the curls off her forehead. "If you are, I'll say right now, I don't plan to marry for a long, long time—maybe never." Ana stirred and cleared her throat as Sara Elena withdrew her hand.

"You don't understand." Juan looked stunned.

"Oh, so you're not thinking of marriage?" Sara Elena hated the tone of her voice, but couldn't seem to stop.

"Well, I'm not opposed to it," said Juan, "but I don't think the girl is willing." He stared at Sara Elena forever with deep, sad eyes. Then a thought came to him and he assumed a playful manner.

"Say, maybe you can advise me, Sara Elena. You see, I met this red-haired girl with blue eyes and so stubborn she makes a mule seem even-tempered."

"Yes, go on." She sat on the edge of her seat.

"This young woman comes from a loving family and has many talents—she can cook, she can translate documents—"

"Oh, really?" Sara Elena rolled her eyes.

"Yes, but she's had many tragedies in her life, and especially a string of odd marriage proposals, so she's scared." Juan leaned forward, hands clasped on the table.

"Scared? Or realistic?" Sara Elena's face grew taut and her jaw locked solid.

"Afraid—afraid to give her heart away to anyone." He nodded.

"So, what will you do, Doctor Sanchez?"

"I thought you could advise me, Sara Elena." Juan glanced at her.

"You'll just have to be patient, and wait for her." Sara Elena gazed back.

"Wait for her to love me?" His face looked bleak.

"Yes, if she ever will."

"How long will it take?" Now he was staring.

"Maybe a long time." She dropped her eyes.

"I will wait however long it takes." Juan gazed at Sara Elena so long she felt his intensity. "Until then, I'll continue as I am."

"And what is that?"

"A friend and helper of the family—and a doctor." Juan's mouth creased in a smile.

Sara Elena blinked and grinned. "Can we just be friends, then? It would be lovely just to discuss problems with you." Ana nodded her approval.

"Yes, I'll be your friend. Now, let's talk." He rubbed his temples. "Although conversing with you is like wrestling a tiger."

They ordered soup and bread. Sara Elena asked the first question.

"Tell me a little about yourself. You're from Córdoba, right?"

"Yes. My parents still live there. My Father is a merchant, trading in leathers."

"How did you become a surgeon? Did your Father oppose it?"

"I always enjoyed learning—had a knack with herbs and potions."

"Where did you learn your skills?"

"I learned about herbs from an old monk. People brought the sick to him. My mother often went to the monastery infirmary to help care for the ill and dying. I followed along. After my Father saw that I was good at it, he didn't oppose my choice."

"And now, you're the surgeon for the great Columbus venture. Why?"

"I needed a job—and wanted to try something new." Juan Sanchez pushed away from the table and uncrossed his legs. "That's enough about me. Come on, let's walk to the plaza. Then I'll ask you all my questions." He dropped some coins for the meal beside his plate, helped Sara Elena out of her chair, and guided her through the street. Ana trotted along behind.

The next day dawned clear as transparent silk. The sun began its morning duty of warming the house's rosy sandstone blocks. Cobblestones in the street baked like bread rolls in an oven. A light breeze filtered through the windows.

Raul and Beata stood near the door, their bags piled around them. "We really must go now or the caravan will leave without us." Sadness crept into Raul's eyes as he looked at his beloved father and sister who needed his help now more than ever.

"How long did you say it will take to get to the coast?" said Sara Elena.

"Not long," said Beata.

"I hate to see you go," said Sara Elena. "We will miss you so much." Don Alonzo nodded while tears streaked down his cheeks. The family hugged and kissed one another and a silence fell upon the room.

Raul looked at Beata and took her hand. "We want you to know our good news before we leave. Beata is with child." He put his arm around her.

"The babe will be born about January. We should be settled in Jerusalem by then." Beata's face glowed with a new radiance Sara hadn't seen before.

"As soon as we reach the Holy Land we'll send word, and then later when the babe is born." Raul reached for his cloak and travel bag. "I hate to say it, but we really must leave now—it's getting late."

After more embraces and tears, they hurried out to meet the horse caravan.

"*Vaya con Dios*," Luis called after them.

"They are in God's hands now," said Sara Elena.

"Yes, and only God knows when we'll see them again," said Ana.

Chapter 18

❋

The next few weeks sped by, filled with the daily visits of Juan Sanchez. Sara Elena looked forward to hearing his deep voice each day, encouraging Father to try one more new thing or to walk farther than the day before. During the early days, he and Sara Elena struggled just to get Don Alonzo out of bed.

"Father, please sit up." Sara Elena grasped one arm and Juan the other. Pillows stuffed behind his back kept him in upright position, but he slumped to one side.

"Don Alonzo, you look like the least thing could push you over—a feather or a gust of wind," said Juan. "If you're going to walk again, we need to strengthen your muscles. Here, let me show you what to do." Juan bent and raised one arm up and down from the elbow. "Now, Sara Elena, help him with the other arm." Sara Elena followed his example.

"Now, Father, try to do it yourself." Sara Elena looked at him with sympathy and encouragement. His face grimaced with determination as he bent and lifted his left arm. But as he lifted his right arm, it became clear he had lost almost all of its control and mobility. He could barely move it at all. Sweat poured off his face with the effort. He grunted and let his hand drop.

"That's fine, Don Alonzo," said Juan. "It will take some time to regain your strength."

"He's so weak," Sara Elena said under her breath. Deep creases zigzagged across her forehead.

"It's not unusual for such an illness." Juan glanced at Sara Elena. "He may or may not regain the full use of his right arm."

"Well, what use is it to work with him, then?" Sara's eyes welled with frustration.

"I believe your father will get weaker if we do nothing, but he may improve if we try to help him."

"Of course, you're right. But it's so tedious." Sara took a deep breath. "Here, Father, try it again." Sara Elena smiled as she coaxed the infirm man to move his limbs once more.

"Tomorrow, we'll work your legs, also, Don Alonzo." Juan clapped him on the shoulder. Don Alonzo peered up at him and smiled.

Father winced as he lifted his useless right arm from the shoulder a few inches off the bed covers. After a while, he let his arms drop and closed his eyes.

"Yes, you rest now, Don Alonzo. You've worked hard. You've earned a *siesta*."

Sara Elena removed the extra pillows from behind Alonzo's back and helped him lean back into a horizontal posture. She arranged the covers around his shoulders, and motioned for Juan to follow her out of the room.

"He's naturally weak right now, but I believe your father can improve by moving his muscles again." Juan wiped his forehead with a handkerchief.

"I've never heard of such a treatment before."

"I told you it's just an idea of mine, based on my observations of several people who have recovered from this affliction."

"What's the alternative?" Sara Elena looked up to see the green marbled eyes watching her. She jumped back a step.

"Like I said, if we do nothing, he will only get weaker and waste away. Remember, his progress will vary. Some days a lot, and some days it will seem he's going backwards."

"I guess we have no choice, then." Sara Elena blew auburn coils off her face and shone a smile in Juan's direction. "Will you stay for lunch, doctor?"

"Call me Juan—and yes, I will stay. I've heard you're a good cook, but I must test the claim by direct observation." He flashed a smile back that reached all the way to his eyes, and then turned to the wash basin to clean his hands.

The next several days, Juan and Sara Elena worked at getting Don Alonzo to raise his legs, first straight out and then to bend the knee and curl it as close to his chest as he could. The right leg also refused to work normally, hanging limp and lifeless from his hip. Only with clenched teeth and a fierce determination did Alonzo raise his leg a few inches off the bed sheets.

"Good, Father—wonderful." Sara Elena exclaimed over each small triumph.

"Wonderful—marvelous," added Juan, standing alongside to support Don Alonzo's frail body.

"Think of all the progress you've made, sir." said Juan one day, as he watched Don Alonzo lift each leg ten times before sinking back against the pillows. "I think you're ready to begin walking." He grinned at Sara Elena.

"Wonderful! Are you ready?" She beamed at her father and then back at Juan, showing her delight. Her gaze lengthened and lingered on that rugged and now familiar face. She dropped her eyes as she saw an unguarded longing in his eyes.

"You love Juan." The words came out so clear and sure from Alonzo's lips, more a statement than a question. Sara Elena dropped her eyes as her face heated.

"Father, you said a whole sentence." She avoided Juan's look, but heard his chuckle.

"Very good, Don Alonzo. You notice your surroundings—that's a sign you're getting well." His deep laugh bubbled out. "What I notice is your father's strength and endurance returning." Juan looked at Father with serious eyes.

"Yes." Don Alonzo nodded and nodded as his words became clearer.

"Yes."

More weeks passed. Each day, Juan arrived to give the muscle training treatments. Gradually, Don Alonzo's labored steps became stronger and steadier. From the first feeble paces, he progressed to walks around the room, and then down the hall.

"Father's right foot still drags and doesn't work properly yet," sighed Sara Elena after a vigorous workout one day. "His right hand, either. What can be done?"

"I can't promise it will return to normal function," said Juan, "but perhaps we can make it easier for him to walk. I brought something that will help." Juan went to the door and produced a stout pole carved with a lion's head for the handle and wrapped with leather strips.

"A cane?"

"Yes, someday he will need to walk on his own power, so a sturdy cane might be the solution." He looked at the old man. "You are improving every day, Don Alonzo," said Juan Sanchez. "Do you feel stronger?"

Father bobbed his head in assent. Straightening his back, he looked Juan in the eye, willing words to come. "Thanksh—"

"It's my pleasure, sir." He handed Don Alonzo the cane.

"Father, how about taking a few steps on your own?" Sara Elena looked at Juan.

"Without our support? Yes, I agree. I think it's time." Juan's eyes roved her face and shone with the answer they saw there.

"Rest . . . first." They had been walking along the street in front of the house. He leaned against a sandstone wall and sank down on a protruding ledge. Summer sun radiated off the golden walls, creating an unrelenting heat. Don Alonzo wiped his face with the back of his sleeve. People dashed up and down the streets preparing for the forthcoming mass departure. They jostled the old man and his helpers.

"Let's hurry. It's getting too hot—almost time to go in for lunch."

"Here . . . I go." Father pushed himself to a standing position. Juan and Sara Elena hovered on each side.

"Five steps down the street on your own, Don Alonzo. That's your goal today." Juan smiled his encouragement.

"One." Father heaved a foot forward and leaned hard on the cane. Sweat hovered on his brow.

"Two . . . three . . . four." Sara Elena let her arms fall away. He lumbered ahead, the cane stumping a rhythm on the pavement.

"Five." Juan Sanchez grabbed his elbow as Don Alonzo wavered on the last step.

"Did it." His smile shone triumphant.

"Wonderful, Father." Sara Elena kissed his moist cheek. "And your words are returning, too." Tears shone in her eyes.

"Now, let's get you home." Juan steered him toward the house.

After they got Father in the house and settled in a comfortable chair, Ana announced:

"It's lunch time. Doctor Sanchez, will you be eating with us?"

"Thank you, but no, Ana. I have a great many tasks to accomplish today."

"Surely you won't work through *siesta* time, Juan. And you do need food." Sara Elena turned toward him.

"I like to hear you say my name," he said to Sara. "However, I really must check my list of supplies and medicines for the voyage against what has already been purchased. I've been neglecting my duties. I need to buy everything and have it delivered to the ships in Palos quickly. Sorry, but I must decline."

"You're preparing for Columbus' great expedition, aren't you? But, don't you leave at the end of summer?"

"Yes." Juan's face became serious. "That day is soon."

Sara Elena gasped and looked away. She clasped her hands and turned her back.

"We knew the day was coming, but we dread it," said Ana. "Both you and Luis will leave us for who knows how long?" Ana clucked her tongue. "We'll miss you."

"Thank you, Ana." Juan bowed to her. "I will miss all of you." He scanned the room and found Sara Elena in the corner. He addressed her softly.

"Could I speak with you about a matter of importance, Sara Elena?"

"Don Alonzo, let me help you." Ana helped the old man stand and started him toward the dining room. "Sara Elena, the stew can simmer for a while. Take Doctor Sanchez into the study, where you both can have some privacy." Her eyes twinkled.

Sara Elena led Juan into Alonzo's study. Heavy tapestry drapes swept across the corners of the window like giant eyebrows. The midday sun streaked through, burning bright squares on the tile floor. Sara slid onto a cool leather divan away from the window, where Juan joined her.

"What did you want to tell me?" Her voice was thin and tight.

"What's the date today?" He turned toward her.

"July twenty-first. Why?"

"The time is shorter than I thought. Columbus wants to leave Palos on the third of August."

"The same day the Jews must leave Spain?"

"One day after."

"Isn't that foolish? It will be impossibly chaotic."

"Columbus thinks the flurry will subside by the next morning. And he wants to leave as soon as possible. He doesn't want any of his crew delayed by the mass emigration. That's why we have to be there and on the boat by August first."

"What are you telling me?"

"Luis and I must leave tomorrow. Palos is a week's journey by horse."

"I didn't want this day to come."

"Neither did I, Sara Elena. I've come to know your family—and you—these last few weeks. I admire all of you for your courage. Living as a *converso* is degrading and difficult, but you manage so well. And your father, he digs deep into his soul and exerts all his strength toward getting better."

"Thank you. I'm grateful for how Father has improved."

"But, it will get more difficult for you soon. With Luis and Raul gone, what will you do? How will you take care of your father by yourself and keep up the family business? How many documents have you translated lately?"

"Not enough. All my time is taken up with Papa's care."

"So, what will you do?"

"Ana and I will manage. We'll plant a big garden in the back. And the Queen gave me some money."

"You must leave Spain." Juan grasped her arm. "Take your father. It's not safe for you alone. And that filthy dog, Morales—he'll keep hounding you."

"I can't go. Father couldn't survive such a long trip. Besides, I'll be fine."

"That's what I love about you, Sara Elena—your foolish, reckless spirit."

"And do you—?" Her deep eyes revealed both questions and more.

"What?"

"Love me?"

"Yes, I do." He placed his hands on her shoulders. "Don't you know that by now? In spite of this precarious time in history and all our differences, I've come to care for you deeply. You delight, you dazzle—and you inspire the best in me." He leaned forward and kissed her, his lips tender and gentle. As the kiss deepened, Sara felt her heart race.

"It's really impossible, you know." Her cheeks burned and her breath came in ragged gulps as she pulled away. "I'm nobody, saddled with an invalid father, and with very little dowry. I'm selfish, impetuous, and stubborn. And the world is falling apart." She paused. "But, I love you, too." She clasped her arms around Juan's neck and pulled him to her for another kiss.

"I've been waiting for you to say that," he said as he drew away finally to speak "Marry me, dear Sara Elena. It's not impossible if we love each other." He caressed her cheek and pulled at a stray curl.

"Yes, it is. You're leaving soon." She pulled back and took his hands in hers. "Nobody knows where you'll end up, or if you'll return."

"Columbus says six months, at most. We can marry when I return."

"I may be arrested by the Inquisition before you get back. Are you prepared to deal with that?"

"Morales? What evidence does that old meddler have on you?"

"Nothing really, but he suggested something lewd the day you rescued me—remember?"

"What?"

"His protection in exchange for certain personal favors."

"If he tries, I'll kill him!" The depth of hate in his voice startled Sara Elena.

"Don't do that. No, I must find another way to satisfy him—give him information he wants, perhaps."

"You mean betray your friends and neighbors?"

"No, I didn't mean that. Oh, I don't know—I'll think of something." She looked away.

"Promise me you won't do anything foolish."

"Maybe I could appeal to Queen Isabella. Tell her Morales is threatening me."

"Sara Elena. I must go. What do you think about what I've said today?" His hand turned her face back toward him.

"You really did propose, didn't you?" Sara Elena hugged herself. "It's wonderful to get a real offer of marriage. But, I'm afraid. Once before I got betrothed to someone—Diego

Amargo—just before he went off to war. He never came back. I don't want that to happen again."

"Who did you say—Diego Amargo? I knew someone by that name. I was surgeon to the armies gathered for battle at Huelva. I remember him talking about his *novia*."

"You remember him?" Her mouth dropped open.

"Yes, he fought bravely, as I remember. The battle was fierce and our side outnumbered. He and his men held their position all day, but finally, he received a mortal blow to the chest."

"Didn't last long—died quickly, they told me." She sobbed.

"Yes. Sara Elena. I'm so sorry." He sat beside her and gathered her into his arms.

"I couldn't face that again." She closed her eyes to keep the tears from falling.

"I won't die on this voyage. I'm not a fighting man, I'm a doctor."

"I don't know. It's all happening so fast."

"Sara, promise me you'll marry me when I return."

"I guess so—of course." She threw herself into his arms once more.

"Wonderful!" A smile transformed his face. "Then, we agree. And here's a kiss to seal it." Juan pulled her face close. His lips encompassed hers, speaking of promises deeper than words.

"Don't you have to ask my father?" Sara Elena burrowed her head against his chest. His fine linen doublet smelled of pine forests.

"I'll be back tomorrow to do that. Until then, I love you."

"*Te amo, también.* Now, let me show you out." Sara Elena grabbed his hand and pulled him after her. They walked into the dining room. Ana looked at them both.

"Tomorrow I must speak with you, Don Alonzo, and then bid you all farewell. Luis and I leave for Palos." He bowed to Don Alonzo.

"No, no, not 'bye." Father shook his head.

"*Hasta luego, mi amor.*" Juan kissed Sara Elena's hand and departed.

Chapter 19

With the dawning of the new day, a new reality settled on the Torres house. The sky glowed cobalt and the whitewashed buildings shimmered like the snowy peaks of the towering Sierra Nevada above them. Red geraniums flamed from countless patios and terraces. But Juan had come to say his goodbyes.

"Here, Sara Elena, take this money I've saved. Use it to care for yourself and your father till I return." Juan placed a heavy pouch in her hands.

"Juan, what are you doing? I can't take your money." She pushed it back.

"Since you are too stubborn to leave the country, how else can I protect you? After all, you are both my beloved and my betrothed now."

"Did Father consent?"

"Gave . . . blessing." Alonzo walked out of his study, supporting himself on the sturdy, lion-handled cane. Sara Elena ran to him and placed a kiss on his pallid cheek. Then she returned to Juan.

"You see, you need to do as I ask. We are *novios* now." He pressed the coin-filled pouch into her right hand, concealing it from Don Alonzo. She took it, and suddenly felt her knees give way.

"I don't know what to say."

Juan gripped her waist and helped her sit down. He whispered into her ear. "Has my love overcome you that much, or is it the weight of my purse?"

"I guess I have been anxious about our situation—Father's and mine. I didn't realize it until now."

"Don't tell him about it," whispered Juan. "It's our secret."

"I can hardly believe how good you are to me. Thank you, dear Juan." She concealed the pouch among the folds of her skirt. "I'll take it to my room and put it in a safe place." She kissed him on the cheek, then rose and turned to go.

"Sara Elena, come into the dining room for lunch. Everyone's waiting." Ana stood in the doorway. A rare smile brightened her face. "Bring your *novio*, too." She scuffled over to Don Alonzo and began leading him toward the other room.

"How did she know?" Juan whispered.

"She misses nothing." Sara Elena squeezed his hand.

"I'll be there in a moment, Ana." Sara Elena ran to her room and placed the money in a carved wooden box that had belonged to her mother. Then she hid the box in the back of her wardrobe under some folded clothing.

Sara Elena and Juan joined the others at the table and as she looked at Luis and Juan she knew the family was gathered for a final meal together.

First Raul and Beata left. Now it's Luis and Juan. Why are there so many good-byes?

Ana had outdone herself today with roasted chicken and vegetables, rice and juicy melons. During the meal, Luis told of last-minute preparations for the voyage.

"Columbus continues to have difficulties getting supplies and crew members because of the impending Jewish migration. He frets and complains constantly."

"Yes, I know. He asks me everyday about the medical supplies."

"And have you found all that you need?"

"Now, that's an appropriate and timely question. The answer is yes, but let me explain." Everyone turned their attention to Juan as he stood.

"This sounds ominous," said Luis. He winked at Sara Elena.

"All my life I've been looking for someone who understands me—someone who keeps me from my tendency to melancholia. I have found all that in this wonderful woman." He took Sara Elena's hand. "Sara Elena and I would like to announce our betrothal." He kissed her hand.

Amid congratulations by all, Alonzo struggled to his feet to propose a toast.

"B-b-blessings . . . all." His slow, deliberate words filled the room. "Trust God's . . . m—mercy. *Shalom.*" With clinking glasses the only sound in the room, they all raised their cups and drank. Father sank down, tired from the exertion of his speech. Flickering candles bathed them all in a golden light.

"A caravan of horses and carts leaves at seven," said Luis. "I have arranged for two horses for Juan and me. We'll be leaving out of Palos, since Columbus will sail west. We'll be riding hard to get there sooner."

"Will you see Raul and Beata?" said Ana.

"No, Raul and Beata left from Almería. That's to the east and much closer to Granada, only takes two or three days by horse. Our journey is west, twice as distant, so we must make haste."

"Promise you'll send us a message that you arrived safely," said Sara Elena. She looked to Luis and then Juan. "The roads are dangerous through the mountains between here and Palos."

"We promise," said Juan. "I'll personally dispatch a message just before the three caravels set sail."

"Now we must go, sister." Luis got up from the table and kissed his sister on the cheek. Next he folded his arms around his father. "Goodbye, Father. We will meet again soon."

"*V-V-Vaya . . . con Dios.*"

Don Alonzo's words came out clearly but with great effort. Luis pulled himself away from the lingering embraces and the many tears. His muscles twitched.

"Let's go, Juan."

"Give me a minute with my *novia*. You understand." He leveled his gaze at his jumpy partner in travel.

Juan led Sara Elena to a private corner. He folded her in his bulky arms. "Living here in Spain will be precarious now. I wish you'd go join Raul and Beata."

"Father's too ill."

"It's better than staying here."

"It's too late to book passage."

"There are ways to acquire a place. You could hide on board until you get out to sea. The captain wouldn't turn back then."

"That's a desperate plan. I hardly think an invalid man could slip aboard without being noticed."

"Use the money I gave you to persuade the captain." Juan's eyes locked with hers.

"A bribe? You don't mean that, do you?" Sara Elena held his gaze for a long time. "Besides, I must stay here to care for Father."

"Then promise me you'll live quietly and not stir up the notice of anyone."

"I'll do my best."

"I guess that's all I can hope for. Dearest Sara Elena, wait for my return. I'll be back before a year is out—six months, more likely. Once I've fulfilled my contract to Columbus, we'll be wed."

"I'll be waiting, *mi querido*."

After Juan left, Sara Elena still felt the pressure of his embrace and the warmth of his kisses. She shivered. Love was a new sensation to her—exhilarating—full of unexpected delight. She thought about it as she cleared the table for Ana.

I can hope again. I have a future. And someday I'll have a home of my own. This has been a happy day. I wish it could go on forever. She sank into a chair, like a sagging pillow. *Silly girl! Everything changes tomorrow. All the people I care about are leaving, and Spain will spend all its time chasing heretics. How can anyone endure that?*

Ana came in. "Your father's taking a siesta. He felt tired after all the events of the day. How are you, child?"

"Oh, Ana. I'm overflowing with joy and at the same time I'm sad. How can life be so up and down at once?

"You've found yourself a handsome *novio*. Steady and caring. He'll make a good husband."

"I think so, too."

"*Dios te bendiga.* You are truly fortunate."

"Thank you. But now that the world is falling down around us, what will happen? How will we live—two women and a frail, old man.?"

"It's impossible without the help of the Almighty."

"I need a real answer."

"I'm telling the truth. What can we do but live one day the best we can, and then commit the next day to God's keeping? We'll plant a garden, let people know the Torres family still does translation work, and keep up the routine Doctor Sanchez began. And we'll share with others in need. We're not the only ones facing hardship."

"I know. But, you should go back to Ramon's."

"No, I need to stay here. Do you remember the story in the Holy Writings about a widow woman who used her last oil and flour to feed the prophet?"

"I think so. Because she gave freely, her flour jar and oil pot never ran out until the drought ended."

"Yes. So, let that be our example." Ana turned, and shuffled toward the kitchen. "Now, come and get the packet of food I've prepared for Margarita."

Sara Elena delivered the food to the prison. Margarita gobbled the stew and wiped the sides of the bowl with the last crust of bread. Sara noticed her flesh had wasted away these last weeks.

"How are you, Margarita? When will the Inquisition decide your case?"

"Soon. I'm bearing up, but I'm not so sure about Alfredo."

"Have you heard from him?"

"Remember old Juanita? She sent me a message that my husband is in hiding. Says he's afraid to come see me."

"He'd be put in irons if he showed up here."

"Yes. Alfredo's deathly afraid of enclosure. Gets a wild look in his eyes—and sweats all over. I'm frightened he will do something rash to avoid capture." She wrung her hands.

"I'll see what I can find out. Do you have a message I can take to him?"

"Tell him I love him—tell him to keep safe no matter what happens."

"I will." Sara Elena embraced Margarita and said goodbye.

Will I ever see her again? She kicked at a stone as she walked along toward home. *What about my family—and*

Juan? What will become of us? I need your help, God. My problems are too many.

By the time she got home, Sara Elena's mood had lifted. The bright sun glowing in the sapphire sky meant summer had fully arrived, and it was time for a light heart and a merry manner.

Nothing can spoil the rest of this day. I'll take Papa for a walk before dinner, so he can enjoy the fine weather, also. With her plan fixed, she reached her front door and walked in.

"Sara Elena, you're finally here."

"What's wrong, Ana?"

"It's your father. When I went to get him up—well, he's very weak. Come and look. Hurry!"

"Papa!" Sara Elena raced into the bedroom and knelt by the bed. Heavy curtains shrouded the windows. In the velvety darkness, she took her ailing father's hand. She saw his lips move and leaned closer to hear.

"Sara Elena."

"I'm here."

"Love."

"I love you, too, Father." She squeezed the parchment skin stretched over the bones of his hand. He stirred, and his eyelids fluttered. Reaching for each shallow breath, he rasped:

"You and Juan—love?"

"Yes, Papa. I do love him."

"Good. You, Luis, Raul, Beata—love not hate." He sank back into bed, panting for air.

"Don't talk now. Save your breath." She plumped the covers around him. "I'll be back in a moment." She ducked out of the room "Ana, have Luis and Juan left Granada yet?"

"The caravan leaves soon—it's almost seven."

"See if you can get word to them before they go."

"What shall I tell them?"

"Tell them Father is dying."

"I'm on my way, Sarita." Ana trotted out of the house, heading for the plaza where the horses and carts assembled. Travel between towns, though difficult, had now become routine. You could hire a horse or a cart if you had baggage, and expect a guide to lead you down rocky passes, over muddy streams and across grassy plains to your destination. The caravan stopped at pensions along the way, where for a few *maravedis* you could eat a bowl of lamb stew and sleep on rough homespun sheets. Not luxury, but respectable.

"*Vaya con Dios*, Ana. Go swiftly." Sara watched until Ana disappeared around the corner. She had just shut the door and turned back toward her father's room, when she heard a knock and a voice.

"Señorita Torres."

"Who is it?"

"Don Antonio Morales."

"You couldn't have chosen a worse time to come." She opened the door.

"Your summons to appear before the Inquisition." He handed Sara Elena a scroll rolled and sealed with red wax. "Perhaps this will persuade you to reconsider my offer."

"I don't care about your summons. My father is dying." She threw down the scroll and slammed the heavy oak door.

"You have twenty-four hours to arrange your affairs and present yourself to the tribunal." Morales' voice commanded her attention from beyond the door. "See that you appear without fail. Goodbye."

"*Un momento.*" Sara Elena opened the door again. "What if I consented to your arrangement? Would you do anything I asked?"

"Now you are making sense," said Don Antonio, a smile slithering across his stony face.

"Well—would you?"

"What?"

"Grant me a special request."

"Yes. If you promise to become my consort, then I'll do whatever you ask." Morales' smile slid across his face like a puddle of olive oil.

"Promise?"

"Yes, I promise." Don Antonio's eyes gleamed.

"Then, I accept your proposal."

"Splendid. And what is your special request? Name it—a new gown, perhaps?" He reached out, grasped her hand and petted it.

"I request that you release Margarita Martinez from prison, and absolve her from any charges by the Inquisition. And bring no charges against her husband, Alfredo." Sara Elena pulled her hand back and looked straight at Don Antonio.

"That's a daring wish."

"You promised, sir."

"You ask too much—" The words sputtered out.

"Then I retract my promise, too." She cast him a look that hinted more.

"I'll see what I can do—it won't be easy." Beads of sweat popped out on his wrinkled brow. "You are a shrewd woman."

"You said you had considerable influence, as I recall."

"She will be released tomorrow morning."

"Tonight—by midnight." The firm tone of her voice surprised Sara Elena.

"Ruthless bargainer," he spat out. "Very well—by midnight."

"And her husband?"

"No charges will be made. I guarantee it. And I shall send for you in the morning. Good night, my love." Don Antonio slid his hand over Sara Elena's shoulder, coughed, bowed, and left.

Sara Elena shuddered. *Will my bargain save my friend?*

Sara Elena ran to her father's room just as she heard a rattling sigh.

"Oh, no, Father. Don't die—wait." She ran to him. His eyes held the straight-ahead look of one embarking on a long journey. His skin still felt warm.

He's gone.

She sat down in the bedside chair and wrapped her arms around herself to control the trembling. She rocked back and forth feeling waves of involuntary shudders wrack her body.

Oh my dear father, my father.

She rocked and rocked. Great sobs came, and tears washed down her face. After a while, the sobs subsided and the trembling eased. She closed her eyes.

Chapter 20

"Sara Elena, where are you?"

Ana's back.

Sara stirred but didn't answer.

"Sara Elena, what's this I found outside the door?"

Ana walked into the bedroom, carrying the scroll. "How are you, dear Sarita? And your father?" She looked at Sara Elena's face and then at Don Alonzo's form lying in the bed. She dropped the scroll then crossed over the room to embrace Sara Elena. "I'm so sorry." Ana's sympathy brought a fresh round of sobs.

"I'm soaking your shoulder with my tears." Sara Elena sniffed after a while. She rubbed at her eyes.

"*No importa.* It's not important. Come and sit with me in the other room. We'll prepare the body later." Ana led her to the table. She dropped into one chair and Sara another.

"Tell me what happened here, and I'll tell you what I've done. I've only been gone half an hour, and yet I think the whole world has changed again."

"It has, Ana. Papa breathed his last just after you ran out the door. At the same time, Don Antonio, the Inquisitor, brought a summons to the Inquisition tribunal. That's the scroll you found." She shivered. "What am I to do now?"

"First, I have some bad news. The caravan left before I got there." Ana hung her head. "I am just an old woman, Sarita. Too slow."

"It's all right, Ana." Sara Elena put her arm around Ana's shoulders.

"What about Juan and Luis? How can we get word to them?"

"That's a bit of good news. Tomorrow, early in the morning, another caravan leaves."

"Why so soon?"

"The caravan driver says there's a great demand right now—so many people leaving for the coast in the next few days."

"How can we get them back—Juan and Luis?"

"We can't—there's no time. And there's no reason to come back—your father is already gone."

"Yes."

"And now there's something else. We must arrange a proper burial for Don Alonzo."

"Yes. And then I must leave Spain."

"What—?" Ana's head rocked back as if she had just been slapped on the cheek.

"Listen, Ana. I promised to become Don Antonio's consort in exchange for the release of Margarita."

"Sarita, no!" Ana shrieked.

"I won't go through with it, of course. Don't worry. But I must leave Granada before tomorrow morning. Don Antonio expects me to come to him then."

"How do you know he will release Margarita?"

"If he doesn't let her out by midnight tonight, then our agreement is broken. He wants me enough to do what I ask." Sara Elena shivered. "But I think I have a plan." She explained it all to Ana.

Listening carefully, Ana finally said, "Your plan is strange and desperate. There's no doubt it's risky, but now is the time for us all to have courage. The need is urgent."

"What will you do, Ana? Will you leave Spain, too?"

"No. I'll go back to live with Ramón now. He needs me—I'm still his mother."

"Take care that Don Antonio won't find you."

"Ramón will see to that."

"Thank you, Ana". Sara Elena leaned over and embraced her. "You have been such a blessing to our family."

"It's not ended yet. I'll go out and make the burial arrangements quietly. Nobody must know you are leaving. Word could get to Don Antonio fast." Ana got up with difficulty. "These old legs are not so reliable anymore, but I still have strong arms. Let me help move your father's body into proper position for cleansing, and then I'll have to go if I plan to get everything done."

"Remember," said Sara Elena. "Ask the caravan driver if there's space available for tomorrow. It must be tomorrow, you understand."

Ana nodded. She and Ana straightened the bedclothes and stretched out Don Alonzo's body, folding his hands over his heart.

"I will. I'll be back as soon as I can." Ana opened the door a crack and looked out. "God is our only help now. Pray that all our plans succeed." She disappeared into the growing dark.

I will pray.

"Thank you, dear friend, for all your help." Sara Elena said as Ana left. "Now I must work like a mad woman to accomplish all my tasks tonight." Sara Elena moved to the hearth and took the iron kettle off a hook hanging over the fire. She poured some in a crockery bowl and grabbed a clean cloth.

First, I'll prepare the body. Then, I'll spend the night in vigil, until it's time to go.

Sara Elena entered the bedroom and reached out to bathe her dear father's body. She flinched once before setting about her task.

His skin is cooling—and fragile as the old manuscripts he loved. Sara Elena worked with care, wiping face, arms, and legs. *Forgive me; I have to remove your doublet now. I mean no disrespect. I just need to prepare you for the burial shroud.* When she saw his shrunken chest and wasted muscles, fresh tears spilled down her cheeks.

This is the worst night of my life. I have loved you with all of my heart and now you are gone. What will I do, Father? Juan is far away—and Luis, Raul and Beata, also. All gone. Will I ever see any of them again?

Sara Elena walked to the closet and found a fresh doublet of snowy linen to put on her father. Then she carried the dirty water outside and dumped it. Returning to the bedroom, she found a pillow to kneel on. Wiping the tears off her face, she prepared to pray. Her mind found no rest as she knelt there. Every muscle tightened and her feet started to tingle.

I don't have time to think about my troubles now. I'll keep silent my fears and grief until there is time to indulge them—later. Goodbye, dear Father. I see only a long road of danger and uncertainty ahead. I have nobody but my Heavenly Father now.

What did Mama teach me when I was a child, and afraid of night noises?

She shifted her weight off her feet and thought for a while, listening in the stillness.

'I will trust and not be afraid.' Thank you, Heavenly Father, for that reminder.

Sara Elena took a deep breath and settled down to keep her vigil, releasing her grief and fears to the Almighty above.

Ana returned and knelt next to Sara Elena. She whispered in her ear.

"All the funeral arrangements are made. I'll attend and say you are overcome with emotion. By then, you will be gone. The caravan leaves at dawn. I reserved a horse for you."

"Thank you. At least a few details are settled."

"And one more thing—" Ana turned away and rubbed her eyes.

"Yes?"

"I heard a rumor on the street that Margarita's husband is dead."

"No!" Sara Elena flung her head back and roared the word.

"Yes, he jumped from the city wall yesterday. They found his body earlier today, in a crumpled heap. The remains are already buried."

"I thought I could help Margarita, but now there's just heartache for her." Sara Elena arose.

"Ana, could you keep the vigil for a while? I must pack a few things for my journey."

"Of course, Sarita." Ana bowed her head and clasped her hands under her chin.

Sara Elena ran to the wardrobe, reached to the back for the carved box, and retrieved the bag of coins. It included the *maravedis* the Queen had given her.

I have enough to secure a place in the caravan and then some. I think Margarita will come here when she's released. But how will I smuggle the coins out of Spain?

She threw a few gowns into a tapestry bag, as well as a few other necessities. Last of all, she put in her mother's hairbrush and mirror, and a scroll Alonzo had been copying before he fell ill.

I'll need to reserve enough coins for passage on a ship, also. Maybe for two. Margarita, dear friend, can I persuade you to go with me? There's nothing left for you or me in Spain. You and I are bound for Jerusalem.

Sara Elena expected a knock on the door at any moment. But who would it be?

"If Margarita comes to the door, Ana, let her in. But if it's Don Antonio, tell him I'm keeping vigil and can't be disturbed." She shuddered.

"You don't expect him tonight, do you? Remember, he said he won't come until tomorrow, and then he'll just send a carriage. After all, he must be discreet about his *pecados*—his sins." Ana sniffed, as if the mere thought were unsavory.

"I suppose." Sara Elena shifted her position. She had returned to her vigil after packing. Kneeling for hours had made her legs tingle and swell.

"Sara Elena, get up for a while and come talk with me." Ana leaned back off her knees and scrambled to get up. "Come, join me at the table." Sara Elena followed her.

"Now, Sarita, I imagine you have lots of thoughts flying around in that active mind of yours." Sara Elena nodded.

"You've always had big plans and ambitions. The way seems dangerous right now, but somehow I know you will find your way onto a ship bound for the Holy Land. How will you locate Raul and Beata?"

"I don't know yet." Sara sighed. "May be we can send a message with the next group going to Almería."

"More immediately, how will you get to Palos in time to see Juan and Luis before they leave?"

"Only God knows that, too."

"I'm proud of you." Ana patted Sara Elena's hand. "I've seen changes in you these last few months. You have become a woman of faith and courage. It showed in your patience with your Father, and in your love for Juan." Ana brushed a wisp of hair from her forehead. "Before all this happened, you were a selfish girl."

"Oh, Ana. I don't feel mature or confident at all. I have so many fears for the future." Sara Elena shuddered.

"It's the same for everyone now—our security has been pulled from under us like a dirty carpet. But, you will survive."

"How?"

"For this moment in life, all we can do is follow honor and gather courage. Your heart will discover the way."

A knock on the door!

"Go hide in the bedroom, Sarita. I'll answer that." Sara tiptoed out of the room. Ana heaved her body up and tottered to the door.

"Who comes at this time of night?" Ana spoke through the door.

"It's Margarita. Hurry, open the door."

Ana removed the bolt and Margarita pushed her way in. Her tattered skirt dragged along the tiles as she strode across the floor and sank into a chair.

"Where's Sara Elena?"

"Here I am." Sara Elena ran into the living room. Margarita caught both her hands and squeezed them hard.

"It's seems I have you to thank for my release."

"I wasn't sure Don Antonio would actually go through with it. Tell me how it happened." She sat in a chair next to Margarita. Ana went to fetch some refreshment.

"About an hour ago—the guard said it was eleven o'clock—a messenger came from the Inquisition tribunal. He brought a full pardon from Torquemada himself. Told me I was free to go, but that I must present myself to you by midnight." She looked around. "Have I come here on time?"

"Yes, it's just midnight now." Ana handed goblets to Margarita and Sara Elena.

"Why did he say that?" Both women turned to Sara Elena.

"I persuaded Don Antonio to let you go. And not charge your husband."

"How? He's not one to make deals. Stubborn, that's what he is."

"I promised him something."

"Not a bribe—not money, I hope." Margarita's eyes widened and her eyebrows shot up. "That could get you in trouble later."

"No."

"What, then? Why are you reluctant to tell me?"

"I'm not reluctant; it's just difficult to tell." Sara swallowed hard. "I promised to become his paramour in exchange for your freedom." Sara Elena let out a big sigh.

"What have you done? You're a crazy woman—*Sara la Loca*." Margarita jumped up waving her arms and began to pace the floor.

"Don't worry, Margarita. I'll be leaving Granada by dawn. I don't plan to let Don Antonio get his hands on me." Sara Elena shivered.

"I don't understand a thing you're saying. What about your father? Who will care for him?"

"Sit down, Margarita," said Ana. "Much has occurred in the last day. Let Sara and me tell you what's happened."

"I can only stay a little while. I've been trying to find my husband during the last hour, before I came here. Nobody will tell me anything."

"We'll tell you about that, too, dear Margarita, although it's not good news." The three women huddled together and began a long conversation, punctuated several times by Margarita's wails. Ana and Sara Elena held her as she clutched her middle, each bit of news a physical insult. Convulsing sobs shook her body, and tears flowed. Finally, Margarita rested her head on Ana's shoulder then lay down and slept for a while.

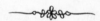

"I need to wash, and get some clean clothes." Margarita stirred and got up. "And, I must go and find Alfredo's grave."

"Let me get you some hot water," said Ana, instantly attentive. She bustled to the hearth to fetch the kettle.

"I'll find you a clean gown. We're about the same size." Sara Elena headed for the wardrobe.

Ana poured steaming water into a crockery bowl. Margarita reached for a sliver of soap and began to lather her hands and arms, and then her face and neck. She soaped her hair last and used several pitchers of water to rinse it.

"That feels so much better," she said as she rinsed and reached for a bit of toweling. "I could never keep clean in prison." She rubbed her hair dry with the towel and brushed it smooth. "There, I'll let it dry in the air—can't waste time on anything more. I have much to do before dawn." She put on a fresh gown and looked toward the fading ebony sky. "It couldn't be more than a few hours till then."

After dressing, Margarita slipped out into the night and returned about an hour later, eyes red but face composed and calm.

"How did you find Alfredo's grave?" said Sara Elena.

"Asked a guard by the city wall—he pointed me to the right place, a pauper's graveyard." She sighed. "I'm glad I found it and said my final goodbyes. Someone had marked it with a wooden cross bearing his name—bless them!" She covered her eyes and tottered on her feet. "To think, I'll never see my sweet Alfredo again!"

"Oh, dear Margarita. Come and sit down." Sara Elena reached out and guided her exhausted friend to the table. "Come and eat. A little food may help revive you."

"Will you really go with me?" said Sara Elena after Margarita had eaten some bread and cheese.

"Yes, of course." She set her mouth firm as two bricks mortared together. "What else can we do? There's no life left here for me, now that Alfredo's gone, so let's get ready to go." She brushed crumbs from her lap and got up.

"Sara Elena, you get ready, too," scolded Ana, as she picked up the dirty dishes. "Go put on your costume."

"Yes, Ana. I remember. I'll be ready in a few minutes." Sara Elena strolled into the bedroom, and saw the clothes Ana had put out. Taking off her dress but not her shift, she reached for her costume. She plopped the brunette wig on her head, the one she had borrowed from the palace. She added a few more touches to the garb.

I hope this works.

When she came out into the living room a few minutes later, Margarita laughed. "Look at you. *Embarazada—!*"

"I need to take some coins out of the country, and I thought this might work." She turned to the side, revealing the swollen belly of a pregnant woman. "Nobody will search me in this condition—will they?"

"Maybe not, but I hope you can convince the patrols you can ride a horse."

"In my delicate condition? This belly sure itches—and it's heavy. I have a lot of coins hidden inside this blanket." She scratched and readjusted her middle.

"I hope you don't jingle when you walk.' Margarita chuckled.

"I've heard stories that some travelers swallow their coins. And they get very sick."

"You won't do that, will you?' said Ana.

"That's why I'm trying the 'pregnant woman' disguise."

"You are clever, but two women alone can become targets for all kinds of treachery."

"I know, but most men will treat a pregnant woman with kindness," said Sara Elena. "I'm depending on it." She patted her stomach and walked around the room.

"You'll have to practice walking with a different gait. You know how expectant mothers waddle." Margarita muffled a snicker as Sara Elena took short, wobbling steps back and forth.

"How's this?"

"Fine, but hold your belly, too, like it's too heavy."

"It is too heavy."

Sara Elena followed Ana's directions and started puffing like she really was pregnant.

"This is more difficult than I thought."

"Keep trying until it's a habit. This disguise may be our salvation yet," said Margarita. Under her breath she said, "I hope we don't see anyone we know along the way."

Sara Elena paced around the kitchen and the hall until she swayed and stepped in just the right way. She stopped and spread out her arms.

"Margarita, meet your new daughter-in-law." She curtsied and almost lost her balance. "Now, let's hurry and leave Granada. The sun is about to rise."

Chapter 21

Two fine chestnut horses pranced down the narrow street, pulling a shiny black carriage behind them. No herald or insignia appeared on the side to identify who had sent it. Their hooves drummed a staccato cadence in the early-morning stillness. When the coachman stopped and rapped on the heavy oak door, furtive eyes peeped from behind windows and doors up and down the street to see who had received such an important visitor.

"Yes, who is it?"

"I'm here to collect Señorita Torres. Open up, please." The crisp words came more as a demand than a request.

"One moment." Ana struggled to lift the latch and slide the door open.

"May I come in, señora?"

"Who are you, sir, and who has sent you?" Ana planted her feet and folded her arms across her chest, manlike.

"Surely you must know." The coachman stepped forward and pushed past the old woman without waiting for her reply.

Ana played ignorant. The coachman jammed his hands on his hips and spoke.

"By pre-arrangement, Señorita Torres has consented to come to the house of Don Antonio Morales. I am Alexo, his driver, sent on his orders." He jerked his chin up and brought his heels together.

"Well, you've come at the wrong time," said Ana. "Señorita Torres is mourning her father Don Alonzo. She's unavailable for the rest of the day." Ana nodded once and set her mouth firm.

"We were not informed of his death." The driver frowned. "When did this happen?"

"During the night. There's been no time to spread the word."

"I must tell my master." His eyes narrowed. "Are you telling the truth?"

"Of course. You can view the body in the next room."

"That won't be necessary." He cleared his throat. "Where is the funeral taking place?"

"At the cathedral, in one of the side chapels. It's a private affair—small."

"Very well." The coachman turned on his heel. "You will hear from Don Antonio soon." He marched out of the house and jumped into the driver's seat again.

Ana let out her breath, latching the door as the carriage rolled away.

"Remember the plan, Ana," she said to herself. *"Sara Elena and I talked about what to do."* She took a long, shuddering breath. *"I must be strong and courageous. Now, I must go to Ramón's, and leave this house just as it is—as if someone had just stepped out to go to market. It must look as if the family could return at any minute."* Ana scurried around, tidying up a few dishes and sweeping the floor. She folded the freshly washed linens and put them away.

"I hope this is as you want it, Sara Elena. I've done my best." Ana swept a stray wisp of grey hair back from her face and wiped her forehead. *"Oh, I forgot the most important part."* Ana ran to the towering wardrobe and reached her hand inside, her fingers searching for what she wanted. She grabbed a leather pouch.

"The money belonging to Doctor Sanchez. My, it's heavy."
She shoved it into one sleeve and tied it flat against her arm with a rag as best she could. Ana peeked out the door; the early morning light warmed her cheeks. Stepping out onto the smooth cobblestones, she shut the heavy oak door behind her without a sound.

"I promised Sara Elena I would guard this until Juan or Sara returns, and I will—with my life, if necessary." Ana drew her shawl over her head and around her shoulders, letting it trail over her bulging sleeve. She padded down the silent street and turned toward her destination on top of the hill. *"That poor girl needs someone on her side right now. Lord, protect her."*

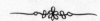

"What trickery is this?" roared Don Antonio and pounded on the desk where he sat. The coachman cowered and stepped back.

"It's true, sir. The housekeeper said she was mourning her father, who passed on just last night."

"We'll see about that," hissed Morales. "She could be telling the truth, but somehow, I don't trust Señorita Torres. I thought her bargain was too good to be true." The black-clad figure gathered up bits and pieces of documents and books strewn across his desk. Shoving his chair back with a screech of wood on tile, he reached for his cloak and hat.

"Is the carriage still hitched up?"

"Yes. I came in to report as soon as I got back—before seeing to the horses."

"Good. Come with me."

"What would you have me do?" The coachman bowed low.

"We're off to attend a funeral," said Don Antonio, striding down the hall, "and to collect a prize that is rightfully mine."

"Sir, which church?" He sprinted to keep up.

"I know, I know, there are several in Granada. Too bad you didn't find out which one."

"I didn't think—"

"Yes, you didn't think, so now we have to search the city. This may take some time." Don Antonio climbed into the black carriage as the coachman latched the door behind him. "Go to the cathedral nearest the Torres house. We'll start there."

The sleek black carriage clattered up and down the city streets, stopping at one church and then another. Discreet inquiries of the resident clergy met with negative replies. Don Antonio hid behind the black-curtained windows, not wanting anyone to recognize his face and see his growing rage.

Finally, one curate said,

"The Torres funeral will be held here later today. Nobody is here now."

"Where is that double-crossing woman?" Don Antonio mopped his forehead with a soft linen handkerchief. He thumped on the roof of the carriage with a clenched fist till it lurched to a halt. The coachman leaped down and opened the carriage door.

"Sir?"

"Take me by the Torres house. I want to check on something."

"Right away, sir."

"And do it quietly."

The chestnut horses pranced up the ancient cobblestones and stopped at the big oak door. The driver tapped on the door, once, twice and then a third time. He opened the door. "Is anyone home?" he called as he looked around.

No answer.

"Nobody's here, Don Antonio, but it looks like they'll return soon."

"Just as I feared. Get back aboard, and take me to wherever they arrange horse caravans." Don Antonio leaned back into the soft velvet upholstery. "Could it be my little bird has flown?"

Joselito tipped the grimy wine bag and let the bitter red liquid stream into his mouth. He wiped crimson drops off his bushy beard with the back of his coarse tunic. The stables where he lived and worked smelled of rotten straw and manure.

"Your establishment stinks!" The carriage driver pinched his nose and turned away.

"All because we're running twice as many caravans these days. Everyone wants to leave the country, you know. No time to clean out the muck." Joselito yawned and scratched his belly. "What help would you be wanting, sir?"

"Never mind, Alexo. I'll handle this." Don Antonio waved the driver away, and stepped down from the carriage, drawing his cloak around bony shoulders. He coughed and sputtered in the foul air of the enclosure. After a few wheezing breaths, he covered his nose with a handkerchief and went on.

"We need information. When did the last caravan leave here?"

"Early this morning. A full group."

"Any young women?"

"Oh, you're looking for a runaway, are you?" A smirk twitched the corners of his mouth. "A lover's quarrel, perhaps?" He winked at the cleric.

"No, just an unfortunate misunderstanding. I need to catch up with her and apologize." Don Antonio Morales put on his most contrite expression.

"Isn't that sweet?" Joselito spat and ran rough fingers through his thinning head of hair. "And you a church man, too." Color rose up Morales' neck and reached his cheeks.

"Well, were there any young women? Someone pretty— with auburn hair and blue eyes, perhaps?"

"No, I wouldn't say that. Some women joined the group, of course, but none that might catch your eye. Several women, all dark-haired; and one lady with a belly out to here." He held his hands out in front of him.

"In a family way—pregnant?"

"Yeah, pregnant. But not red-haired, and not pretty."

"And where was that caravan heading?"

"To the coast—Palos. It's the farthest of the departure points around here for all the Jews leaving the country. It's a madhouse right now, but I mean to make a few *maravedis* on it by ferrying as many poor souls as possible in the next couple of weeks." Pinching one nostril, Joselito blew hard through the other one, sending a glob of mucus to the rancid straw below. He rubbed his hand on a pant leg and smiled a yellow-toothed grin.

"Are there any other stables that arrange caravans?"

"Yeah, there's one or two. You can check with them just across the street." He pointed. "I couldn't tell when their last caravans left—don't pay much attention." He pointed out two other dark doorways across the way.

"That will be twenty *maravedis* for the information, sir." He held out his hand.

217

"Pay the man, Alexo." Don Antonio twitched his nose and retreated to the sanctuary of his spotless carriage.

"What now, sir?" said Alexo after dropping a few coins in Joselito's greasy hand.

"Take me home, and then come back and question the other stable owners across the way. I need time to think—and to breathe."

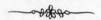

The realization came hard to Don Antonio, but all the signs pointed in one direction. Alexo reported back in the afternoon that none of the other stables in Granada had sent out a caravan in the last two days.

"We don't have much to go on, Alexo. We're not even sure Señorita Torres took Joeselito's cursed caravan."

"Sir, all our other options are exhausted. She must have taken it."

"You're probably right. Now I'm forced to take the only action I can."

"What's that?"

"I want you to arrange a caravan for me—for me alone—I don't want any other travelers with us. You will go with me, of course—and get one other servant—perhaps Paco, my valet—to go along."

"Where can I rent horses in a hurry?"

"That's not my problem. Just find some. And pack all the things we need. We need to leave immediately to catch up with that caravan."

"But, sir—don't you need permission from Bishop Torquemada?"

"Never mind him. He's busy with the King and Queen and the edict deadline right now. He won't know I'm gone."

"We won't be back for three weeks."

"It doesn't matter. Leave word if necessary that I'm on the trail of a wayward heretic." Don Antonio poured some red wine into a crystal goblet and waved him off.

"Very good, sir." Alexo hurried to make ready for the journey.

"There was little to choose from, with all the best horses reserved already."

"Don't give me excuses. What did you get?" Morales drew the curtain back and eyed the early-morning scene outside.

"I hired two horses, adequate for our purposes, and three sturdy donkeys. One will carry our supplies. The guide has brought them here for packing."

"Adequate?" Don Antonio coughed.

"Yes, sir. Older but still serviceable."

"Hmm. They look like used-up beasts to me." The proud priest eyed the animals outside and then looked back at his restless servant. "I'm still angry we didn't get off yesterday."

"Don Antonio, it was not humanly possible—with all the cooking and washing and fetching of things. Besides, I had to pay a pretty price to get the horses and donkeys I did, and a guide to lead us. Most people have to walk to Palos now."

Alexo shifted his weight from one foot to the other.

"May I take your leave and finish the preparations?"

"Yes, yes. Hurry and get ready. We've lost too much time already. I guess there's nothing to be done but take what we can get." Morales tore off a piece of bread from the crusty loaf in front of him, and popped it into his mouth. "Tell

Rosa and the rest of the household I leave in one hour." He dismissed Alexo with a careless gesture, and then began drumming his fingers on the polished table.

Rosa had surpassed herself, cooking little cakes and loaves of bread, sending kitchen girls off to buy figs and grapes, and filling a number of animal skins with new red wine. She fetched a leg of *jamón* from the airy lean-to out behind Don Antonio's residence, and wrapped many thick slices in parchment and a tanned goat skin. Several wheels of sheep's cheese rounded out the supplies, and then came the "essentials," as she called them: two pillows of goose feathers, several wool blankets, extra shoes, hats, hosen and doublets. Besides that, a sharp razor for shaving, a looking glass, clean handkerchiefs, a comb and brush, and soap and towels.

"Have I forgotten anything?" said Rosa to Alexo as she stuffed the last small packet in the saddlebags.

"Nothing! We have more than enough." Alexo tipped his cap to Rosa and spoke under his breath. "My thanks to you. You have done well, under the circumstances."

Rosa blushed and nodded to him. She receded to the kitchen while Alexo knocked and entered his master's study.

"All is ready, Don Antonio." Alexo brought his heels together and made a deep bow to his master. "We must go soon—before the sun becomes too hot."

"Finally! We have already lost too much time." Don Antonio jumped up from his seat and marched outside toward the waiting animals. He frowned and whirled toward Alexo.

"No, no!" he said. "I won't ride either of those animals. Saddle my own mare, *Estrella*. I had hoped to spare her but I can't trust these nags to make it all the way."

"Yes, sire." Alexo ran to tell the stable boy, as the others checked their mounts' saddles and cinched the girths once more for the long ride.

They set off, under a barrage of complaints and demands by Don Antonio. Truth be told, Don Antonio had little experience riding a mount. He always relied on his carriage and driver in Granada. This trip would cost him in comfort and convenience. He shifted in his saddle and felt sore spots developing already on his posterior. He called to the caravan guide.

"Tell me again. When did the last caravan leave Granada?"

"Day before yesterday, sire."

"Is there any chance of catching up to it?"

"It could happen, if they make an unexpected stop, or get waylaid. It's hard to tell. Anything can happen along the road to Palos." The muleteer chewed on a piece of grass and pulled his ear.

"That arrogant girl!" Morales spat out the words through clenched teeth. "Señorita Torres will be sorry she ever challenged me."

"Yes, sir."

Chapter 22

✳

"This caravan is so slow! We'll never get to Palos in time," Sara Elena hissed to Margarita. "I don't know if I can endure one more moment!"

"Patience, dear one."

Margarita smiled at her and shifted her weight in the saddle. The mules lurched and rocked forward, picking their way over rocks and through ravines. Six people perched atop scrawny grey animals with large pointed ears. The sandal-shod feet of the taller travelers dangled nearly to the ground. Some pulled up their garments around them to keep from getting road dust on themselves. The dirt-caked hides of the animals reeked of moldy stables and rancid straw. One woman swatted at flies with her scarf. The head muleteer snapped his whip from time to time to keep the mules on the path.

"They promised us horses, but look what we got—" Sara waved her hand at the scabby beast she sat on.

"We had little choice. Joselito didn't have anything else—I checked the stable to be sure." Margarita sneezed and brushed straw out of her hair.

"All the same, they made a promise." Sara lowered her voice and spoke in Margarita's ear. "Besides, what if Don Antonio follows us?"

Margarita groaned. "I hadn't thought of that."

"Well, it's all I can think of right now, and I'm worried." Her whispered words rose loud enough for the others to hear. A dark-skinned woman across from Sara replied,

"Don't worry about the child you're carrying, little mother. The rocking of the mules is just like the cradle you'll be putting it in." She flashed a knowing smile. Something about her face looked familiar. Sara Elena's mouth turned up in a shy smile in spite of herself. She nodded and closed her eyes, signaling an end to the conversation.

"She sleeps all the time these days," said Margarita, then added, "Do you know how much longer it takes to get to Palos?" Perhaps she could divert the conversation.

"We've only been traveling one day, and you already want to know?" The dark-skinned woman laughed. "It'll take a good ten days, I figure. It's best to relax and be patient." She yawned and stretched, then reached out to touch her husband's shoulder. Barely aware of her nearness, his hollow eyes gazed into the distance with a vacant desperation. A slight young woman with frightened eyes, probably the daughter, followed behind. The other traveler, an old man with drooping shoulders, sat still and withdrawn.

"Thanks, I guess you're right." Margarita closed her eyes and let the swaying and lurching of the mule lull her to sleep.

The mules bobbed along in the mid-day sun, the muleteer directing the mules with a light flick of the reins to one side or the other. All the while he spoke encouraging words to the animals.

"You're beauties, my dears. Just a few more bends and we reach a nice cool stream. You can drink your fill when we get there. Just a little while longer." He clucked and whistled to the mules. Their ears twitched and they turned their long faces toward his voice as if taking in every word.

The rocky hills around Granada made slow going. Sometimes the muleteers had each passenger descend from their beast and lead it over rocky cliffs with nothing but cobalt blue sky between them and the ravine below. Often the way ahead looked more like a staircase than a road. The muleteers before and behind the group urged the mules on and scanned the area for any signs of bandits.

After hours of rocking and lurching through endless miles of countryside, the landscape opened out into a wide, grassy plain. They heard sounds of a bubbling stream. The mules picked up the pace, breaking into a trot that jostled the weary travelers. The muleteers led the group up to the flowing brook where the mules lost no time in lapping at the cold water.

"We'll rest here," said Pedro, the lead muleteer. "It's time for the noon meal and a *siesta*." He spread out some large woven cloths under the olive grove for sitting. He and the other muleteer then proceeded to unload provisions for all: a large *bota* full of red wine, *alforjas*, saddle bags filled with loaves of bread, almonds, raisins, figs and olives, a hindquarter of *jamón* for slicing, and even jugs of water to quench the thirst.

"I don't think I can walk anymore," said Margarita, wobbling back and forth a few steps. Sara Elena slid off the mule, taking care not to dislodge her tied-on middle. She groaned.

"I'm stiff as a dried-up sausage." She stretched out her lower back. "I feel like an old grandma."

"Come and sit in the shade," said Margarita, patting a place near her on the ground cloths. Sara Elena eased herself down and kicked off her sandals.

"Ah, that's better." The others sprawled across the colorful textiles spread out for them, leaning on some of the soft bundles they had scattered around them. Pedro came around offering the wine and water jugs to the dusty travelers.

"Everyone, eat what you need. We'll rest here for an hour or two. It's hard to travel in the hottest part of the day."

"I hope we won't stay too long," said Sara to Margarita. "It's urgent we reach our destination as soon as we can." Sara Elena's words cut through the intense afternoon heat like a hot knife through butter.

"We'll stay as long as there's need." Pedro scowled at Sara. "We could all use the rest."

He eyed her belly. "Shouldn't you be napping for the sake of your child?"

"Sorry—yes, of course." Sara dropped her eyes, not willing to challenge the tough muleteer, but hoping she'd made her point.

Pedro pulled out a lute and began to pluck the strings. A gentle melody filled the air. Sara Elena curled up and found a bundle to support her head. She let the plaintive notes float over her. The others sank into silence as well, as Pedro and the other muleteer raised their voices in an undulating Moorish tune. They sang of the beauty of the Alhambra, the valor of fighting knights, the honor of their King and Queen. As her eyes closed, she was transported to a world of dancing water pools, the sweet song of a nightingale, and the ardor of a handsome *hidalgo* courting a dark-haired maiden—a place where pleasure, perfection and joy reigned.

Pedro and the other muleteer began to rouse the travelers.

"Wake up, it's time to go."

Margarita shook Sara Elena's shoulder. Sara Elena rolled over and looked at the startling blue above the trees.

"Oh, no! The sun has moved a long way across the sky already." Sara Elena jumped to her feet and fumbled around gathering up her belongings. "It's getting late. Where are my sandals and my shawl?" She reached for a sandal, strapped it on the wrong foot, then ripped it off and tried again.

"Calm yourself, *señora*" said the muleteer. "The mule caravan will leave when everyone has packed up again." Pedro looked at her with stern and squinting eyes. "Not one minute sooner."

The family of three picked up their bundles and lashed them back on their mules, while the old man struggled to his feet and leaned heavily on a wooden staff.

"Here, old man, let me help you mount your donkey." Pedro guided the silver-haired gentleman back to the gentlest of the donkeys and supported him as he threw a stiff leg over its back.

"Now, ladies—" Pedro's strong arm held Sara's and then Margarita's as they settled themselves for the long trek ahead. The mother and daughter received help from the other muleteer.

"All ready? We travel for some hours, until nightfall, and will find lodging in a small village ahead." Pedro clucked to his donkey and guided it and the others across the dry meadow and through a rocky divide onto a steep path. Far below lay rocks and wild sage. Sara Elena held her breath and tried to ignore her fear of falling.

Nine more days. Will we get to Palos in time to see Juan, or die along the way?

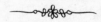

"You fool!"

"These rocks do look familiar," said the guide, stopping his tired beast, and signaling the others to pull up.

He mopped his sweating brow. "Do something."

"We're lost." Don Antonio's face turned from red to purple and his eyes popped.

"We'll stop here and take refreshment. It's almost noon." Tomasito, the guide, dismounted and took a long swig from the water *bota*. Unlike his childish name, his muscular bulk proclaimed him every inch a powerful man. With a neck as thick as a tree trunk and arms like hefty poles, he commanded respect wherever he went. Except from Don Antonio.

"I knew I shouldn't have trusted Alexo to organize this trip," Don Antonio muttered under his breath. "We're losing precious time!"

"Since you did entrust *me* with this caravan, Don Antonio, *I* will make the decisions." Alexo met his master's displeasure with grim determination. He passed the water *bota* around to the others, as they each found a rock to sit on. "Find shade and wait till the guide and I come back." They moved to follow his instructions, while Tomasito climbed on a high rock and looked out over the countryside. Alexo followed behind.

Scanning the jumble of rocks below, he saw a faint trampling of dry grass curving between them. Beyond, the land opened out into a dry plain. Alexo waited as the guide scrambled down the slope and climbed the next craggy boulder to get a better look at the far horizon. Alexo shaded his eyes and thought he saw some trees in the distance.

"Good news," said Tomasito, leaping the crags to get back uphill, agile for a bulky man. "We're not far from a grove of trees. And I'm sure we'll find a stream where we can water the animals. Let's mount up."

Don Antonio and Paco, the other servant, followed Alexo and the guide. When the donkeys heard the sounds of rushing water, they began to trot, and Don Antonio's horse pranced and swished its tail. All four men arrived at the same time under the grove of trees and dismounted, letting their animals drink at the flowing creek.

"Looks like someone has stopped here, and not too long ago," said Alexo. "The grass is still flattened out." He got out a pillow for Don Antonio to sit on. The rest sat on the grass. Alexo passed around the provisions: bread, *jamón*, and dried fruits, followed by the wine sack. Don Antonio's stern presence dampened their natural inclination to chat.

"We'll rest here for an hour. It's too hot to go on now."

"No. We need to push on—hot sun or not." Don Antonio hoisted himself up off the pillow and brushed off his black woolen robes. "We've got to catch up to the caravan ahead." His jaw clamped shut like a great iron trap.

"It will be hard on the animals," said the guide.

"I don't care. You should have considered that when you got us lost."

Alexo clenched his fists until the knuckles bulged. He bit back the angry retort he wanted to spit out and the punch he wanted to place on Don Antonio's chin.

"Yes, sir," said Tomasito through thin lips.

Alexo got up, checked his horse's saddle, and packed the food away, yanking extra hard on the saddlebag straps and buckles. "Let's move on then, everyone." He mounted, clucked to his reluctant mount and steered them all to a shallow ford over the stream.

"Which way now?" Don Antonio squashed a broad-brimmed hat on his head. Alexo rose up in his saddle and looked in all directions.

"We'll take the trail that's right ahead of us. See the trampled grass?" The guide pointed and urged his mule on. "This way."

Each man pulled out a cap and clamped it on his head to shield against the overpowering sun. The horses and mules clopped along without complaint for the first two hours. Picking their way through boulders, ravines, and cliffs slowed them down. Don Antonio closed his eyes when a cliff face dropped off suddenly next to him.

"Trust your animals to get you through," said the guide. "Slow and steady."

"Slow and steady is not what we need," grumbled Don Antonio. "It's speed and action." As soon as he got past the cliff and onto an open plain, he kicked his horse with both heels. The horse jumped ahead, and started to trot.

"Don Antonio, not here! The terrain is too rough—slow down!"

"Your caution only delays us." He spurred his animal again.

"No! Watch out for rocks—this wild country is full of them." Tomasito urged his mule as much as he thought was safe, trying to catch Morales.

"The animals are tired—please, Don Antonio!" Alexo waved his arms and yelled after his master, who trotted on ahead and disappeared through a narrow aisle among giant granite boulders.

"What is that hothead doing?" Alexo muttered under his breath. "Let's keep up the best we can," he said to the others, "and find a way to slow His Grace as soon as possible."

"Let me handle it," said Tomasito. "It's my job." He guided his mount through the narrow parting of rocks. Thistles and briars lined the way, and it was all he could do to get himself and the mule through the long ravine unharmed. As he emerged on the other side, Don Antonio let out a scream, and then fell silent.

"Don Antonio?" The guide dug his heels into his sturdy beast, and trotted forward.

"Where are you, master?" Alexo emerged from the rocky passageway and scanned the countryside for clues. Around a bend, they spied *Estrella*, Don Antonio's horse, at the edge of a precipice. But where was their master? "I never could see beyond ten paces," Alexo complained. As he closed the distance, he heard Don Antonio's weak cries:

"Help me!"

"Coming, Your Grace." Tomasito had already reached the scene of the accident. Alexo reined his weary horse next to the sweating *Estrella*. He saw a tangle of arms and legs waving in the air on the far side of the agitated horse.

"Help me—quick! I'm right on the edge." Alexo heard bits of gravel falling and saw puffs of dust rising. He flung himself down and grabbed Don Antonio's flailing arms. One of his feet was caught in a stirrup and twisted at an odd angle.

"What happened?"

"I think Don Antonio didn't see the cliff, but his horse did." Tomasito grabbed the reins of *Estrella* and patted her muzzle to calm her.

"Hurry, you idiots! I think I broke my ankle." Sweat streamed down Don Antonio's face.

"One minute, sire. Let me pull you away from the cliff." Alexo freed the injured ankle, and dragged Don Antonio by the shoulders till he lay on a patch of dry grass away from danger. Don Antonio moaned and spewed out bad words.

Belligerent braying signaled the arrival of Paco and the pack mule. He catapulted off his animal and ran closer to help.

"Quickly—get me a rope," yelled the guide. Alexo slung the water bag over his shoulder and brought a coiled rope from his saddle. Tomasito wound the rope around Don Antonio's body, securing his arms to his sides.

"Just to protect us from your punches, Don Antonio—no disrespect intended."

Don Antonio growled in reply.

"We'll have to see how bad the damage is first." Alexo cut away the shreds of hosen covering his master's ankle. Yellow and purple bruising already adorned the skin like a stormy sunset. His skin was scraped raw. Paco poured water onto the wound while Alexo brushed away bits of cloth, dirt and gravel with a scrap of hosen. Tomasito pushed and rotated the ankle into various positions.

"Hurry up! I can't take this pain much longer." Don Antonio's voice alternately bawled then squeaked.

"It's not broken, but badly sprained." Tomasito leaned back, let out his foul breath all at once, and stood up. "He'll be all right after a rest." Alexo intervened.

"Brace yourself, sire. We're going to wrap your foot to keep down the swelling." Alexo motioned for Paco to tear some strips of cloth from a pillow case. Don Antonio moaned as Alexo wrapped the soft cloths around his now puffy ankle.

"You're killing me!" Alexo ignored his protests and kept wrapping till several layers of bandages crisscrossed the priest's lower extremity.

"Our work is done for now." Alexo leaned back and inspected his work. "Let's see about making camp nearby. It looks like we'll be here until Don Antonio's ready to travel. That won't be any time soon."

Alexo and Paco set up a comfortable bed for their master under the trees. One pillow for his head and one for the injured ankle plus blankets under and around him brought a look of relief to the proud cleric's face. A dose of poppy juice that Rosa had packed "just in case" put Don Antonio out for the rest of the day, and another dose later would help him sleep all night. The two of them took turns standing guard over the wounded gentleman. Tomasito slept on, his head resting in his saddle.

Overhead, a million flickering stars lit the dark sky, waiting for the flaming sun to once again seize the dawn.

Chapter 23

On the fifth day of travel, a few clouds scudded across the sapphire sky. Wind rippled the dry grass and stirred up the dust into red swirls. Pedro, the lead muleteer signaled for the mules to stop near a clump of bushes. Sara Elena and the others circled around to hear what he had to say.

"Listen, everyone. We've made good progress so far. Only three or four days now to Palos. Let's camp here and have *almuerzo*, our noon meal." The travelers dismounted, glad for a change of position and a little food to fill their empty stomachs.

"At last," said Margarita. "I'm so tired of bobbing along on these beasts."

"And I'm tired of worrying about bandits and other dangers along the road." Sara Elena patted her mule and left it to munch the pale grass just outside the canopy of shade the bushes made. She plopped down on the hard ground after spreading her shawl to sit on.

"You certainly play the part of pregnant lady with flair." Margarita smiled at Sara Elena's feigned awkwardness.

"It's almost second nature now. Besides, all the coins hidden in here are heavy." Sara Elena patted her bulky middle.

"Take care about quick movements. I thought I heard jingling when you sat down just now." Margarita whispered her warning, and then reached out to accept a loaf of bread and a plate of ham making their way around the group. She tore off a large hunk of bread even though it was stale.

"Is this ham all right to eat?" asked Sara Elena, holding up a slice with a blue tinge and gummy surface.

"What choice do we have?" Margarita stuffed a piece in her mouth and started chewing. She washed it down with gulps from the water jug.

"We'll rest here one hour and cover another few miles before dark." Pedro hurled his body down onto a mat he had set out for himself. "Take your ease—close your eyes," he ordered and then promptly followed his own advice.

Little clusters of people whispered a while to each other, and then one by one let their eyelids drop closed. A breeze rustled through the bushes mingling with the quiet sounds of slumber.

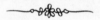

Sara Elena awakened with a moan. She grabbed her stomach and fought the urge to retch. Rolling over on her side, she saw Margarita wince, also.

"Ooh, my insides," complained the dark-skinned woman. "I feel terrible." She got up and ran behind one of the bushes. Although out of sight, everyone heard her get sick. Her groans roused the remaining sleepers.

"What have you done to us, Pedro?" Margarita clutched her middle to hold back the pain.

"Just a little traveler's distress, I reckon." Pedro cradled his considerable belly as if it were a newborn baby. "Could be the food or water back at our last stop. It did have an odd taste." He considered for a minute. His stomach rolled and lurched noticeably. He sprang to his feet and raced behind the bushes just in time. He returned, spitting and wiping his mouth with a dirty sleeve. Whatever the affliction, one by one each of the travelers turned pale, gripped their middles and raced to empty their stomachs behind the bushes.

"People, we'll have to rest here longer till we all recover," said Pedro. "Get comfortable. We'll have to camp here for the night."

"I know, I know," said Pedro as people murmured their complaints. "I promised you a place at the inn up ahead. I'll make it up to you. Ohh." He clenched his stomach once again and rolled on his mat. "I'm not moving."

Everyone lay back, rubbing their distressed abdomens, trying to let sleep relieve their pains.

"Ooh," groaned Sara Elena. "This is terrible. We can't afford any delays."

"Well, just the thought of rocking and bobbing on that mule makes me feel sick all over again." Margarita fanned her face, and took a sip of water. "Someone needs to find fresh water, and throw out that ham. That's what sickened us."

"I hope Pedro takes care of whatever the problem is," said Sara Elena, "but right now, I don't think anyone feels up to it. In fact, Pedro looks the worst of all of us." She gazed over and saw their guide patting his belly with one hand and the other covering his mouth, a picture of sickness and determination to stop vomiting.

"You're right. We may just all have to wait a few hours." Margarita closed her eyes and let out a soft groan, which joined a chorus of others rising from the group.

"It's going to be a while."

The amber afternoon sun dropped into purple night, like a gleaming gem tucked into a velvet bag for safekeeping. Sara Elena opened her eyes and looked around. The whole group slept, filling the dark with soft sighs and whispers. An occasional snort came from a lone guard who struggled to finish his watch. Nearby, Margarita gave a soft groan and turned over.

"Margarita, are you awake?"

"Hmm?"

"What time is it? It must be late at night, or maybe early morning. Does your stomach still hurt? Did you get sick during the night?"

"Hmm—no."

"Me, either. What about the others? Did you hear anyone else during the night?" Sara Elena rubbed her stomach and realized it no longer felt like someone had kicked it. Just a faint tenderness remained.

"Sara, go to sleep. It's too late to talk." She stifled a yawn.

"But it's almost dawn, Margarita."

"All right, it's too early to talk, then." She rolled over, turned her back to Sara, and resumed her rhythmic breathing with the next breath.

Sara Elena rose and grabbed the shawl she'd been sleeping on. The wool around her shoulders eased the chill. She walked over to a giant boulder nearby and sat on it. A thousand stars beckoned her toward heaven.

If I rise to the heavens, you are there. The words of the Psalms say it so well.

Sara Elena hugged her knees to her chest, as much as she could with a big belly, and closed her eyes. Night sounds surrounded her—the wind rattling the dry leaves on the bushes, the howl of one lone wolf, and the suggestion of a gurgling brook nearby. She let the night's quiet seep into her. She sat there until a golden smudge creased the horizon.

Dawn's coming.

In her reverie, Sara Elena became aware of another sound: a twig snapped. Then the dried leaves on a bush rattled.

Wind or a passing animal?

With a light step and a swish, someone advanced on her and pressed a sharp blade to her throat before she had time to cry out.

"Not a sound, señora."

"Who are you?" she gasped.

"All will be revealed." His hot breath scorched her ear and his tight grip made it hard to breathe.

Sara Elena shuddered and thought she might faint. She wobbled to her feet and felt a sting under her chin.

"I said, don't move!"

A trickle of blood oozed from the cut.

"Come with me. My partner and I have a plan." He shoved her forward off the rock, keeping the gleaming blade under her chin. They walked toward the sleeping group.

"Get up, everyone." He and another masked bandit kicked at the sleeping travelers. Irritated at being disturbed, the group soon saw the urgent situation and scrambled to their feet.

Sara Elena thought Pedro might lunge for the robber's dagger, but the bandit noticed his fleeting look and forced an even tighter stranglehold on her.

"Don't do anything stupid."

Everyone turned their eyes on the masked invaders, suddenly fearful.

"Señor Peccadillo and Master One-Eye at your service." The lead bandit saluted.

"No sudden moves. We want no trouble—just your valuables."

"Throw all your jewelry and cash down here." Peccadillo motioned to a rough blanket he spread out before them. He walked among the band of travelers pointing to rings, earrings and necklaces.

"We have no cash, only what we need for food and shelter on our journey. Don't you know Ferdinand and Isabella claimed the rest?" The old man brayed like a donkey in his distress.

"Quiet, old man." One-Eye hit him with the back of his hand, sending him crashing to the ground.

"Coward! You're brave enough when you have a knife!" Pedro's mocking tones got him a fist in the jaw that knocked him backwards. He rubbed his chin and felt blood.

"Sit down." The bandit pushed Pedro to the ground, then yanked his arms behind and wrapped a heavy rope around his joined wrists.

"You won't get away with this. Another caravan is coming through here any minute."

"Shut your mouth." One-Eye kicked him in the middle. Pedro moaned and doubled up.

Peccadillo watched as the travelers dropped their jewelry on the growing stack. One-Eye walked to the mules and unbuckled their packs, letting them drop to the ground.

"Where's the gold?" The bandit pushed the man with the far-away look toward the saddlebags.

"Go ahead, señor. Hurry!" One-Eye goaded the man with his knife, and grabbed a leather pouch he discovered.

"Where's your money, señora?" Peccadillo raked the grimy dagger across Sara Elena's earlobe. She winced but kept from crying out by grinding her teeth.

"I have no money."

"You're lying!" The bandit tightened his hold on Sara Elena. "Maybe we should search you, little mother."

Peccadillo laughed and flipped her around so she faced him. He poked her in the belly with the tip of his knife.

"You're mighty soft," he sneered, as he reached out to pat her down.

"Wait, sir. I'll give you what I have." Sara Elena gulped and stepped back, to keep him from discovering the truth. "Just let me turn my back."

"Not a chance. I'd like to watch you, pretty lady."

Sara Elena pulled slowly at the string that hung around her neck and under her clothing, hoping her padding wouldn't shift as she did so. A leather purse came into view at her neckline. The leering bandit snickered.

"No, Sara Elena!" Margarita gasped.

"That's better." The bandit grabbed and yanked. The bag flew out of his hands and landed on the ground, coins bouncing in every direction.

Sara Elena staggered. Her hand flew to her throat. The rope burns from pulling out the bag stung her neck, but at least the bandit had withdrawn his knife. One-Eye jumped to gather up all the coins.

"Hurry, you idiot," cried Peccadillo, looking at the sky. "The sun's rising. We must get away now."

"I hear horses coming," said Sara Elena.

"You're a pretty nuisance." Peccadillo pinched her face with his bony fingers. He did stop to listen.

"Quick, One-Eye, she's right. Someone is coming. Tie up the rest of them. Let's go!" Hoof beats grew louder as he watched his partner make quick work of knotting rope around the others. Peccadillo snatched up the cloth, tied it into a bundle and slung it over his back. Last of all, One-Eye tied Sara Elena's wrists together.

"Sorry to leave your company, ladies and gentleman, but we must depart." With a bow and a flourish, Peccadillo

239

and One-Eye jumped to the rocks, climbed over the top, and jumped into the thick bushes beyond. The sun cleared the horizon just as two horses trotted into the clearing.

"Oh, no!" Sara Elena whispered to her friend. "Come with me, Margarita—right now!" Sara Elena inched back into the shadows and hid behind some bushes. She peeked through the brittle leaves as a somber figure got off his horse and bowed to the travelers.

"Don Antonio Morales at your service."

"Margarita, come here! Let me untie you." Sara Elena coaxed loose the cords biting into Margarita's wrists. It wasn't easy with her wrists tied, but she kept at it. The older woman rubbed each hand to restore feeling to her fingers.

"Now you, Sara Elena," she whispered. "Your hands are turning blue—he sure tied them tight!" Margarita worked quickly to free her young friend.

"Shh, let's get behind the big boulders over there, and try to hear what Don Antonio is saying."

Sara Elena crawled behind a craggy granite rock large enough to conceal them both. Margarita followed and leaned her ear down close to the rock's surface. From this vantage point, they could see the camp site, and the still morning air carried every word straight to them.

"Welcome, Don Antonio. I am Pedro, the muleteer and guide for this caravan." He rolled over and onto his knees before struggling to his feet. "Could one of your men free us?"

Don Antonio motioned to Paco and Tomasito, who had now caught up with Alexo and his master. Tomasito pulled out a knife and made quick work of cutting the ropes, while everyone murmured their thanks.

"Now, Your Grace, what do you want with our band of travelers? As you can see, we've already been relieved of our valuables." Pedro massaged his wrists as he talked. He moved toward each member of his group, checking them for cuts and bruises, while he waited for Don Antonio's answer.

"How dare you insinuate I'm here to rob you! I'm a Holy Father of the church—and a member of the Inquisition." Don Antonio's eyebrows shot up like black horseshoes held above the smoldering embers of his eyes.

The members of the traveling party shrank back when he identified himself. The mother and daughter re-arranged their shawls to obscure their faces. The old man hung his head. Don Antonio composed himself and took on a more friendly tone.

"Actually, I've come to rescue a runaway woman. I wonder if you've seen her, or if she's been traveling with you."

"Liar!" hissed Sara Elena. She stomped her foot in the dirt near the boulder.

"Quiet, Sarita. I want to hear what Pedro says." Margarita rubbed Sara Elena's back to comfort her, and then turned her attention back to the conversation.

"A runaway, you say? Or someone you're collecting for the *quemadero*?" Pedro's words hit Don Antonio with a burst of hatred and a spray of spit.

"See here, Master Muleteer. I could have you arrested for talking to me that way."

"What do I care? You and your kind burned my only brother already. I have nothing left to lose." Pedro set his mouth in a tight line and punched a hefty fist into his other hand.

Don Antonio took a step back and considered his reply.

"Look here, *hombre*, I'm not here to fight or argue. I just need to find a woman who disappeared from my household.

241

She's young, has auburn hair—full and wavy—and blue eyes. She may be traveling with an older woman."

Pedro stroked his chin and sank deep into thought.

"No woman here with auburn hair, only black. As far as blue eyes—I usually don't pay attention to that. Couldn't say—"

"I see you have some extra mules. Did someone leave suddenly when we rode into camp?" Don Antonio looked around, trying to assess the guarded countenances of the other travelers. A momentary panic flickered across the daughter's face.

"You're hiding something. What is it?" He strode toward the young woman.

Pedro intercepted Don Antonio and tapped his chest.

"You're too late. Bandits have already taken our two ladies traveling together, plus a lot of loot. Those are their mounts, the two extra mules you see."

"When did they strike? When did they ride off?" Don Antonio leaned forward with an eager face.

"Oh, I'd say they left eight hours ago, or more. Attacked at sunset and made off with the ladies as hostages." Pedro looked at the others. "Isn't that right?"

"Why, yes. Yes, of course," they all chimed in. "You'd better hurry if you want to catch them. They're long gone." Each member of the traveling party added a bit to the tale.

"Why aren't you rescuing them?" said Alexo.

"We'll do that. Finally, some reliable information," said Don Antonio. "Alexo, Paco, Tomasito—let's be off. Double the pace—we may catch the little bird yet." Don Antonio sprang to his horse and spurred it ahead down the path.

"Neither one had auburn hair, sir," yelled Pedro to their backs.

"No matter. At last we have a lead to follow."

The men on mules trotted behind, urging their brave beasts ahead to the chase.

"*Buena suerte*," called Pedro. "You'll need it," he muttered under his breath.

Sara Elena and Margarita came bounding from behind the boulders after Don Antonio's party receded into the distance.

"Pedro, Pedro. Thank you so much." Sara Elena ran to Pedro and touched his arm.

"What did I do, young lady?" He turned his reddened face away from Sara Elena's glowing smile and withdrew a few paces.

"You saved us both, by sending Don Antonio on a wild chase." She and Margarita beamed at him.

"It was nothing. I really didn't know anything, and I certainly wouldn't tell the truth to a member of the Inquisition." Pedro massaged his raw wrists.

"Where have you been, anyway?" He searched their eyes with piercing intensity.

"When I saw you'd disappeared, I thought the bandits took you off as hostages when they escaped."

"We hid because we were afraid."

"Afraid of Don Antonio?"

"Yes."

"You're not a wayward maiden with auburn hair. But you do have bewitching eyes, blue as the sea at Palos." Pedro scanned Sara Elena up and down, and then grabbed at her belly.

"What's this?" He pulled at the wad of blankets and padding covering her middle. It bulged out and shifted beneath her gown. A leather bag fell to the ground.

Sara Elena slapped his hands away and clutched at the unraveling mass.

Margarita scooped up the bag and the coins, and hid them away.

The others stood open-mouthed in stunned silence.

"So, you're not a pregnant woman traveling to meet your husband." Pedro said it as a fact, not a question.

"No, I'm not. I'm only trying to protect my money from confiscation when I get to Palos. I thought nobody would search an expectant mother."

"Are you, also, the woman Don Antonio seeks? Perhaps you have auburn hair after all?" Pedro grabbed at her hair and lifted the dark wig off amid more gasps.

"Yes, I am Sara Elena Torres," she said, and shook out her no-longer-confined glowing hair. "And I can explain everything." Her eyes narrowed and her lips curled in challenge.

"Let's hope you can. I'm ready for a good tale." Pedro's laugh bounced among the rocks like a rabbit gone mad.

Chapter 24

"So, you see, I have reason to flee from Don Antonio." Sara Elena finished telling her story and leaned back against the rock she used as a back rest. She and the others sat on the ground as the story unfolded.

"That's an exciting tale, for sure," said Pedro. "Did you really make such a bargain with Father Morales?"

"Yes—but I never intended to go through with it. I was just so desperate to free Margarita." She squeezed her friend's arm and smiled.

"You're a brave young woman." The dark-skinned woman looked at Sara Elena, her eyebrows arched in a questioning look.

"You're reckless—and stupid." The husband's words slashed the air.

"Why the stinging words, sir?" Sara Elena bristled.

Have I met these people before?

"Because sooner or later, the Inquisition will catch up with you."

"Diego—stop! She has no idea." The dark woman touched his arm, and then turned toward Sara Elena. "Young woman—"

"My name's Sara Elena."

"Sara Elena—all of you—" Her gesture brought in the whole group. "Perhaps it would be good if we shared our story now." She received a nod from her husband to go ahead.

"We are the Romero family. I'm Mara, my husband is Diego, and this is our daughter, Alma." Each one inclined their head when introduced.

"We are on our way to the coast to escape the Inquisition, and especially the fiend Morales." She spit out the words and shuddered.

"About two years ago, that evil man came around our neighborhood rustling in his fine garments and making inquiries about us. He accused us of reading the Holy Writings in Spanish instead of going to church to hear the priest."

"Was that true?"

"We're translators—we had original manuscripts in our hands—Of course, we read the parchments. We had to, in order to translate them."

Sara Elena sucked in her breath.

"What happened next?"

"We explained our situation to the Holy Office, and thought that would be the end of it. But Morales kept nosing around, whispering questions—seeking scandal. Soon, a so-called friend—we don't know who—maybe Gonzalez who owes us money—made a complaint about us. Anyway, soon they called us back and threw us all in prison. No explanation. No way to explain our innocence—we're God-fearing people!" She made the sign of the cross over her face.

"You're Jewish, aren't you?" said Sara Elena. "*Conversos,* maybe?"

"Yes." A wild panic filled Señora Romero's face.

"That's enough to bring the Inquisition to your door. They don't trust *us*." Sara Elena reached for Mara's hand and squeezed it.

"Then, you, too, are one of us?" She looked at Sara Elena, a spark of hope in her eyes, and received an acknowledging nod.

"Yes."

"We shouldn't speak of it here. Too dangerous."

"Did you practice your faith and observe the sacred holy days, Señora Romero?"

"We tried to maintain the traditions quietly. It's difficult." She sighed. "We were tortured, of course, and confessed in order to stop the torture. Sentenced to die on the wood pile, but Jehovah intervened. Praise his holy name." She raised her hands heavenward.

"Do you remember I said I was present at the time of your day of burning?"

"Yes, you said that. But I don't remember you, of course. I was occupied." Her eyebrows slanted down and over her nose.

"My father said something startling that day." Sara whispered in Señora Romero's ear. "I was standing with my father and he mentioned that you and Señor Romero would help me if ever I found myself in a tight place. Do you know what he meant?"

"Remind me of your father's name again."

"Don Alonzo de Torres."

"Where's your family from?"

"Toledo at first, and now Granada. You don't remember him?"

"We lived in Toledo for a while. You should ask my husband—Diego!" Mara waved to her husband.

Diego heard his wife and sidled over to them. "Yes, my dear?"

"I was there at your time of burning," said Sara Elena. "I remember the rain started just as the flames caught hold. The crowd got the idea that God wanted you to live." Sara Elena smiled. "I remember the stamping and shouting to let you go."

"You were there?"

"Yes, with my father, Don Alonzo. Justice prevailed that day."

247

"Praise the Holy One! Your words warm my heart." Small lines around Señora Romero's eyes crinkled when she smiled.

"And now you run from the reach of the Inquisition—hiding in the smallest villages—making your way to the ships that go to Jerusalem—to freedom," said Sara Elena.

"You understand!"

"We all do—and we'll help you get to freedom." The old man spoke with conviction.

Everyone nodded and murmured their agreement.

"Here, have some bread." Pedro brought some loaves and got out a hunk of cheese. Scraping the surface mold off, he cut several slices and placed them on a wooden platter filled with figs and raisins. A thin red stream shot into his mouth as he raised the wine bag high.

"You'll pay dearly for crossing Morales." The old man joined the conversation, stroking his beard.

"You're as good as dead." Pedro concurred.

Sara Elena looked around the group in wonder.

Why such pessimism from all of them?

"Believe me, I know. It happened to my brother." Pedro pounded a powerful fist into his palm.

"And I know, too," said the old man. "They humiliated me in front of the whole town. I wore a *sanbenito* for a whole year." The old man looked down, remembering his shame.

"And we nearly burned at the stake as heretics—all for reading a banned book." Alma's lips pursed into a fine thread, and her eyes glowed with cold fire.

"Have you ever heard of the water torture?" She looked at her parents and received the slightest nod of the head from her mother.

"Tell me, Alma. I want to understand your suffering."

"The Inquisition has devised an ingenious torture to get a person to confess—to anything. After your hands are tied, the holy brothers pour water into your mouth, without stopping. You choke, you gasp, you can't get a breath—but still they pour water. Soon, it gets in your nose as well, and you cough and sputter. The water keeps coming. It's enough to make you scream and agree to anything, just to stop it!" Alma threw up her hands. She was shrieking in her remembrance of the horror.

"I'm so sorry!" Sara Elena leaped up and moved to embrace Alma. Alma sank into her arms and trembled.

"It was so horrible, so horrible! I cannot bear to think of it again."

"You have endured so much—"

Sara Elena stroked Alma's long hair and rubbed her back. Then, she looked around as a new thought came to her.

"Are we saying, all of us, that each has met up with the Inquisition in some way?"

They nodded.

"Amazing!" Sara Elena let out a long breath. "How did we all find our way to the same caravan, and arrive here at just this point in time?"

"Just a lucky coincidence."

"But, all of us victims of the Inquisition?"

"Victims of Morales, you mean."

"We're all refugees trying to find a way out of Spain. And you know, don't you, that Italian ships leave from Palos and go to the Eastern Mediterranean, but Spanish ships don't."

"No, I didn't know." Sara's eyes met Margarita's own. She raised her eyebrows.

"And we're facing a deadline."

It's remarkable."

"No, God has arranged it," said Margarita, and all heads turned to hear her.

"What I mean is, well, I guess it could happen—seven people mistreated by one man in the name of God—accused, tortured, and condemned. But, it's not likely. We all have something in common. We came together for a reason."

"Right. We can help each other survive the rest of this journey, and, if we travel beyond Spain—well, that's even better."

"Yes. We do need each other. If we combine forces, maybe we can keep our meager possessions and whatever money we've managed to hold onto."

"It's too late—the bandits took it all."

"Is that true?" said Sara Elena. "Did the bandits get away with all your things?" She looked around to all the members of the groups, searching their eyes to discover the truth.

"No, not everything," said the dark-skinned woman. "I didn't give them my mother's jewels."

"Good for you!" Sara Elena smiled at the pride and defiance in her voice.

"I didn't throw in all my coins." The old man held up his chin.

"Those thieves didn't get all my valuables," said Margarita. "I have a few secrets intact."

"I'm so happy."

"I still have—" Alma began.

"I hate to break in on this little chat, but we really should get on the road," said Pedro. He slapped the dirt off his pants and got to his feet.

"Get your gear together, and mount up. It's still a long way to Palos, and the day slips away while we chat." He ambled over to attend to the animals.

Sara Elena jumped to follow Pedro's instructions. She noticed the other members of the caravan also hurrying to get ready, as if encouraged by their discussion. A few smiles exchanged, a helping hand extended to someone lagging behind, served to speed the process along. It was strange how she hadn't paid much attention to the others on the journey before. Now, everyone wanted to help each other. Within fifteen minutes, all had prepared for travel and arranged themselves in their saddles.

The sun rose over the rocks and vaulted into the cobalt sky as each one urged their mules forward. The animals didn't protest, for they had found shade and adequate grass at their camp spot. Soon, they came to a rocky outcropping, where the vista opened up. Ahead, the road sliced through rolling country, leaving a scar like an old sword wound. Shading his eyes to take in the situation, Pedro scowled and motioned for them to stop talking.

"See that cloud far ahead on the horizon. That's Morales and his group. They're traveling like demons to reach their prey." He smiled at Sara Elena.

"But, they'll never catch us," said Sara Elena with a triumphant lilt.

"No, never," said Margarita.

"We need to stay out of their sight, but keep them in our view. Don't want to get too close to them."

"What do you propose?"

"Be quiet—no unnecessary talking—and follow me. I'll lead us on a more private path." He motioned for them to move forward. "It may take a little longer."

In the raw silence, a single raven swooped above and crowed its annoyance.

They skirted the villages along the route that day, avoiding any place Don Antonio's group might stop. Finally, in the late afternoon, they stopped at a well outside an inn on the edge of a pine forest. The travelers slid off their mules, shook their numb legs, and rubbed their sore behinds.

"Pedro, can't we please stay the night here?" One by one they pleaded.

"It's been days since we washed properly, and slept in a bed."

"I could use a good, hot meal."

"All right," he conceded. "I don't see our pursuers here, so I guess it is safe enough. The mules could use a rest, too."

Pedro walked to the stable and procured lodging for the mounts, and then walked into the inn to find rooms for his group. He returned in a few minutes, smiling.

"Good news: Don Antonio's group passed by here before noon. The innkeeper said they wasted no time—didn't even stop for a meal."

"Good! As long as they think we're ahead of them, we're fine."

Pedro cocked his head and grinned.

"The other bit of good news is there's lodging available for all of us. It's not a fancy place, but it's clean. The Romero family has a room. The two ladies come next, and there's a smaller room with several beds for the rest of us *hombres*."

"I can hardly wait to wash my face."

"To kick off my boots and sleep on a soft mattress—that's what I'm looking for."

"Come in with me and get your rooms. Supper's at nine o'clock. Smells like mutton stew."

Pedro grabbed his saddlebags and some of the other baggage of the travelers and strode through the door. The others followed, chatting with animation at the prospect of sleeping indoors at last.

"Let me show you to your rooms." The short, round woman waddled along in front of them. With her ample girth and toddling steps, she looked like a stout ship rocking in the waves.

She ushered them to their doors, repeating instructions about towels and meals to each set of people.

"Take a *siesta*, dears, and come down for supper at nine. It's warm in the *comedor*. There's extra blankets draped over the beds, if you need them. If you want to wash up, let me know and I'll bring a basin. Enjoy your rest."

She left them with a curtsy and a hearty smile.

That night, they all slept without a worry—secure, warm, and fed.

Don Antonio ground his teeth and snarled.

"Where is that infernal woman? We've been driving ourselves to exhaustion and yet we never seem to catch up to her."

"Let's stop here, sire," said Alexo. "Perhaps a little refreshment would help." He reined in his horse, dismounted and spread out a heavy robe for a resting place. He withdrew the *bota* bag and a loaf of crusty bread and a knife from a saddlebag while Don Antonio dismounted with a grimace and settled himself on the robe.

"Leave me for a while, Alexo. I need time to think." He waved his servant off. Don Antonio felt angry and frustrated. How could such a slip of a woman evade him and his men? How dare Sara Elena Torres promise something so tantalizing as her own body, and the next moment laugh in his face and run away from him?

The middle-aged cleric tipped the *bota* and let the cool, red liquid stream into his mouth. So enticing! Almost the way I feel about this elusive young woman.

My pursuit borders on obsession, I know. I want her but can't seem to possess her. The fantasies of an aging, lovesick man . . . It's not as if a man of the church hasn't taken a woman before. If she would only come to me willingly and give herself freely, I believe I could truly be good to her. But no! She disregards my authority—my dignity! She manipulated me to gain freedom for her friend.

Don Antonio stabbed the loaf of bread with the knife he'd used to cut it before. Again and again he slashed at it until the loaf split into a dozen pieces.

I must control myself. Why does this young woman make me so angry?

Don Antonio felt his heart pounding. He shifted his weight to a new position and let his thoughts drift down old pathways. His mother's voice still echoed in his mind.

'*Antonio! Stop that, Antonio. You foolish boy!*'

'*Can we take care of it, Mother?*'

I came into her sitting room, clothes rumpled, twigs in my hair. I placed the quivering bird on her lap. Shrieking, she'd shaken her skirts until the bird dropped to the floor.

'*Kindly take that creature away, Antonio. You must never do that again,*' *said Mother.* '*Never! I won't have filth in my house. And that includes you, Antonio. Never come into my room unless you are properly groomed and dressed. Someday, you'll be an important member of the clergy. It's time you learned proper behavior.*'

So, that started it. In that and other ways Mother let me know sentiment mattered not at all . . . . I mattered not at all.

Now I'm just a stilted old clergyman, impeccably dressed but hollow inside. I've never loved anyone or anything. Maybe I'm only capable of hate. Yet, I'm pursuing a young woman with hopes of loving her. Or at least I'll possess her.

Don Antonio got up, stretched his legs, and watched his faithful servant shake the crumbs from the robe and fold it away in his saddlebag.

But, if I catch Sara Elena, it will be my ruin! She has an opinion about everything and her willingness to express it attracts attention.

"Alexo, we need to move on. When will we ever catch up with Sara Elena? It's as if they've vanished."

"Perhaps they hid in the woods along the way—or tricked us into running ahead of them." Alexo mounted and coaxed his beast onward.

The strange suggestion gripped Don Antonio with an icy certainty. *She tricked me!*

Chapter 25

"Rodrigo Galvan, at your service." The old man straightened his back, made a sweeping flourish with his hat, and bowed to the group. He looked and acted more robust than he had at any time on the trip so far.

Pedro had asked them all to assemble outside the inn by nine o'clock in the morning.

"I wanted to get an early start," said Pedro, "but now it seems Señor Galvan would like to tell us his life history." Pedro cast a hard look his direction.

"Can't you tell us on the road?" Sara Elena interrupted. "We'll have many tedious hours ahead that you can fill with your story."

"I guess I could, young lady. A tedious story for a tedious journey?"

"I didn't mean that." Sara's cheeks colored.

Señor Galvan chuckled. "No insult taken, señorita." His eyes crinkled up at the outer corners.

"Let's be off, then." Pedro swung into his saddle and kicked his animal into action. The others followed, now expert in riding the plodding mules.

"Tell us your interesting tale when we get out on the road," said Margarita.

To start, Pedro led the group along at a quick clip, making conversation impossible.

The travelers jabbed heels into their animals' ribs to keep up, the promised story forgotten.

The late July sun, like a squeezed grapefruit, shot a yellow-orange stream through clumps of bushes dotting the road. Soon, hot African winds would blast through for the day, scorching the stubborn plant life and shriveling creeks to thin blue ribbons.

The mule caravan carried on for several hours over parched grass, pebbled roads, and rolling hills. Always the cobalt sky stretched above, a deep beauty.

Sara Elena scanned the horizon, or what she could see through the clouds of dust. She hoped she'd never meet up with her pursuer again. Her dread of Don Antonio grew each day.

Don Antonio must be doubly angry now. Will he realize I've tricked him again?

Señor and Señora Romero stayed close to Pedro. Sara Elena and Margarita followed, and then came Señor Galvan, with Alma Romero, and the other muleteers trailed along behind them. The mules trotted down a dusty pathway and clopped across a wood bridge spanning a dry creek bed.

"Could we stop here?" said Señor Galvan. "My mule is limping."

"Everyone, pull over and rest your animals. Perhaps, señor, you could tell your story now—may it not delay us too long." Pedro shrugged his shoulders and grinned.

"It won't take but a few minutes." Rodrigo Galvan dismounted and tied his mule to a dry bush by the dusty creek bed.

The others followed his example and then settled themselves on the robes they had draped on the ground. Señor Galvan paced back and forth in front of them, trying to sequence his tale just so. His straggly gray brows dropped low over his eyes.

"I come from Córboba. My aristocratic parents insisted I receive the best education available. When I finished my studies, I secured a teaching position at the same place I spent so many happy hours studying. You know, Córdoba was the capital of Andalucía in its glory days. So many learned minds gathered there over the years—Samuel the Nagid, Judah Halevi, Averröes, and Maimonides, for example—and everyone seemed to get along. Jews, Arabs, and Christians coexisted in relative harmony—and all prospered." His eyes looked up as if gathering the memories from afar.

"Just imagine the libraries—over 400,000 volumes in the caliph's collection! Imagine! Nine hundred baths, thousands of shops. Everything in Córdoba set the highest standard of culture and civilization. It was truly 'the ornament of the world.'"

"Yes, Don Rodrigo," said Pedro. "I've heard of the wonders of Córdoba. But tell us how you encountered the wrath of the Inquisition."

"Sorry. I'm proud of my historic city."

"As you should be. It was a miracle—"

"But, let me continue. Like I said, I received the finest education and became intoxicated with the intellectual environment of Andalucía. Of course, we all spoke Arabic, the language of philosophy and poetry. I immersed myself in Moorish culture—it is so rich! But my own heritage suffered. I lost interest in Latin and the learning of the west. In fact, I began to criticize it loudly. Like Judah Halevi, that great twelfth-century poet, said,

'My heart is in the East, and I in the West
As far in the west as west can be!
How can I enjoy my food?
What flavor can it have for me?
How can I fulfill my vows
Or do the things I've sworn to do,
While Zion is in Christian hands
And I am trapped in Arab lands?'

258

"This displeased the authorities, of course. They warned me, and then when I wouldn't stop, they brought me before the tribunal."

"I know that terror," interrupted Margarita. She folded her arms across her chest and squeezed them tight to control her shivering.

"You do?" Señor Galvan shot a questioning look at her.

"Oh, yes. In Granada I worked among the people awaiting trial by the Inquisition—helped them get messages to loved ones and found out about the charges laid against them. For this, I was accused of disloyalty to the Holy Church. Who knows what would have happened to me if Sara Elena hadn't intervened."

Margarita flashed a tender look at the young woman who had saved her.

"You have much for which to give thanks." Señor Galvan nodded his head toward Margarita.

"Sara Elena is the daughter I never had. She's precious to me."

"Indeed she is."

"Finish your story, Don Rodrigo." Sara Elena hoped to divert the conversation away from her crimson face.

"There's not much else to say. I was treated well, because of the prestige of my family. Instead of torture and death, I only had to wear that suit of shame, the *sanbenito*, for three years."

He rubbed his eyes. "The humiliation alone is a kind of death that never goes away." His voice trailed off. People spit at you, shun you, and whisper behind your back."

"Then we all have suffered under the Inquisition." Pedro got up and brushed off his dusty pants.

"Yes." They all assented.

"I will get you safely to the sea coast and onto a ship departing this cursed country—whatever the cost." Pedro clenched both fists and crossed them over his chest. "Now, let's get going. Time is short." Pedro dropped his arms and swung into his saddle. The others followed his lead.

"Mara, may I ask you a question?" Sara Elena worked her way closer to Señora Romero on the trail.

"I don't know what I can offer as information, but you may ask." She gave a sideways glance and clucked at her mule.

"I'm still curious about what my father said—"

"And you'd like to hear the whole story."

"Yes."

"I'll tell you all I can. Your father was our rescuer at a very bad time. We are forever grateful." She shifted her position on the mule and closed her eyes a moment."

"Let me think how to start—Yes, I know. To start at the beginning: our family lived for many years in Toledo. After all, it was a center for language study and translation. Diego, my husband, worked sometimes with your father Don Alonzo. Always a pleasure. We enjoyed living in that ancient city. So many learned people contributed to that stimulating city atmosphere! Do you remember any of this? You were probably a young girl then."

"I recall a few cloudy memories, but not much. We left when I was ten or so."

"Your father excelled in translation and became the favorite of the aristocrats and city officials. He kept busy and out of trouble mostly. We all tried to conduct our business and not get caught in controversy. But it was hard, because we were Jews, after all, and therefore, noticeable."

"It's always that way, isn't it?" Sara Elena smiled a corners-down arch.

"Yes, and we're easy to blame for any trouble that comes along." Mara sighed. "Well, one day Diego took his latest copied document to the mayor. Came in and was received in a polite manner. The mayor had a fever and a large sore on his arm. 'I feel miserable,' he said. 'What can you do to help me?' Well, Diego touched the sore and suggested a poultice to draw out the poison. He had a painful boil before and it eased his discomfort. Diego received payment and left, thinking no more about it."

"I think I know what happened next." Sara Elena leaned forward on her mule.

"Yes, it's predictable, no? We heard the next day that the mayor was much worse, and that his wife and young son had contracted the same symptoms. The fever, the bumps, or bubos, that spread over the body like bubbles in a stew. The mayor was near death two days later, but had Diego arrested for spreading the disease. Just because he touched him once." She shrugged her shoulders and rolled her eyes.

"My mother got sick then, too. It was the black plague, right?"

"Of course. The mayor ordered that Diego be put to death as soon as the mayor died. It looked bleak for us all. We would be forced to leave the city we loved, too."

"What happened?"

"Your father stepped in. He pled for Diego, asking he be released, that nobody causes a disease. It's just the will of God. It just happens."

"That didn't work, did it?"

"No, angry and sick men want their revenge. Next, your father offered money to ransom Diego out of confinement. That didn't work, either. The mayor knew he'd never live long enough to enjoy spending it."

"So, what happened?" Sara Elena was as curious as a mouse looking for a crust of bread.

"I don't know for sure, but I think your father stole into the jail, gave the guard a sleeping potion I think, and got Diego out of there. He put him on a horse and sent him out of town immediately. Then Don Alonzo went back home, sent us a message. When investigators came around, he acted as if he knew nothing. Mara and I left the next morning with a few belongings. By then, the mayor had died and others in Toledo had fallen ill. So, people forgot about Diego and responded to the general panic by running to their families and isolating themselves behind barred doors."

"How did you find your husband?"

"He waited outside of town and watched for us until we came by. It was a miracle we were reunited. We thank your father, Don Alonzo, every time we think of that dreadful time."

Sara wiped away the spilling tears. "Thank you a million times. That story is precious to me."

"You are welcome. God bless you, Sara Elena." Sara retreated to her thoughts for a long time afterward.

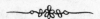

Señor Galvan made his way forward on the trail until his mule plodded alongside Margarita's.

"The monotony of the trip shows on your face."

"What? Oh, pardon me. I was deep in my thoughts." Margarita flashed a smile in his direction.

"May I ask you some questions, señora?"

"Margarita. Please call me Margarita. After all, we have all gone through much together. We're family now."

"Margarita—and you must call me Rodrigo." He compressed his lips as she nodded.

"If you wish."

"Margarita, you are a fearless woman. To work with victims of the Inquisition, when everyone else avoids them—that is courage."

"Thank you, but perhaps it is foolhardy."

"No—courageous, definitely. How long did you work for the rights and comfort of the accused?"

"Several years, before I was noticed and caught." She brushed a hand across her forehead.

"And your husband—did he help you with your work?"

"My husband was a timid man, and fearful. He retreated to a safer world—his own work, and nothing else." She sighed and gazed into the distance.

"He spent the last months in hiding."

"But now you are going to meet him and be united once again?" Señor Galvan pressed her for answers.

"My husband is dead. He jumped from the city wall because he couldn't bear the thought of torture and death when the Inquisition caught him."

"I'm sorry." Señor Galvan looked away to hide his discomfort. Margarita's face betrayed raw grief.

"It's all right, Rodrigo. It was only a matter of time. Alberto couldn't abide being caught and caged—never could tolerate enclosed spaces for long."

"Nevertheless, it must be a double sadness that he took his own life."

"I don't fault him. I only hope God receives his tortured soul in Paradise."

Rodrigo Galvan lapsed into silence as he rode side by side with Margarita along the rocky path through the granite boulders.

"My wife died three years ago. Now I'm making my way to Jerusalem, the heart of our faith."

"We also plan to go to Jerusalem—Sara Elena and I."

"Perhaps I could be of service, and escort you there."

"Perhaps you could. I will discuss it with Sara Elena."

The caravan trotted along in silence. An angry sun glared at them from the cloudless sky. Hot breezes washed over the members of the caravan and each in turn felt its drying effects.

Sara Elena reached for a water bag slung over the horn of her saddle. She had fallen back to ride with Alma.

"Will this heat ever stop?" She tilted the bag for a sip and gave it to Alma.

"Perhaps in October." Alma took a long gulp as the cool stream shot into her mouth. She licked her lips and splashed a few drops on her face.

They laughed and continued their rhythmic swaying and bobbing on the mules.

"Was it really awful?"

"What?"

"Was it awful being tortured by the Inquisition?"

"Yes—worse than you can ever imagine." Alma closed her eyes.

"I didn't mean to make you relive it."

"No, it's all right. I dream about it every night still. I can never get away from it."

"That could make you bitter—oh, sorry." Sara Elena clamped her mouth shut.

"The reason I'm bitter," said Alma, "has nothing to do with the torture. Something else happened." She looked away.

"What—is it all right to ask?"

"I may as well tell you. After I was tortured, I said I'd confess. I wanted the pain to go away." She covered her eyes with a trembling hand.

"Don Antonio said he'd personally take my confession, and brought me into a private room. Nobody else was there. I wondered about his intentions—but he soon revealed himself, you might say. He threw me down on a small cot in the corner—and violated me."

Alma shuddered and let out a groan. A tear streamed down each cheek.

"No!" Sara Elena reached out for Alma's arm.

"Yes, that supposed man of God is nothing but a fiend." Alma turned away from Sara's touch.

"Has he done this before to other girls, do you think?"

"The guards seemed to know—left the room immediately instead of staying to stand guard."

"Is there no way to make him pay for his wrongdoing?"

"My word against a respected member of the Holy Office?"

"No way to prove this outrage?"

"I'm not pregnant, if that's what you mean. At least, God was merciful in that respect."

"But you are forever scarred, in mind and body."

"Yes. And I'll never forgive that lowly coward."

"Somehow—someday—you shall receive justice." Sara Elena gritted her teeth and clenched her fists.

"You are kind to say so."

"I will see to it."

Alma urged her mule ahead to join her mother. She looked back and laughed at Sara Elena.

"It will never happen—but you're a dear friend to say it."

Chapter 26

"The finest cheese in the kingdom—come and buy."

"Warm blankets for the voyage—100 *maravedis!*"

"Get your rice and beans—right here."

"Look at these prices. Outrageous!" said Margarita, as she and Sara Elena wandered through the various stalls set up in Palos' central plaza.

"What choice does anyone have? If they didn't bring provisions with them, they'll have to buy here at double the price."

The caravan had arrived in Palos late the day before and settled in a quiet inn at the edge of town. Pedro bade them all farewell, after pointing out the best and safest ship in the fleet moored in the harbor. In fact, he personally bargained with the captain and procured passage for all six members of the caravan.

"It's a miracle," said Señor Galvan. "How did you do it?"

"I still have some friends," smiled Pedro.

"However you got our passages, we thank you." Everyone shook Pedro's hand or slapped him on the back.

"I bid you goodbye and may God keep you safe." He saluted them with tip of his hat and was gone. "By the way, this Italian ship is headed up the coast for Lisbon before it heads south again."

After Pedro left, they slept well and by ten o'clock the next morning, curiosity propelled them all out to the streets. They spread out in separate directions to perform their errands.

Palos swarmed with activity. Like ants preparing for a long winter, people rushed through the streets of the once tranquil coastal town. Frenzied travelers ran from wharf to wharf trying to find the best price on passage out of Spain, or for that matter, any available space on any ship. Merchants peddled shoes, blankets, air-cured hams, wheels of sheep's cheese, dried figs and dates, candles, rice and beans, and anything else travelers might need on a long sea voyage.

Sara Elena adjusted her shawl over her head. Wearing the black wig made her head itch, but without it disguising her hair, she'd be easily noticed in a crowd. Sara's belly bulged out and she held it to keep the padding from shifting in the crush of people.

"Do you think I look unremarkable? Would Don Antonio spot me here?"

"You're never unremarkable, Sarita, but I think you blend in. You look like just any other weary traveler."

Margarita pulled her black shawl low on her forehead, to just above her eyebrows.

"I feel like I a need a disguise, too. This town has a thousand eyes."

"Nonsense. There's no reason Don Antonio or his men will recognize you."

"No, he only saw my face once, at the market. He's always sent a subordinate to deal with me. But if we're seen together, they might suspect something. They did hear from Pedro about a pregnant woman traveling with an older woman in the caravan."

"That's true. We should be extra careful." Sara Elena put her hand up to her face to conceal it further.

Margarita wrapped the ends of her scarf around her neck and pulled a fold up over her mouth.

"A scarf hides many secrets." She winked at Sara Elena, and her eyes crinkled.

"I'm smiling behind this shawl."

"Just keep your head down and let's get to the ship Pedro told us about."

Babies wailed, chickens squawked, and goats nattered as Sara and Margarita shoved through the crowds. Haggling vendors arguing with irritable travelers made it hard to get through. The marketplace smelled of manure and sweat, and the heat was steamy for a summer day on the coast.

Sara Elena and Margarita shouldered heavy tapestry bags carrying their precious belongings and moved through the crowds. They planned to go back for another load later. Last night's innkeeper promised to safeguard their things until they returned.

"I wonder if the captain would send a boy to fetch the rest of our things."

"That's not likely. We're not nobility."

"You're right. We'll be fortunate to find a clean bed to sleep in on the boat."

"Maybe we can send a message to Juan and Luis on their ship—or arrange a meeting."

"A meeting would be risky."

"But wonderful," sighed Sara Elena.

"Do you have your coins hidden away? In this crowd, anyone could brush by and lift a purse—and who would even notice?" Margarita lowered her voice so passersby wouldn't overhear their conversation.

"Don't worry—it's safe."

They reached the far side of the plaza, re-adjusted their shawls and bags, and headed down a cobblestone street that led to the harbor.

"What's that stink?" Sara Elena wrinkled her nose.

"Silly, that's sea air—the briny ocean—salt water gives it that aroma."

"It smells rotten to me. Is that what we'll be breathing on this voyage?"

"Yes, indeed."

"Oh, dear." Sara pinched her nose.

Margarita chuckled. Sara Elena pushed forward and came to the docks. Sturdy planks were placed side by side along the shore in either direction from where the street ended.

"Where is Juan's ship, do you think?"

"Over there, to the left are the *Niña*, the *Pinta*, and the *Santa Maria*, two caravels and a *nao*, sometimes called a carrack, hired by Columbus. The *Santa Maria* is the flagship."

"Where did you find out all this information?"

"Rodrigo. He told me they had a devilish time finding enough vessels for the expedition."

"Rodrigo?" Sara Elena rolled her eyes as Margarita pursed her lips and looked away.

They watched furious activity surround the three ships. Scores of men handed boxes and bundles up a human line to the next pair of hands. They juggled supplies for the voyage, and trinkets for anyone they might encounter on their trip.

"I wish I could find Juan. Do you think he's here somewhere?" Sara Elena scanned the sea of faces.

"I'm sure he is. Maybe we can approach the *Santa Maria* after we stow our own bags. Let's go."

They turned right and zigzagged their way through scurrying people, loads of boxes and barrels, and a few barking dogs. Here and there, a cat darted between boxes, chasing after a mouse. Hundreds of people crowded one end of the dock, clambering up gangplanks, arguing with the sea captains, and hauling their precious belongings to a safe place on board.

"Here's the *Veronica*," said Margarita. "That's our ship."

"It looks like everyone stows their own belongings," said Sara Elena as she reached the main deck.

"Aye, that's right, pretty lady," said the captain.

"Are you Captain Ferlandini, sir?" Sara Elena dropped her bags and looked up at a tall, bulky man with long curling black locks and eyebrows thick as hairbrushes.

"Aye. And who are you two ladies?"

"Pedro sent us. He purchased our passages yesterday."

"Names?"

"Margarita Martinez and Sara Elena Torres."

Captain Ferlandini held out a sheaf of papers and ran his finger down the list of names.

"Here you be. Just pay your passage to the purser and find yourself a sleeping spot below." He tipped two fingers to his hat in an informal salute then turned to the next passenger.

"Captain—could I ask a favor?" Sara Elena grabbed the man's arm.

"What might that be?" He peered down at her with hard eyes.

"If someone comes asking about us, could you say we're not on board?"

"Oh? In trouble with the law, or perhaps the Inquisition, are you?"

Sara shrugged her shoulders and didn't answer.

"Well, you're not the only one on the boat that's running away." He laughed.

"Don't worry, señora, I don't tell anything to people who come snooping into people's private affairs. Your secret's safe on board the *Veronica*." He turned toward the next passenger.

Sara Elena and Margarita grabbed their bags and walked to the nearest doorway. A sailor stood guard there.

"Go one flight down—turn left. You can have any room or bunk still available. Watch your belongings—we'll not be responsible if they're stolen."

Suddenly his gruff tone changed.

"Let me help you, signora. Will your husband be joining you later?"

"Thank you. We can manage."

"By the way, what day is it, sailor?"

"What day, signora? It's August first." He tucked his thumbs into the top of his breeches.

"Thank you."

"Glad to be of service, signora."

Sara Elena backed her way down the ladder and reached up for her bags. Margarita handed them down, as well as her own, then backed down the ladder, also. They hurried through the dark, narrow passageway past several occupied cabins. In a narrow alcove, they found two straw mattresses covered with heavy canvas, laid on two wooden frames with ropes that crisscrossed each other. A homespun curtain hung nearby to be used as a privacy screen.

"We can put our bags under the beds and against the far wall. One of us will have to stay here and guard our things all the time, though."

Sara Elena shoved her bags under the bed and pushed them with her foot.

"If we leave the cabin area, someone else will claim it, don't you think?" She sat down on a mattress. It sagged but held her weight.

"The straw is new, and it doesn't smell of mold or mildew. If we're lucky, there'll be no bed bugs, either."

"That's too much to hope for." Sara scratched herself.

They looked at each other and laughed.

"We just need to avoid being seen by Don Antonio before the ship leaves."

"We'll be safe here."

They leaned back, sank into the mattresses and soon both women fell asleep.

Sara Elena was the first to hear voices, coming from the main deck. She sat up and listened.

"Is Sara Elena Torres a passenger on this vessel?"

"Who wants to know?"

"Don Antonio Morales, of the Holy Office of the Inquisition."

"Well, well. Welcome to my ship."

"I'm looking for her—she's a runaway."

"Do you think I'd tell you who's on my ship?"

"I don't like your attitude, captain."

"This is my ship and I can say who comes and goes." He paused. "You, sir, must go."

"Very well, I'll go, but you'll be sorry you said no to me."

"I doubt it. Now leave my ship."

The sound of footsteps faded away. Sara Elena shook Margarita.

"Did you hear that, Margarita?"

"What was it, Sarita?"

"Don Antonio was just here—on this boat—just above us on the main deck!"

"What did he say?"

"Wanted to know if I was on the *Veronica*."

"Did the captain tell him anything?"

"No, he just ordered him off the ship"

"Good for him. I like Captain Ferlandini."

"What'll I do if Don Antonio finds us?"

"Well, it hasn't happened yet—I imagine he's checking all the passenger ships in Palos. He knows you were headed this way."

"I'm scared."

"Be calm, and don't step out of this cabin until the *Veronica* sets sail. Captain Ferlandini will keep all the curious away."

"I hope you're right, but we have to go back for the rest of our belongings."

"I'll go for them," said Margarita. "You stay here."

Margarita jumped up and grabbed her shawl.

"Whatever you do, don't leave this ship!" Margarita ran down the passageway before Sara Elena could object. She climbed the ship's ladder to the main deck.

"Be careful. Keep your face covered," Sara called after her.

Margarita ran down the gangplank. She hesitated a moment, planning her next move.

"Should I get our bags first, or send word to Luis and Juan? Luis should know about his father's death and sister's change of plans as soon as possible."

On the other hand, Margarita didn't trust the innkeeper to hold their bags much longer. Anything left lying about became plunder these days. People had lost their sense of decency in the mad scramble to survive.

"Baggage first." Margarita headed along the wharves toward the street that led to the plaza. She made her way through the crowds of people and found the inn. "I feel like a fish swimming against the tide." She trotted to the inn.

"I've come to retrieve our bags," she said as she strode into the lobby.

"There's a fee for their safekeeping." The innkeeper looked up from his ledger. Light glistened off his oiled hair, and his nose gleamed with inflamed pustules.

"You offered to keep them for free yesterday."

"Conditions have changed. You have to pay now before you get them. Fifty *maravedis* per bag."

Margarita pulled the necessary coins out of her sleeve and slapped them on the counter.

"It's more than you deserve." She narrowed her eyes and glared at him.

"A pleasure doing business with you, señora. Your bags are in the back room—go and select them." He stuffed the coins in his vest pocket and made a note in his ledger.

Margarita walked back to the *Veronica* with measured steps, and stopped often to rest her sore fingers. When she reached quayside, she looked around. Two small boys sat on a bag of rice, absorbed in fondling a small white ball. Soon the white ball unrolled and walked up one boy's arm all the way to his shoulder.

Margarita stifled a scream.

"Boy. Come here, and leave that mouse behind. I have an errand for you."

"How many coins will you pay me?"

"Twenty *maravedis*—thirty if you come back as quick as an angry bee."

"It must be an important message." The boy jumped forward and tossed the mouse to his friend.

Margarita scratched a few lines on a scrap of parchment she found in one of the bags, folding and handing it into the boy's grimy hands.

"This message must be delivered immediately to Doctor Juan Sanchez on board the *Santa Maria*. Do you know it?"

"The *Santa Maria*? It's right over there." He pointed in the direction of the flagship.

"Can I have my coins now?"

"I'll give you half now and the rest when you return." She pressed some coins in his palm. "Go now, quickly, and bring me my answer. You can find me on the *Veronica*. It's the brightly painted one on the other end of the pier."

"The *Veronica*—right." He turned to leave then halted. "Who do I ask for?"

"Margarita."

"I'll be back soon with your answer, Señora Margarita."

Margarita smiled as the skinny boy darted among clusters of people and disappeared. She picked up the bags once more and made her way to the *Veronica*. Arriving on deck, she passed by the sailor guarding the hatch to the passenger area.

"I told her not to go by herself."

"What are you saying?" Her heart beat faster.

"I told the young mother not to leave the ship without an escort. She ignored me and kept on going."

"You mean my traveling companion?"

"Yes. The pretty woman, in a family way. You know." He folded his muscular arms and scowled.

"Sara Elena," she said under her breath.

"Told her it's not safe to leave her things below without someone to watch them."

"Did she say where she was going?"

"She asked me a lot about all the boats Columbus is outfitting. She seemed most interested in the *Santa Maria*, though."

"Oh, no!" Margarita turned to back down the ladder to the deck below.

"Sailor, please hand me my bags one by one when I get halfway down. I've got to store these as soon as possible, and go find her."

"You'll stay on the boat, señora. Captain's orders. Doesn't want anyone else wandering about."

"But I need to find Sara Elena."

"Captain's sent out a search party. You stay put and guard your bags."

"If a boy comes with a message in the next half hour, would you send him to me? It's vitally important."

"I can do that. I'll watch for him."

"You are kind." Margarita flashed him a grateful smile and scurried down the passageway, anxious to see if their belonging were still intact.

"Sara Elena, you impetuous girl," she breathed. "What will become of you now?"

Chapter 27

Sara Elena lay back on the mattress to think. Her thoughts careened through her mind with abandon, disturbing her repose.

Don Antonio nearly discovered me just now. That's too close!

Margarita's right. I should stay here and keep out of sight. But, oh how I want to see Juan and talk to him. I miss him so much. And Luis—I need to tell him about Father. My life is such a mess. I don't belong in Spain anymore, and I don't know where I'm going. No home, family scattered. How will I ever find any of them?

Juan always had such good sense. He listened when I explained my problems, and always gave wise advice. I wish I could discuss things with him now.

She rolled to one side and propped herself on one elbow.

Perhaps I can. I could make my way to the Santa Maria if I walk without drawing notice. Quietly—not in a rush—with my disguise intact. If challenged, I could say I need to see the doctor. It's true. I desperately need to see Juan.

"It's decided," said Sara Elena and stood up. "I'm going to see Juan."

She pushed the wig back into place, brushed the bits of straw off her dress and strode to the ship's ladder.

"Won't Juan be surprised?"

Sara Elena climbed the ship's ladder to the main deck.

"It's a fine day, isn't it, *marinero*?"

"*Sí, signora*." He nodded and smiled.

"Tell me about the ships Columbus readies for voyage." She gave him her most engaging smile.

"What would you like to know?"

"How large the ships are, what they can carry, how far can they go—those kinds of things."

"Captain Columbus had difficulty finding vessels in this whirlwind of time. The King and Queen commanded the city of Palos to provide two caravels, which they did. But the smallest they could find. Unsatisfactory, according to Columbus' complaint.

"What about the flagship?" said Sara Elena.

"The third vessel, the *Santa Maria*, was hired by the Crown. It was made in Galicia, in the northwest corner of Iberia, and is slower and smaller than Columbus wanted. It's a *nao*, and not fast like the caravels. Hard to maneuver, and more suitable for sailing the Mediterranean than the wild open sea."

"I suppose you've heard lots of stories about the expedition?"

"Yes, signora. It's taken ten weeks, not ten days like they said, to outfit the boats. Quite an ordeal. But now, they're ready—anxious to be off." He rubbed the stubble on his chin.

"Fascinating." Sara Elena swept her eyes over to look the young sailor in the face.

"I imagine you'd like the chance to prove yourself on such an adventure—strong and capable as you are."

The young mariner thought a moment.

"Yes, I reckon I would." He puffed out his chest and crossed his brawny arms.

"Well, thank you, *marinero*. I'll be off now to see to an errand. Thank you for the information." She swept her shawl around her shoulders.

"Signora, you shouldn't leave the vessel. Someone is looking for you."

"Don't worry. I'm going to meet my husband. He'll protect me."

Sara Elena looked back and waved as she exited the *Veronica*.

"The captain will not be pleased," the young mariner called out after her.

"I can't hear you," she mouthed the words. Then she turned toward the area of the harbor where the *Nina*, *Pinta* and *Santa Maria* sat anchored.

"Juan Sanchez, here I come."

The sky washed blue like a hillside of lupines shone above as she scuffled down the long pier. Salty air and creosote logs prickled her nostrils, and the sounds of dogs barking, vendors hawking, and boats creaking filled her ears. She walked along swinging her arms and smiling.

"Oh, I forgot. I need to walk as if I'm invisible. I hope nobody's noticed me yet."

She glanced around and caught the eyes of a young man dressed in black. She dropped her head and put the shawl over her head and wig.

Why is that man interested in me?

Sara Elena began to walk faster. She brushed through tangles of people littering the quay. She looked back and noticed the man had left his spot across the street from the *Veronica*.

Where is that man?

She felt a presence behind her.

Strange, how even in the middle of a crowd, I know someone is following me. Is that one of Don Antonio's subordinates?

Sara Elena picked up her pace.

So much for a quiet walk to the Santa Maria.

She glanced behind her once again, and then broke into a trot. The man in black loped behind her. *Why did I decide to go out and find Juan?*

She broke into a run, and heard footsteps behind keeping pace with her. She neared the anchored *Santa Maria.* Just a few more paces and she would reach the gangplank. A knot of men stood talking nearby.

I don't want to get caught.

She ran with a last burst of energy. Someone grabbed at her shawl.

"Please, help me," she said as she burst through the cluster of men. "Someone is chasing me." Tears streamed from her eyes and her wig slipped off.

"What's this?" A deep voice sounded. "Sara Elena?" Strong arms grabbed her, and she glanced up to see granite green eyes.

"Oh, Juan. It's you. Thank goodness," she murmured, and then collapsed.

Sara Elena gradually became aware of his presence, but didn't know where she was.

"Hello, *querida.* I never thought I'd see you here. You're quite a sight."

Juan leaned forward and caressed her cheek. He grasped her hand and planted a kiss on it.

In the semi-darkness, Sara Elena's eyes darted around. She was lying on a soft bed. The walls contained nautical charts. She touched her head. The wig was gone. Then she touched her middle. The wadding had also been removed.

"Where am I?"

"You're in my quarters aboard the *Santa Maria*. You've been resting for a while. I think you were quite exhausted when you ran into my arms. I imagine you have quite a story to tell me, too." He kissed her hand again and squeezed it.

"I don't know where to begin."

"At the beginning, of course."

"So much has happened. So much has changed since I saw you last." She closed her eyes and shuddered.

"What have you endured? You seem distracted, undone." Juan wrapped his arms around her and stroked her hair. Sara Elena felt her body relax.

"Father died. Then, I made a bargain with Don Antonio, and Margarita was released from prison. I had to leave Granada. Don Antonio has pursued me all the way to Palos, and now he's trying to catch me." She gulped for air.

"Wait! Slow down! What you say is fantastic!"

"It's all true."

"Just tell me one thing at a time." He leaned over and planted a gentle kiss on her forehead and then moved to cover her lips. Sara Elena sighed and returned his kiss with all the emotion she had bottled up these last perilous days.

Juan broke away, his breathing ragged.

"I've missed you, too." He laughed and stroked her cheek again.

"Much as I'd love to kiss you, we do need to talk. Please tell me about all the things that have happened to you—every last detail."

Sara Elena sat up and straightened her clothes. She swung her legs out onto the floor and faced Juan.

"There is much to tell. I hope you have time to listen."

"All the time we need." He grasped her hands and leaned forward to hear it all.

"I can hardly believe what you're telling me. It's incredible!" Juan held her and rubbed her back to comfort her.

Sara Elena sniffled and mopped her tear-stained cheeks. She leaned into Juan's chest and felt his warm nearness.

"But, it is true. All of it."

"So, your father had another attack and passed away just after we left?"

"Yes."

And, on the same day you made a bargain with the devil—Father Morales?"

"Yes, I was desperate to save Margarita, so I promised my body in exchange for her freedom."

Juan squeezed her tighter to him.

"I can't believe you did that. Were you crazy?" His voice bellowed in her ear.

"I never intended to go through with it. You do believe me, don't you?" She pulled back to look into his eyes.

The smoldering fire she saw there subsided to glowing embers.

"I believe you, Sara. But, you're so foolish. In fact, Morales is still hoping to claim you. The man in black is one of his minions—we can be sure."

"I thought I could trick Don Antonio long enough to get away. I almost made it."

"Morales is evil, and he never gives up. That's his reputation. How could you risk—"

"Juan, let me explain—"

Their argument was interrupted by a knock on the door.

"Is Sara Elena in here?" Luis barged into the room and ran to her side, enveloping her in a giant embrace.

"Luis."

"How are you, little sister?" His words rushed out. "I'm so glad to see you're all right. I heard from the crew that someone chased you all the way to the *Santa Maria*. Would have caught you, too, in another second."

"Yes," said Juan, "she created a scene. Here was this dark-haired, pregnant woman running like her life was in danger straight toward the ship. A man in black pursued her and had grasped one elbow when she plunged through a group of us standing by the gangplank, and fell into my arms."

"How did you recognize her?" Her brother's face showed both disbelief and amazement at the tale.

"Sara Elena recognized me—said my name and then collapsed."

"And then—"

"Well, her wig had slipped and the padding in her middle dropped to the ground."

"So, you're not pregnant?" Luis barely contained his brotherly rage.

"No, of course not. How could I be?"

"Well, I thought maybe you and—" Luis let his voice trail off.

"You thought I had been with her?" Juan stood up and shoved him away. "I'm not that kind of man."

Luis gathered his dignity, and pushed him back. The two men stood nose to nose, ready for someone to make the next move.

"Would you stop it, please?" Sara Elena strode over to them and interposed herself between them. "Let me explain."

"When I knew I had to leave Granada, I tried to think of a way to disguise myself. I first thought of dressing like a man—wearing some of your clothes, Luis—and cutting my hair short."

"No! Not your hair." They both shouted.

"I decided I just couldn't cut my long hair. Anyway, auburn hair of any length is still noticeable."

She let them go and began circling the room while relating her story.

"Then, I thought I would try to take all the money I'd got from the Queen and from Juan. How could I do it with inspectors waiting at the borders to keep cash from flowing out of Spain?"

She stopped and held up her index finger to make a point.

"I decided to disguise myself as a pregnant woman and to cover my red hair. Do you remember when I spied for the Queen?"

Luis and Juan nodded.

"Part of the disguise was a black wig. I never returned the wig so I put it on, and then tied the coins in several bags around my waist and neck. I divided it up, so nobody would find it all. I added lots of padding—old blankets and such— and behold, there was a black-haired mother-to-be." She held up her hands and shrugged.

"It was my best idea at the time."

"Clever, unusual—." Luis came over and patted her back. "Just like you."

"Everywhere, I've received courteous treatment. Except from the bandits."

"What bandits?"

"About three days before we got to Palos, a couple of bumbling bandits attacked our caravan. One of them grabbed my middle and discovered the stuffing."

"What?" Juan clenched his fists.

"It's all right. Just they then, he was interrupted by the arrival of Don Antonio and his caravan. Margarita and I ran and hid. Morales never actually saw us."

"And nobody in the caravan reported you?"

"No. We're a united group. Everyone hated the Inquisition, and especially they hated Morales. The whole caravan had something against him."

"Once again, rescued at the last moment." Luis shook his head.

"Your timing is perfect," said Juan, "but now the rumors will fly that I'm the father and left you abandoned to go on Columbus' expedition."

"That's ridiculous. Everyone saw my disguise fall apart."

"That may be true, but it doesn't stop the rumor mongers." Juan stroked his chin.

"You know Morales will try again to catch Sara Elena. Will she be safe aboard the *Veronica*?"

"No, I fear not," said Juan. "There's really no man to protect her. The crew can't keep Morales away forever." He came to Sara Elena and folded her in his arms.

"You don't need to worry about me. I can take care of myself," Sara protested.

"That worked for a while, but now Morales knows you're here and you're on the *Veronica*. He'll make a move tonight."

"Yes, he's desperate enough to do anything." Luis looked at Sara Elena.

"Why is he obsessed with you?"

"I have no idea."

"You've never encouraged him?"

"Don't be ridiculous! He's the enemy, the wolf who can hand you over to torture and death by fire."

"Well, he's mad at you, then."

"Could be. I've tricked him twice. Once, when I promised to become his mistress, and then vanished. Also, on the road to Palos, our muleteer sent him off on a wild chase in the wrong direction to pursue me." Sara Elena laughed. "I think he's humiliated and just plain furious that I fooled him."

"You've played a dangerous game, frustrating a powerful man like Morales." Juan looked worried. "What can we do to keep you safe?" He puzzled for a moment, and then grinned.

"I have it—a plan to thwart Morales. It's brilliant!" He rubbed his hands together and laughed heartily.

Sara Elena and Luis looked at him, puzzled by his glee.

"Well? Are you going to tell us, or not?

Chapter 28

"Leave it all to me," Juan yelled as he bolted out the door. Sara Elena and Luis looked at each other.

"What is he planning?"

"I have no idea."

"If he's trying to get out of his commitment to this expedition, he'll be disappointed."

"Why is that?" Sara Elena brushed a loose curl back from her face.

"Columbus has told us leaving now is the same as desertion. It's an affront to the Crown. We'll be thrown in jail."

"Juan wouldn't offend Their Majesties. He's thoroughly dependable. I found that out when he worked with Father."

"Not a chance he's running away right now?" Luis arched an eyebrow.

"Never! No, he's taking the voyage to make his fortune. He'll come right back, you'll see."

"Well, I wonder what excited him so much, then. What's this great plan of his?"

"It could be any number of things."

"Name one."

"Well, Juan could be rousing the local authorities to call off Morales and his stalkers."

"That won't happen. Morales commands higher authority than the constables of Palos. He's a church man, and a favorite of Torquemada, remember."

"He could say I died?" Sara struggled to find a possible idea.

"You fainted earlier, but you're too young to die."

"Juan might devise a plan to lure Morales away from the docks—maybe even out of Palos in the other direction."

"What would make Morales leave Palos?" Luis's voice grated like a dry mill wheel.

"Maybe he'll spread a rumor I've fled to a nunnery for sanctuary."

"Where?"

"Santa Clara, maybe."

"That's a creative idea. He might send someone to investigate, but he won't go himself. After all, you've tricked him twice already."

"But that could take half a day."

"Chances are he'd send his men, but stay in Palos himself to watch the wharves."

"Then, Juan should be finding me a secure place to hide until tomorrow."

"Yes," said Luis. "Somewhere in plain sight, but where Morales has no authority."

"Each captain is sovereign on his own ship," Sara said more to herself than Luis.

"That's brilliant, Sara Elena." Luis rushed to her and gave her a quick hug.

"I'll wager he's talking to Captain Columbus right now. In fact, I'm sure of it."

"I hope you're right. Whatever it is, Juan's plan must succeed. It's our best hope."

"Wait and see."

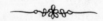

Juan dashed out of his quarters, leaving Sara Elena and Luis slack-jawed. He took the ship's ladder two steps at a time and soon found himself squinting in the bright light of August.

Above deck, all hands labored to prepare for the long and dangerous voyage. Their stony faces showed a stoic acceptance about the undertaking, but their conversation betrayed many misgivings. They went about, securing lines, tying tarps over loads of extra sails, and scrubbing the well-seasoned planks of the quarter deck.

Juan had heard their talk for days, but he listened again as he strode toward the captain's quarters.

"Captain's daft."

"Right. Finding a way to the East—that's crazy."

"You're just jealous you didn't think of it."

"I'd never come up with such a pea-brained idea."

"Well, Captain did and he smooth-talked Queen Isabella and King Ferdinand into paying for it, too."

"*Loco*, that's what it is."

"Whatever it is, you're all bound to go." Juan interrupted the tirade. "Best you not bellyache about it anymore."

Juan reached the captain's quarters and hesitated outside a minute. He straightened his vest and slicked back his hair, and then he knocked.

"Enter."

Christopher Columbus looked up from his desk, quill poised above his work.

"Ah, Sanchez, come in. I'm just finishing a report to the Queen."

"Sorry to interrupt."

"Don't worry. I've reached an impasse. Can't think of what to say next about our progress, such as it is."

He set down the quill and rubbed his thumb and finger on the bridge of his nose.

"What's wrong, sir?"

"Plans have stalled again. Problems with the provisions and getting all the men boarded." Columbus shook off his ill humor. "But, enough of my concerns. What can I do for you, Doctor?"

"Sir, I have a problem." He stepped forward." Yes?"

"I met a young woman a few months ago—Sara Elena." Columbus chuckled.

"Sir?"

"I see why you have problems."

"But I also have a solution."

"Sit down, Sanchez, and tell me all about it."

Juan dropped onto a hard chair and sat at attention as he related all that Sara Elena had told him and all that he knew of her himself.

Columbus directed terse questions at intervals and nodded his head as Juan answered. He pressed his spread fingers against those of his other hand and leaned back giving his full attention to Juan.

"What can I do to help, Sanchez?" Columbus interjected at tale's end.

"Sir, I thought if I marry Sara Elena today—this evening—she would come under my protection. You could add your authority as captain to mine as husband, and we could keep her safe from the clutches of Morales."

"Morales is a devil, but that plan might thwart him just long enough."

"We're talking about sixteen hours or so until the *Veronica* hoists anchor."

"You couldn't bring her with us, you know."

"No, sir. I wouldn't allow her to come on such a dangerous voyage."

"How would you get her to the *Veronica* without incident?"

"I have an idea." He told Columbus, who nodded in agreement.

"That might just work. Don't give Morales a chance to get his hands on her."

"Do I have your approval to carry out my plan?" Juan leaned forward on the chair.

"Where will she stay tonight? On this vessel, I presume?"

"Yes, sir."

"Do you have honorable intentions, Sanchez?"

"That's the other part of the plan."

"All right, tell me all of it. I'm bound to help you now."

The usually gloomy Columbus listened and flashed a rare smile.

"Where's Luis?" Juan burst into his quarters, where Sara Elena was resting. The sun shone at a lower angle through the one porthole.

"Remembered a task he needed to carry out. Left a few minutes ago."

"Bless him. Now I can talk to you privately. I have some important news."

"Will you tell me about your brilliant plan now?"

"Yes, *querida*. All in good time."

Juan gathered Sara Elena into his arms and placed his lips over hers. All the urgency and longing of the day flowed through him. He opened his mouth and sought her tongue with his.

"Juan, you're scaring me."

"Forgive me, dear one, but I'm anticipating a time when I can fully express my love."

"But that won't be anytime soon."

"You might be surprised." His grin spread wide like a melon slice.

"What do you mean?"

"Columbus is making all the arrangements."

"I don't understand."

"Let's just say I plan to make an honest woman of you."

"What?"

"I've sent for Margarita. She'll explain everything. Meanwhile, I must attend to my duties as ship's surgeon."

He planted a kiss on her forehead and exited before she could get in a word.

Sara Elena sat bewildered on the bed, pondering on a million possibilities, until a noise at the doorway caught her attention.

"Sara Elena?"

"Margarita!"

She ran to welcome her friend, who was loaded down with bundles.

"What are you doing here, dear one? You certainly know how to attract trouble."

"As usual," said Sara. "Did you hear what happened?"

"Yes, and I'm disappointed you neglected my advice." She scowled. "As always."

"I just had to see Juan—I just had to!"

"And once again, you barely escaped whole."

Margarita sighed and dropped her bundles. "You are blessed, a hundred times over."

"Blessed—I like that. But tell me why you're here."

"I sent a message to Juan today. He sent back a message to come to the *Santa Maria* and bring your best gown and finery."

"He's planning something, but I'm not sure what." She paused.

"Can't you figure it out?"

"He said he wants to make an honest woman out of me."

Margarita caught her breath. "I knew it. Come, prepare yourself." Margarita held out Sara Elena's moss green gown and laid it on the bed. She went to the door and called up the stairs.

"Bring a basin of hot water, sailor—quickly."

"Aye, señora." Sara saluted her.

"What are you thinking, Margarita? Do I need to bathe?"

"Yes, for a start. And then you need to brush your hair and put creams on your skin and redden your cheeks and lips."

She continued to pull things out of the bundles—a fine horsehair brush, a jar of red cochineal, a jar of blended oils and fragrance, a necklace and bracelets.

"What's the occasion? Look's like you're planning a wedding."

"Perhaps I am."

"Don't tease me, Margarita. What is Juan planning this evening that demands I must wear my finest?"

"Sarita, don't you understand? Juan plans to marry you tonight—truly he does. He's running around now getting a priest or rabbi—whoever he can find—and all the trappings for a proper ceremony."

"What? It can't be! There's no time—we can't get married." Sara Elena stammered out her words of amazement.

"Why not? You are betrothed already. If the priest will waive the requirement of announcing the wedding ahead of time, then the wedding can go ahead. I think it will go forward."

Margarita grabbed both of her hands and squeezed them.

"If all the details work out, you could become Juan's wife tonight!"

"Tonight!" The truth registered on her face, and then her body responded with a sudden spasm.

"Wait! I don't have enough time to get ready."

Sara flew across the room and received the basin of hot water a boy brought to the door. Margarita cleared a space on Juan's desk.

"Be careful not to splash on Juan's papers. Let me help you."

Margarita unlaced the back of Sara Elena's dress and helped her slip out of it. Sara Elena took the chunk of rough soap and lathered up a bit of toweling.

"It's been ages since I bathed. I almost forgot how." She continued washing and rinsing in the hot water till it became cloudy. She set it aside and dried herself.

"Let me brush your hair, Sara Elena. I'll take out your hair pins."

Down tumbled the long auburn waves across Sara Elena's shoulders. Margarita drew the brush through the glowing masses.

"Such glorious hair. I'm glad you didn't cut it when we left Granada."

"So am I." Sara Elena let Margarita arrange her tresses in an upswept style.

"Now, put on this green frock. It favors you so."

"Will I not have the traditional gown and *chuppah*—the marriage canopy?"

"Not this day. But you shall have your groom and his love. That's what matters."

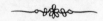

Juan returned just as Sara Elena finished enhancing her face. Margarita slipped a necklace over her head and disappeared out the door.

"I'll let you two be together a moment."

Juan intended to say something, for his mouth had opened. But, now he couldn't think what it was.

"Sara Elena, you are so beautiful, it takes my breath away." He came across the room and gathered her to himself.

"Careful not to damage my face and my hair." She pretended to beat him off.

"You'll not get away from me without a kiss." He covered her bright lips with his moist mouth. He enjoyed feeling her lips part and her body relax into his.

"Juan, you'll ruin me."

"That's my plan," he said under his breath, then smiled. "Have you discovered what my brilliant plan involves?"

"Yes, you silly. We're getting married."

"It's only right, you know, since you're 'pregnant.' Such a scandalous girl you are." He stroked her rosy cheeks and saw a blaze of color rise.

"You know I'm not pregnant." She pulled away and stamped her feet.

"Rumors fly. Better to get married now and make all things right."

"You shouldn't joke about such things. Maybe you started the rumors. I have my reputation to maintain."

"*Querida,* I would never damage your reputation." He laughed. "But, if you'd like, I'd be more than willing to make the rumors true." He looked at her with urgency in his eyes.

"Oh, Juan." Sara Elena's face turned scarlet. She buried her face into Juan's chest to hide her embarrassment and excitement.

"Come, my love, to Captain Columbus' quarters. I have some surprises for you."

Juan took her hand and drew her up the ladder and across the main deck. He was dressed in a fine, frilly silk shirt and black breeches with black hosen, and an embroidered doublet, and with stars in his eyes, looked every bit the eager bridegroom. He and Sara Elena turned heads as they swished toward the upper cabin.

"What's happenin', sir?" said a sailor.

"Meet my bride, mate."

"She's fair beautiful, that's for sure."

"Aye, she is." Juan winked at Sara Elena. She turned and curtsied toward the gawking sailor. He took off his cap and bowed low in return. "Best wishes, young lady."

Juan knocked on Captain Columbus' door and ushered her in without waiting for a reply.

Sara Elena gasped.

"It's wonderful—beautiful!" She breathed deeply of the perfumed air.

Sara Elena's eyes swept the room. She saw a large bouquet of roses—red for love—and, to one side, a priest waited. And Luis had returned.

"Hello, Sarita. Congratulations on your wedding day. I found the roses for the wedding." He kissed her on both cheeks.

Columbus turned around and adjusted a woolen waistcoat over his fitted grey hosen.

"Special occasions demand our best finery." He stepped to one side and joined Margarita who sat in a straight back chair.

"Yes, indeed." Margarita had put on a fine frock and worked with her hair. She looked as elegant as Sara Elena had ever seen her.

"Señora Martinez and I will be your witnesses. The priest is willing to perform a ceremony—sorry to say, no rabbi would show his face today."

"We understand," said Juan, and then looked to Sara Elena.

"Are you ready, *querida?*"

"I've been waiting all my life for this moment."

Juan and Sara Elena joined hands and took a step toward the priest as he donned his chasuble and made ready to repeat the wedding vows to two excited participants.

Chapter 29

Sara Elena awoke to the gentle rocking of the boat. In the darkness, she couldn't identify her surroundings. Sparsely furnished room, desk with maps and documents, burned-down candle—The fine linen sheets caressed her body. Half in sleep still, she remembered enjoying that gentle touch, whispers and sighs—

With a jolt, she sat upright. Someone lay next to her!

"Juan?"

"Mmm?"

"Oh, Juan, it's you." She fell back to the pillow and turned toward him.

"Yes, my love. Who else would it be?" He reached out and traced a finger along her chin, then pulled himself nearer to lower his moist lips on hers.

Sara Elena groaned with pleasure, and welcomed his hands as he explored her body once more.

"Are we really married?" She shuddered with desire as Juan's lips moved to her breasts.

"If we're not, my love, we have committed many sins this night already."

"We did say our vows in the captain's quarters, right? I'm not dreaming?"

"Yes, we did. But, perhaps you're dreaming of me? I can hope—"

"Stop—no, don't," Sara Elena pleaded. She remembered last night now. Juan's gentle touches awakened emotions she never knew before.

"We need to talk, Juan."

"Just one more kiss, *querida*."

He trembled with desire as she turned toward him and wrapped her arms around his neck, planting kisses all over his face.

"Maybe just one more."

She relaxed and opened her body to him, and he entered with a quiver of anticipation. Their passions rose together, and soon his desire overtook him. She in turn tightened and released with a deep sigh. They held each other, not wanting the feeling to end, but soon fell asleep.

"Sara Elena, you need to get up." Juan stroked her face and shook her shoulder.

Sara Elena opened her eyes and yawned. "It's barely dawn."

"Yes, but I need to get you back to the *Veronica* before sun-up." Juan was all business now. He pulled on his hosen and shirt.

"How can we do it? If I step on dry land, Don Antonio will catch me, for sure."

"Then I'll take you by sea." Juan grinned, and adjusted the ties of his doublet.

"What do you mean?" Sara bolted out of bed, threw on her shift, and washed her face with some fresh water from the basin.

"I've got permission to use one of the small boats from the *Santa Maria*. We'll lower it into the sea, and paddle over to the *Veronica*."

"What if nobody knows we're coming? How will I get aboard?"

"I thought of that, too. Captain Ferlandini is expecting us."

Juan drew on his waistcoat and threw a dark cape over his shoulders.

Sara Elena pulled on her green gown and attempted to arrange her hair.

"I can't see anything in the dark. How does my hair look?"

"Beautiful." Juan touched the hastily arranged knot, and it tumbled down.

"Oh, no!"

"Don't worry about your hair. What's important is getting you safely back to your ship. You can slip into bed when you get there—no need to have a fancy hair dressing."

"Juan! We need to talk—make plans."

Sara Elena grabbed Juan by the arms.

"Such as?"

"When will I see you again? Where can we meet when you return? I won't be in Spain anymore, you know."

"Yes, my love. Where shall we meet—say about six months to a year from now?"

"Is that when you return from the expedition?"

"Columbus says it'll be before spring."

"You'll return to Palos?"

"That, or along the western coast of Iberia somewhere."

"I'll be in the Holy Land by then."

"How about meeting in Jerusalem on some major feast day—Easter or Christmas, maybe?"

"Jerusalem? You're a long way from getting there. Will any ship get you from Palos to the Holy Land?"

"I hope so. Everyone in our caravan wants to go there. They say Italian ships go that direction. All desperate people, I guess. We'll find a way. To answer your question, then—Christmas would be better. By that time, I'll have been there for a while and found permanent residence and employment."

"Where could we meet?"

"At the Wailing Wall—or maybe the Church of the Nativity in Bethlehem?"

"Let's make it the Church of the Nativity."

"Why in Bethlehem?"

"Because there are not as many inquiring eyes there."

"That's a distance from Jerusalem. I've heard it mentioned in stories of the Crusades."

"Built by Constantine centuries ago. That's the one."

"Let's meet at the Church of the Nativity, Christmas Eve, 1493. That sounds appropriate."

"I think so." Juan smiled. "Do we have all our arrangements worked out now?"

"Yes."

"All right, let's get you back to ship before I change my mind and desert this ship."

Juan grabbed Sara Elena's hand, and motioned for her to be quiet. They tiptoed up the ladder and past a dozing guard. Then, Juan led Sara Elena to a small boat near the starboard side of the vessel. He maneuvered it over the railing and lowered it from its hoist into the slate black water below. It hit the sea with a gentle splash.

Juan threw a rope ladder overboard, and took the first steps.

"Wait till I get to the bottom, then climb down."

It took forever for Juan to call up to her.

"Sara, come on down. Grip the ropes and don't let go, even if you rock from side to side. I'll help you when you get close."

Sara Elena made her way down the rope ladder, swaying back and forth with each step. Sometimes the ladder swung over the indigo waters, and it looked like she had stepped into a black abyss.

"Ooh, I can't do this!"

"Shh, you're almost there. Quiet!"

Juan caught her by the waist and lowered her to the swaying boat. He pushed off, and rowed toward the hull of the *Veronica*.

"It's hard to see anything in the darkness."

"Shh, nobody must hear us, or see us." Juan kept rowing.

"It's freezing out here." Sara Elena wrapped her shawl close around her shoulders

"Almost there."

The prow of the boat bumped into a larger boat.

"We're here."

"What's the signal?"

"Columbus is here." Juan called softly toward the deck far above.

"Go west," came the reply, and then a ladder cascaded down the side.

"You first, Sara Elena." Juan followed her up the ladder. A callused hand reached out and helped them onto deck.

"Thanks, mate," said Juan. "This is Sara Elena Torres—no, it's Sanchez. Sara Elena Sanchez. She's a paid passenger on the *Veronica*."

"Right you are, sir. Captain Ferlandini explained it all to me. I'll show you to quarters, and then bid you goodnight."

The sailor led the way to the alcove where Sara Elena and Margarita had first claimed a space. Margarita lay on one of the mattresses, but sat up when she saw them coming.

"*Bienvenida*, married lady."

"Hello, Margarita. Is there a place for me to sleep?"

"Come rest. You've had a busy night." She winked at Sara, whose cheeks went rosy.

"I can't bear to say good-bye, Juan." Sara Elena turned to her husband with tears filling her eyes again. "I can't believe how many tears I've shed lately."

"This is what we must do for now. I'll count the days until I return and seek you out in the Holy Land." He kissed her with tenderness and held her long in his embrace. Pulling away, he said,

"Take good care of her, Margarita."

"I will, Doctor Sanchez. And God keep you until we meet again."

"Goodbye, dearest Juan." Tears glistened in Sara Elena's eyes.

Margarita took Sara Elena by the shoulders and guided her to her pallet. Juan strode over and placed a tender kiss on her forehead, and then another on her lips.

"Go! You must get back! This ship leaves at dawn—the captain told me."

Juan tore himself away and strode to the ladder.

"Remember our arrangement, Sarita."

"I won't forget." She blew him a kiss.

"*Te quiero.*"

"*Vaya con Dios.*"

"God be with you till we are re-united, *querida.*" Juan turned, bounded up the steps and down the rope ladder in record time. He jumped into the little boat and shoved off toward the *Santa Maria*.

Sara watched him go, aching to touch him again. *A whole new chapter in my life begins now.*

The little boat bumped into the hull of the *Santa Maria* with a resounding thud.

"Hey, mate, toss me the ladder."

The rope ladder plummeted over the railing and landed on top of Juan, who grabbed it and secured the little boat before climbing to the creaking deck.

"Help me pull up the boat, sailor."

"Aye, doctor. Up it comes." The two men braced their feet and began reeling in the boat Juan had attached to the hoisting mechanism.

"Anything happen on board, mate?" Juan puffed between hauls on the ropes.

"It's right quiet, sir, except for those men waiting out front by the pier."

"What men?"

"Well, they look like they're up to no good, they do."

The sailor led Juan over to the far railing, motioning for him to be quiet.

"See over there, sir? A man in black and two other scoundrels have been there since sundown." His rough whisper grated like a rusty anchor pulley.

Juan's eyes pierced through the thick fog of early morning. He saw two men wrapped in black cloaks watching from the pier. Another one—hidden in shadow—loomed in a corner near sacks of grain.

"Could that be Don Antonio?"

"Who?"

"Deputy of the Holy Office of the Inquisition."

"Why's such an important man of the Church after you?"

"Not me. He's after my wife."

Juan ducked down below the railing too late—Don Antonio spotted him. Immediately, he called his henchmen, and all three moved toward the lowered gangplank.

"Doctor Sanchez. Kindly hand over Señorita Torres to me, and there'll be no trouble."

Two black-cloaked figures grabbed and restrained Juan before he could get away. The sailor faded back and ran for the captain's quarters.

"If only I had my sword. I'd soon rid the world of you vermin."

Juan spat out his defiant words and tried in vain to wrestle free of his captors.

"Slow down, Sanchez. You're not going anywhere."

"How do you know who I am? I've never met you."

"I make it my business to know." Don Antonio curled his lip in a half smile and rubbed his hands together in glee.

"What do you want with this—what's her name—Señorita Torres?"

"You don't fool me!" Don Antonio shouted, his face suddenly next to Juan's. "Sara Elena's your betrothed."

"No, she's not." Juan's spit landed on Don Antonio's nose.

"Liar!"

"She's not, I tell you." Juan lurched and pulled against his restrainers.

"So, you admit you know her."

"Yes."

"But she's not your *novia?*"

"No."

"I don't understand."

"She's my wife, you fool, and if you lay a hand on her, I'll kill you!"

"What's the trouble here? You two, step away from Doctor Sanchez." Captain Columbus jumped between the arguing men, and took command.

"What's the trouble here?" he repeated.

"Don Antonio Morales, at your service, captain." The cleric made a cursory bow and a patronizing bow.

"Now tell me, sir, why you came aboard without permission."

"An urgent mission," Don Antonio rushed on. "Sara Elena Torres has fled my jurisdiction. I must retrieve her before the Jews leave Spain forever." He thought a moment, then added,

"She's one of them, you know."

"I see. A bit of property you wish to appropriate."

Captain Columbus looked down his hawksbill nose and cleared his throat. Don Antonio made no reply but color rose up his neck. "Well?"

"Where is she? I must have her."

"What makes you think she's here?"

"I've had people watching the *Santa Maria*, and nobody's seen her leave the ship since yesterday."

Juan broke in.

"You're too late, man. She's safely aboard her own vessel, which is already pulling out of the harbor. Look." He pointed out the *Veronica*, a bobbing silhouette on the horizon.

"You tricked me, Sanchez. You'll be sorry." Don Antonio pointed a long bony finger at Juan.

"Just remember what I said, Morales."

Juan lifted his chin and shrugged off Morales' accusing gesture.

Don Antonio turned heel and strode off the ship, calling to his cronies. "Get to it! We must reach the *Veronica* before it sets off."

Juan lurched forward to follow, but Columbus pulled him back.

"Stop! No telling what you'd do if you went after him now."

"Let me go! I've got to save Sara Elena." Columbus restrained him with difficulty.

306

"Let Captain Ferlandini argue with Morales. He's tough enough to stand up to the lot of them."

"At least signal the *Veronica* that they're coming, captain. Won't you do that?"

Columbus gestured to two deck hands standing watch. "Sailors, escort Doctor Sanchez to his quarters."

"Don't bother. I'll stand right here and not leave the *Santa Maria*. I promise."

Juan shrugged off the captain's hold and walked across deck to look toward the *Veronica*, hands clasped behind his back.

"Very well, Sanchez. You two, see that he doesn't leave ship. He might just desert the whole expedition."

Columbus pointed to the sailors waiting his orders, and then pivoted and strode back to his cabin.

"Aye, captain. You can count on us." The sailors took up posts on each side of Juan and watched Morales shout out orders to his servants.

"I must get Sara Elena without fail." Don Antonio ran down the long pier, his desperation outpacing his strides. His lungs burned from the exertion, and he ran like he had two wooden legs.

"Quick, Get to the ship. I can't keep up the pace." He clutched his chest.

"All this exertion could bring on a coughing spell."

Don Antonio slowed as the first fit of wheezing wracked his body. His servants raced on toward the ship at the far end of the quay.

"I'll just stand here and—catch—my breath."

Chapter 30

Sara Elena couldn't sleep. After Juan left, she lay gazing at the wooden beams above her. A spider dangled on its delicate thread, swaying with the gentle rocking of the boat. Thoughts tumbled in and out of her brain, wrestling each other for supremacy.

What will I do without Juan for almost a year and a half? I miss his touch already. And those kisses—I've never known such pleasure! God keep you, Juan, on your perilous journey. God keep me, too. Where will I end up? How will I live? Is there a safe place for me anywhere? Will I ever have a home and family? Will Don Antonio chase me to the farthest corner of the earth? Will he knock on my door one day?

Sara Elena scratched her head and rolled back and forth, trying to shut out the confusion and desolation of the moment.

"Are you awake, Margarita?"

"Mmm?"

"I was just thinking—"

"Yes?" Margarita rolled over and propped herself on one elbow.

"About Juan." Sara Elena let out a long sigh.

"I'm not surprised—a new bride dreaming about her husband."

"No, not about that—at least not at this moment." Her cheeks colored, and she giggled. "I'm concerned for his safety."

"Are you?"

"It'll be a long voyage—and they don't even know for sure where Columbus will end up. Cipangu or India, maybe."

"Juan can take care of himself. I'm sure he will, for your sake."

"He's just so important to me. I need him desperately."

"Listen to you! Such a change—you've always been so independent before."

"But it's true. I need him!" She pulled the covers up to her chin.

"So, Sara Elena, my young friend, has become a woman now."

"Yes. And I'm worried."

"Worry about yourself, dear one. We haven't left the harbor. You are not yet out of the clutches of His Eminence."

"Don Antonio?"

"Aren't you concerned?"

"I'm terrified. I—what's that noise?"

Sara Elena sat up and cocked her head.

"Something's happening up on deck."

"Are we leaving the harbor now?"

"Hurry, get dressed. Let's go see."

Margarita catapulted off her mattress and threw on a simple gown. Sara Elena followed, and once again tried to arrange her wavy locks. In frustration, she brought all her hair together and tied a ribbon around it, so it fell down her back like a horse's tail.

Shouts and running feet multiplied, both above deck and below.

"I think everyone else wants to see what's happening, too," said Sara Elena. "Listen to all the scurrying feet."

"Like mice after a party."

"Let's go."

Margarita raced up the ship's ladder to the top deck, with Sara Elena right at her heels. They popped up the hatch just in time to see people emerging from all the open hatches.

"Like squirrels popping out of knot holes," laughed Margarita.

"Oh, look, there's the Romero family, and Señor Galvan."

"*Hola, amigos.* Over here, it's Sara Elena and Margarita."

Sara Elena waved and tried to join them, but felt rough hands grab her.

"So, here you are."

Two men caught her arms and began to tie her wrists together.

"What are you doing?"

Margarita flailed at them with both hands.

"Let go of her. Who are you?"

One of the men grabbed Margarita's arms, leaving Sara Elena to the other man.

"Are you her mother?"

"She's like a daughter to me, and I won't give her up!"

"Why defend her? She's wanted by the Inquisition."

"Don Antonio's obsessed with her. That's the real truth."

Margarita kicked the man in the shins and then stomped on his other foot.

"*Ay, bruja!* I'm just following orders."

Scores of people now milled around on deck, watching the proceedings. Just for a moment, nobody knew what to do. Sailors stood in a clump awaiting orders. An assortment of Jews stood to one side, hesitant to get involved in a matter controlled by the Inquisition.

"Someone, get the captain," yelled Margarita.

Instantly, two sailors ran off to captain's quarters. Everyone looked that direction and saw Captain Ferlandini already emerging, cloak over his shoulder, hat in hand.

"What's the uproar about?"

"Sir, these men seized Señora Sara Elena, and want to haul her away to the Inquisition."

"Release her. Don't you know you have no authority here?"

"Wait," rasped a voice. "She's—my prisoner—and I will have her!"

Don Antonio's voice commanded obedience even now. He dragged himself up the ramp to the main deck of the *Veronica*, coughing and gasping and holding his chest.

Sara Elena stopped struggling and Margarita quit kicking. Alexo and Paco, the two men in black, relaxed their tight grip on the women and looked toward Morales.

Captain Ferlandini assessed the situation. "You again?" The sailors formed a barrier between the passengers and the action. The Jewish passengers surged forward, taunting Morales and his men. "Can't find anyone to persecute on land, Don Antonio? Thought you'd take a new bride away from her husband?"

The shouts grew more and more biting.

"Hold the line, *marineros*," said Ferlandini.

Don Antonio saw his opportunity. "Take her away—now!"

Alexo pushed the wrist-bound Sara Elena forward, while Paco slapped Margarita, knocking her onto the deck. They ran across deck and down the gangplank while Don Antonio panted and coughed, following after them.

The Jewish crowd let out a roar and shoved with all their might. Someone cracked a sailor in the skull and another punched one in the jaw. Several grabbed sailors and threw them down and sat on them. Other ran to get rope to tie them up.

Meanwhile, half a dozen shot forward after the retreating Morales.

"Do something about these thugs, captain," called the first mate.

"Not much I can do," said Captain Ferlandini. "Let the Jews have their way. I agree with them, actually."

He smiled and ambled over to watch what would happen next.

"Should we go after them?"

"Let them have their justice."

At the bottom of the gangplank, the skirmish heated up. The Jews, still a little hesitant about openly confronting a holy father, formed a circle around Morales and his men. Nobody actually touched anyone. They just pressed in closer, preventing their progress.

"Let me go. Out of my way," shouted Morales, turning red then purple in the face. He yelled curses between shallow, gasping breaths.

"Curse all of you. I promise the Inquisition will get every last one of you."

He sputtered and heaved another breath.

"Too late," yelled someone. "You've already ruined our lives."

"You and the King and Queen."

"Treason!"

"We won't let you free until you release Sara Elena."

"Let her go now!"

"Never!"

A tall figure parted the crowd, green eyes flashing.

"Let her go, Morales, or you're a dead man." Juan Sanchez grabbed the frightened cleric by the throat and squeezed. Sara screamed.

"Mercy—can't breathe." Don Antonio wheezed and gasped. His face had a bluish cast.

"Release Sara Elena."

Morales resisted. Juan squeezed harder. "I could crush your throat so easily."

"No!" coughed Don Antonio.

"Let her go," cried the crowd.

"Now," said Juan.

Morales nodded to his servants, who immediately dropped their hands. Alma Romero ran through the circle and untied Sara Elena.

"Thank you. Thank you all," Sara began.

"Stop this foolishness," commanded a voice from above. Captain Ferlandini peered from the main deck of the *Veronica*.

"Must I send men to break up this brawl?"

At the sound of the captain's voice, the crowd dispersed, Jews flowing back onto the ship. Other bystanders turned heel and walked away.

Juan kept his hold on Morales' throat, while looking toward his wife.

"Let him go, Juan. I'm all right now."

Juan heaved a sigh and dropped his hand. Morales slumped to his knees, all the while coughing and gasping. He waved his hands wildly.

"Can't breathe—can't get air."

He sputtered and fell into a heap on the gritty pier.

"Juan, I love you!"

Sara Elena ran to embrace her man.

"*Querida,* I thought I had lost you to the evil Morales just now."

Juan planted kisses on his wife's lips, and drew her within the circle of his strong arms.

313

"Is he dead?"

"I don't know."

"What shall we do?"

"I'm staying with you."

Juan looked into Sara Elena's eyes.

"Curse Columbus and his voyage. You need protection."

"I'm afraid for you. Juan. Desertion is serious."

"I don't care—I'm staying."

"You'll do nothing of the kind." Two sailors grabbed him and shoved Sara Elena aside.

"Captain Columbus needs you. He'll not give you up, even for a new bride."

They dragged him off toward the *Santa Maria*, struggling to keep hold of the thrashing body.

"Wait."

Just then, Margarita took Sara Elena's arm and started toward the *Veronica*.

"Come Sarita. Let him go. He has obligations to fulfill."

"But, I need to be with him."

"You know that's not possible—not on that uncertain voyage."

Sara Elena looked back at the clot of men struggling with each other while retreating to the *Santa Maria*.

"What about Don Antonio?"

"His servants will attend to him."

"But, what if he's dead?"

"If he's dead there's nothing we can do. Come, dear one."

"But—"

Margarita eased Sara Elena up the gangplank.

"You'll be arrested if you delay much longer."

As if to validate the statement, a contingent of mounted constables trotted up to the scene of the struggle. They dismounted and began questioning one lone man who sat on a sack of grain. The man pointed to the *Veronica*.

Sara Elena covered her face and walked across the deck.

"Weigh anchor, mates," called Captain Ferlandini. "Time to set sail."

Sailors scurried to follow orders. Several hauled up the anchor and cast off the lines holding the boat to the dock. The *Veronica* creaked and groaned to life as it eased out of its berth.

"Stop that vessel!" yelled a constable from the quay.

Captain cupped a hand to his ear.

"Sorry—can't hear you."

Margarita let out a nervous laugh.

"You stir up danger wherever you go, Sara Elena."

"I just want an ordinary life—home and family."

"Your life will never be ordinary, dear one."

"What will happen to us now, Margarita? How will I survive?"

"The way you always have: by your courage, and with the Almighty's protection. Both of which you have in abundance, it seems."

"May God bless you, too, Margarita—always."

Spanish Words and Other Phrases

adios—goodbye

alforjas—saddle bags

almuerzo—lunch

alubias—large, white beans used to make soup

amantes—lovers

amargo—bitter

amor—love

Antilia—mythical city in the Pacific Ocean

auto de fé—long ceremony held by the Inquisition
    leading to a public burning

besito—little kiss

bien—good

bienvenida—welcome

bodas—wedding

bonita—pretty

bolsa—purse or bag

bota—leather bag to hold water or wine

Cathay—China

chuppah—Jewish wedding canopy

Cipangu—Japan

¿Cómo estás?—How are you?

con mucho gusto—with much joy

converso—person of Jewish descent, who has converted
    to the Catholic faith

Dios te bendiga—God bless you

enfermera—nurse

esposo/esposa—spouse

estrella—star

familia—family gracias—thank you

hasta la vista—until I see you

hasta luego—until then

hija—daughter

Iberia—the landmass comprising Spain and Portugal

jamón serrano—air-cured ham

jarrón—terracotta urn

loco—crazy

maravedi—a measurement for money in 15th century

marinero—sailor

mil gracias—a thousand thanks

no importa—it's not important

novio/novia—betrothed

orgulloso—proud

peccadillo—little sin

perdon—pardon me

querido/querida—dear one

quizás—perhaps

Quinsay—Hangzhou, a city in China

sala—room

sanbenito—pointed cap and tabard with devils and flames on it, used by the Inquisition

también—also

te amo—I love you

te quiero—I love you

tocino de cielo—a thick custard with dark caramel (heavenly bacon)

un momento—one moment

vaya con Dios—go with God

viudo—widower